DATE DUE		
NOV 29 2016	MAY 24 2021	
JAN 26 2017		
FEB 16 2017		
JUN 22 2017		
JUL 15 2017		
JUN 19 2018		
JUL 12 2018		
SEP 07 2019		
JUL 23 2020		

WITHDRAWN

THE FIRST MOUNTAIN MAN
PREACHER'S
BLOOD HUNT

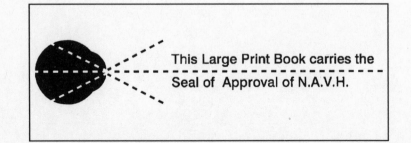

This Large Print Book carries the
Seal of Approval of N.A.V.H.

THE FIRST MOUNTAIN MAN
PREACHER'S
BLOOD HUNT

WILLIAM W. JOHNSTONE
WITH J.A. JOHNSTONE

THORNDIKE PRESS

A part of Gale, Cengage Learning

GALE
CENGAGE Learning·

Farmington Hills, Mich • San Francisco • New York • Waterville, Maine
Meriden, Conn • Mason, Ohio • Chicago

GALE
CENGAGE Learning®

LIBRARY OF CONGRESS CATALOGING-IN-PUBLICATION DATA

Johnstone, William W.
    The first mountain man : Preacher's blood hunt / by William W. Johnstone with J. A. Johnstone. — Large print edition.
    pages ; cm. — (Thorndike Press large print western)
    ISBN 978-1-4104-6706-5 (hardcover) — ISBN 1-4104-6706-6 (hardcover)
    1. Outlaws—Fiction. 2. Rocky Mountains—Fiction. 3. Fur traders—Fiction. 4. Large type books. I. Johnson, J. A. II. Title. III. Title: Preacher's blood hunt.
    PS3560.O415F5726 2014
    813'.54—dc23   2014007319

Published in 2014 by arrangement with Pinnacle Books, an imprint of Kensington Publishing Corp.

Printed in the United States of America
1 2 3 4 5 6 7 18 17 16 15 14

THE FIRST MOUNTAIN MAN
PREACHER'S
BLOOD HUNT

CHAPTER 1

Preacher smashed a knobby-knuckled fist into the face of one of the men attacking him and wondered why the hell he ever came to St. Louis in the first place. He could have sold his furs at one of the trading posts in the mountains and not even made the long journey back down the Missouri River.

But then he would miss out on all this entertainment and excitement, he thought wryly as he ducked under a wildly looping punch and hooked a hard left into his opponent's belly. The man's breath, laden with rum fumes, gusted in Preacher's face.

Something smashed into the small of his back, driving him forward with a grunt of pain, and he couldn't avoid the next punch aimed at his face. The fist landed on his right cheekbone and rocked his head to the side.

"Grab him!" a man yelled in the darkness.

"Put him on the ground!"

Preacher knew he faced eight or ten men, maybe a few more. It was so dark it was hard to tell.

Overwhelming odds, no matter how anyone looked at it, even for a veteran frontiersman like him who had been in countless bare knuckles brawls. If the attackers ever got him on the ground, they could stomp the life out of him.

The ruckus had gotten serious in a hurry.

Preacher yanked his big hunting knife from its stiff leather sheath and slashed from left to right in front of him. To a certain extent, he struck out blindly. The shadows were so thick beside the riverfront tavern where he'd been drinking earlier in the evening that he couldn't see the men who had jumped him as he left. They were shapeless lumps in the darkness.

One of them howled in pain as the razor-keen blade of Preacher's knife sliced through his flesh. Preacher pivoted, still slashing back and forth, and opened a small area around him.

He didn't know why the men had attacked him, but robbery seemed the most likely motive. Gangs of thieves sometimes had spies who kept an eye on the fur company offices, so they would know when a trapper had sold a load of beaver pelts and as a result had money in his pocket.

Preacher had sold a good season's worth of plews earlier that day. He planned to spend a few days in St. Louis, then outfit himself and head back to the mountains.

He never went on a binge when he came to town, like some fellas did. A few drinks, some cards, maybe a visit to one of the fancy houses if he was in the mood . . . that was the extent of the carousing Preacher did.

After walking around some, he had gone into Kilroy's tavern, where he had downed a few beers on previous visits to St. Louis. He'd never had any trouble in the place.

But when he left to go back to the stable where he'd left Horse and Dog and turn in for the night in the hayloft, several men had grabbed him and forced him into the alley. Before he could break free, he was surrounded.

He was far from helpless, though, as the man who had tasted his cold steel had found out. He must have been the leader. In a voice taut with pain, he ordered, "Get that jasper!"

The other men hesitated, realizing their quarry was armed. None of them wanted to

9

be the next to feel the bite of Preacher's blade.

Then one of the men leaped forward and yelled as he swung a club. Preacher tried to get out of the way, but it cracked across his wrist and sent the knife flying from his fingers. His hand went numb.

With his left hand, he pulled one of the flintlock pistols he carried from behind the rawhide belt tied around his waist. He hadn't wanted it to turn into a gun battle, but they weren't giving him any choice.

As the men closed in around him again, he drew back the pistol's hammer, hoping the metallic sound would make them think twice and leave him alone.

That proved to be a forlorn hope, as the man with the club swung it again. The cudgel crashed against Preacher's ribs and staggered him. The man pulled the club back for another blow.

Preacher shot him.

Flame geysered from the pistol's muzzle as the powder charge exploded. At close range, both balls from the double-shotted load slammed into the attacker's chest and blew him backward.

Preacher lunged forward. Sometimes taking the fight to the enemy was the best thing a man could do.

He swung the empty pistol, crashing it against a dimly seen head, and felt bone give under the blow. He'd put a third man out of the fight.

Unfortunately, there were still plenty more, and they piled on, hammering at Preacher with hard fists and booted feet. He tried to stay upright, but the pounding was too much. One foot slipped on the damp cobblestones, and he felt himself falling.

A mountain landed on top of him. That was the way it felt, anyway. Then it lifted up and crashed down on him again. Black waves of pain, shot through with red streaks, rolled through Preacher's brain.

"Teach him a lesson," the leader grated.

Preacher caught a glimpse as the man leaned in, clutching a bloody left arm. He had a craggy, big-nosed face. A black patch covered his left eye.

Then the others closed in around him again, kicking and pounding.

Preacher fought as long as he could, until those waves of pain washed him away.

Preacher had long since learned that sometimes pain was good. Hurting proved that a man was still alive. Dead men didn't hurt. If they did, there was just no blasted justice in this world . . . or the next.

As he became aware of his surroundings again, he lay there motionless for a long time, allowing consciousness to seep back into him. When he felt like he could risk it, he opened his eyes and lifted his head.

That was a mistake. Pain detonated inside his skull. He groaned and let his head drop. The back of it banged against a cobblestone and set off more explosions in his brain.

All right, he thought. Just wait a spell longer.

He waited, and then lifted his head without the whole world spinning crazily around him and trying to throw him off. He was able to roll onto his side, get an elbow underneath him, and gradually push himself up into a sitting position.

The rugged, outdoor life he had lived for almost three decades since leaving his family's farm as a youngster and running off to the mountains had given him a constitution of iron. As he sat there in the alley, he felt strength flowing back into him.

His head throbbed. He lifted a hand to explore it, finding several bloody lumps but no significant damage. He drew in a deep breath and blew it out, checking for the stab of pain that would tell him he had cracked or broken ribs. His sides ached, but that was all. No fractures as far as he could tell.

Preacher was surprised. After cutting one of his attackers, shooting another, and stoving in a third man's skull, he had figured they would kill him. It wouldn't have taken that many men too long to stomp him to death.

Instead, they had allowed him to live. They must have fled because of that shot he had fired. Even though the authorities in St. Louis tended to ignore a lot of violence that occurred along the riverfront, the gunshot could have drawn the attention of a constable.

Whatever the reason, he was alive . . . just not well, mind you. He ached badly all over and figured his rangy, muscular body would be covered with bruises by morning. But he was still drawing breath and there was plenty to be said for that.

He climbed wearily to his feet and checked his poke.

Empty, just as he'd expected. Whatever had caused the robbers to flee, they had tarried long enough to steal all the money he had gotten for his pelts.

Preacher muttered a curse. Normally he would have split up that money and carried it in different places on his person.

But it wouldn't have made any difference,

he realized. The thieves would have searched him from head to foot, and found the coins wherever he tried to hide them.

He asked himself what he was going to do. He still had Horse and Dog, the big stallion and the wolflike cur who were his long-time trail companions, along with his pack horse, his saddle, his possibles bag, his traps, and his long-barreled flintlock rifle, all of which were back at the stable.

But he didn't have money for supplies, including powder and shot, and without that he couldn't venture back up the river into the mountains.

The thought of having to spend months in St. Louis while he worked for wages and saved up enough for a stake made a horrified shiver go through him. A couple years earlier, he had spent a considerable amount of time in the town while he settled a score with an old enemy, and he couldn't bear to do that again.

He would just have to figure out something else.

For the moment, Kilroy would probably give him a beer on the cuff, especially if Preacher pointed out that he had been attacked and robbed right outside the man's place. People in these parts knew Preacher. If he spread the story, it could be bad for

Kilroy's business.

Preacher's broad-brimmed, brown felt hat had gotten knocked off during the struggle. He felt around in the alley until he found it. He brushed it off and put it on his head, grimacing as the hat's pressure against some of the bloody lumps made them throb again. He would just have to get used to it, Preacher told himself, because a man didn't go around without a hat.

His steps were steady as he walked back to the street. Nothing seemed unusual as he looked in one direction and then the other. Obviously, the attack on him hadn't attracted any attention, after all.

St. Louis prided itself on being an outpost of civilization, but robbery and murder, along with plenty of other, lesser vices, were common. If that was civilization, Preacher had mused more than once, folks could have it and welcome to it.

He'd take the vast frontier's endless plains and majestic high country.

He pushed open the tavern door and stepped into its dim, smoky interior. People glanced at him and then looked again as they noticed his scraped, bloody, bruised appearance.

Preacher ignored them and headed for the bar where Kilroy, with his giant, rusty mut-

15

tonchop whiskers, stood talking to a man with his back to Preacher.

Kilroy looked past the man's shoulder and his eyes widened. "Well, speak of the devil. This is the man you were looking for, sir, right here. This is Preacher."

CHAPTER 2

The man at the bar turned to face Preacher. He was middle-aged, with quite a few strands of silver in his dark hair under a fashionable beaver hat. His swallowtail coat, tight trousers, ruffled shirt, and silk ascot were expensive. Lean and handsome, he was clean-shaven and obviously a man who spent most of his time indoors.

That was in direct contrast to Preacher, who wore greasy buckskins and hadn't yet shaved or bathed since arriving in St. Louis earlier that day.

The mountain man's grizzled appearance didn't stop the stranger from extending his hand. "Indeed the man I wanted to meet. My name is Barnabas Pendexter, sir."

Preacher gripped Pendexter's hand and nodded curtly. He was in no mood to palaver with some fancy-dressed fella from back east, but he had a frontiersman's natural politeness. "Pleased to meet you.

What can I do for you?"

"I've heard that you know your way around the Rocky Mountains better than any man alive," Pendexter said.

Preacher shrugged. "Folks can say any damned thing they want to. That don't mean it's true."

"But you *are* quite familiar with the mountains," Pendexter insisted.

"I reckon. I been traipsin' around in 'em for enough years." Preacher's mouth was dry, and his head still hurt. He looked past Pendexter at the tavern's proprietor and said, "I could use a beer, Kilroy."

"Sure," Kilroy said, "but I thought you were done with your drinkin' for the night when you left earlier."

"So did I," Preacher snapped. "Until a bunch of no-good varmints waylaid me right outside your door and handed me a thrashin'."

Kilroy looked surprised again. "How many of the devils were there?"

"Must've been a dozen or more."

"I figured as much. Any less that that and you would've sent 'em packin' with their tails betwixt their legs."

Pendexter said, "Let me understand you, sir. You were assaulted by a dozen men and lived to tell the tale?"

"That's right," Preacher said. "At least one of them didn't, though. You might've heard the shot that killed him."

"Good Lord!" Kilroy exclaimed. "The body's not still out there, is it?"

"No, his friends must've dragged off his worthless carcass. When I came to, the alley was empty except for me." Preacher's eyes narrowed with suspicion. "You're tellin' me you didn't hear the shot, Kilroy?"

He wondered if the tavern keeper might be in cahoots with the robbers. As far as he knew, Kilroy had always been honest . . . or at least no more shady than most tavern owners were.

"I heard what sounded like a gun," Kilroy admitted, "but you know how it is along this riverfront, Preacher. Not a night goes by when you don't hear a gunshot or two. After a while you just don't pay attention to them anymore." He shook his head and added solemnly, "Good seldom comes from a man stickin' his nose in somebody else's business."

Preacher supposed that was true, especially in a neighborhood like this. He decided he would give Kilroy the benefit of the doubt and assume that the man hadn't know about the attack and wouldn't receive a cut of the money that had been stolen from him.

If he ever found out differently, he would take it up with Kilroy then . . . and it would be a conversation the tavern keeper likely wouldn't enjoy.

Barnabas Pendexter said, "This is a dreadful business. You're going to report it to the authorities, aren't you?"

"That'd be a waste of time and breath," Preacher drawled. "The law don't care about every trapper who gets jumped along the riverfront. If they did, they'd never have time for the important things, like takin' graft from all the businesses around here. Anyway, I didn't ever get a good look at the men who robbed me. One of 'em's got a pretty good gash in him from my knife, though. If I run across a fella like that, I might have some hard questions for him." Preacher looked at the tavern keeper again. "Am I gettin' that beer or not, Kilroy? It'll have to be on the cuff."

"Oh yeah, sure. I forgot." Kilroy filled a pewter mug from a barrel sitting on a heavy wooden stand.

"I'll pay for that, my friend." Pendexter slid a coin across the bar.

Preacher wasn't sure if the Easterner was referring to him or Kilroy as his friend. Nor did he care. If Pendexter wanted to pay for the beer, that was fine. Preacher became a mite more tolerant of civilized folks when he was flat broke.

"I'm obliged to you," he told Pendexter with a nod. He picked up the mug Kilroy set on the bar in front of him, took a deep swallow, and dragged the back of his other hand across his mouth and the thick mustache that drooped over it.

"Those men took every bit of your money?"

"Every bit," Preacher confirmed. "They left me my pistols and knife and tomahawk, and I'm a little surprised they did. Must've been in a hurry."

"Such miscreants are usually afraid of being discovered at their nefarious work."

Preacher downed another healthy swallow. "How come you were lookin' for me, Mr. Pendexter?"

"Yes, back to business," Pendexter said briskly. "I have a proposition for you. Shall we adjourn to an empty table and discuss it?"

Preacher didn't think it was very likely he'd be interested in Pendexter's "proposition," but the man had bought him a beer so he figured the only polite thing to do was hear him out. Besides, his throat wasn't nearly as dry, and the beer had helped his

21

headache. He picked up the mug and said, "Sure, I reckon we can do that."

The tavern was fairly loud with laughter and conversation to start with, and while Preacher and Pendexter were making their way across the room to a table in one corner, a couple of old-timers brought out fiddles and started sawing on them.

The music they made, if a person was feeling generous enough to call it that, was shrill and raucous, but it prompted one of the girls who worked in the tavern to lift her skirts around her ankles and start dancing a jig.

Some of the customers began to clap and call out encouragement to her. A burly man in whipcord and homespun stood up and linked arms with her, whirling her around in the impromptu dance. Other men got in line to wait their turn.

Pendexter grinned, sat down at the table, and said loudly enough for Preacher to hear him over the music, "My, this certainly is a colorful place, isn't it?"

"You could call it that," Preacher said.

Pendexter sighed as his expression grew solemn. "I needed something to lift my spirits for a moment. You see, Preacher . . . it's all right to call you Preacher?"

The mountain man gestured with the beer

mug to indicate that it was fine.

"You see," Pendexter went on, "I'm carrying a great burden right now, Preacher. My son William is . . . missing."

"Something happen to him?" Preacher asked, more out of politeness than real interest.

"That's just it. I don't know. He wasn't kidnapped or anything like that. He left home voluntarily. You see, William is fascinated by the mountains. Back home in Philadelphia, we don't have anything quite so spectacular. At least I assume we don't, since I can't speak from personal experience. I've never laid eyes on the Rockies myself. Neither had William, but ever since he read about them, he's wanted to see them for himself."

"I can understand that. When I was a youngster, I used to hear fellas who had been west talkin' about the things they'd seen, and it wasn't long before I was bound and determined to see 'em for myself. How old's your boy?"

"Actually, he's a grown man. Twenty-two." Pendexter paused and a note of anger surfaced in his voice. "Old enough to know better than to run away from home like child."

"So that's what he did? Left on his

and came west?"

"I assume so. We argued, you see. William read Fenimore Cooper's book about the Mohicans and was so taken by the romance of it that he decided to become a woodsman himself. Since every place back east is settled, and since he had such an interest in the mountains, he wanted to come west. I refused to give my blessing to such an ill-advised journey, of course. William would never survive very long on the frontier. He's been pampered and coddled his entire life, I'm ashamed to say. But his mother . . . well, she was very attached to him, and before she passed away she made me promise that I would take care of William the same way she would have. He's suited for carrying on in my business and nothing else."

"What is your business?" Preacher asked, becoming interested in Pendexter's story despite himself.

"Banking," the man replied.

That didn't surprise Preacher. With his expensive clothes and well-groomed appearance, Pendexter looked like a banker.

"So, your boy disappeared and you think he ran off to the Rockies," Preacher said. "Where do I come into this?" He had a pretty good idea what Pendexter's answer would be, but he wanted to hear it anyway.

"It's quite simple, really. I want you to find him."

"And do what? You said yourself that he's a grown man. I can't make a fella do something he don't want to do, not if he ain't hurtin' anybody."

Pendexter nodded. "I know that. It would be enough for you to find him, make sure he's safe, and deliver a message to him for me. I . . . I want him to know that I love him and want him to return home. I want him to know that he's always welcome."

Pendexter looked uncomfortable. Clearly, putting those emotions into words was difficult for him. As a banker, he was more used to dealing with figures in a ledger book than he was with his own feelings.

The two fiddle players had launched into another sprightly tune, which Preacher ignored. He drained the rest of the beer in the mug and set it on the table. "There's a couple things wrong with your idea, Mr. Pendexter. The first and most important is . . . do you have any idea just how big the Rocky Mountains are?"

"I understand that they're vast."

"Vast ain't a strong enough word. They stretch all the way from Canada damn near to Mexico, and there ain't just hundreds of places a fella like your son could be. There

25

are thousands. Maybe more than that. A fella who don't want to be found can disappear into those mountains and never be seen again."

"I'm not sure William doesn't want to be found. Anyway, I've had inquiry agents working here in St. Louis for the past couple months, questioning every man they can find who's been in the mountains recently. I have reports that a young man matching William's description has been seen in an area called . . . what was it again?" Pendexter frowned in thought for a moment. "King's Crown, that was it. Are you familiar with it?"

Now the man really did have Preacher's interest. "Yeah, I know King's Crown. It's a valley, more of a hole, really, with mountains surroundin' it in a circle so that they look sort of like the points on a crown. The valley's a good twenty miles across, with a couple good streams runnin' through it. Prime beaver country."

"That's exactly the sort of place William would seek out. He was convinced that he could be a success as a fur trapper. I'm not sure what made him feel like that, but the obsessions of youth don't always make sense, do they?"

"Been too long since I was young,"

Preacher said. "I've plumb forgot."

"You said there was a second objection. What's that?"

"You want to hire me to find your boy, right?"

"That's what I had in mind, yes."

"But to do that, I'd have to be goin' back to the mountains myself, and right now I can't do that. I don't have a stake, anymore."

"Money to finance the trip, you mean." Pendexter waved a hand. "That's no problem. I'll not only pay you a fee for your help in this matter, I'll supply anything you need."

"Anything within reason, you mean."

"Anything," Pendexter repeated bluntly. "If you say you need something to find William, I'll provide it, no questions asked."

Preacher studied the man's smooth, earnest face for a moment, then said, "Some folks would try to take advantage of anybody who said that."

"But everyone I've talked to says that you're an honest man. And now that I've talked to you myself, Preacher, I can see that they're right. I'm a good judge of character, you see. I know that if you and I come to an agreement, you'll honor it to the very best of your ability." Pendexter held out his hand across the table. "So, can we do that? Can we come to an agreement?"

Preacher didn't shake right away. He spent a couple seconds thinking about the prospect of spending weeks or months in St. Louis, trying to come up with the money for a new outfit. He might be able to find somebody to grubstake him . . . but somebody who wanted to do exactly that sat across the table from him. Running into Pendexter was a stroke of luck. Preacher knew better than to turn his back on good fortune.

He gripped Pendexter's hand. "I reckon we've got a deal."

CHAPTER 3

The ring of snow-capped peaks that formed King's Crown gradually faded from view as night settled down over the mountains. A hint of red lingering from the sunset remained in the western sky. When it disappeared the stars began to appear, millions of brilliant pinpoints of whitish-silver light against the ebony backdrop of the heavens.

Along one of the streams that meandered through the mountain-ringed valley, three men sat around a campfire, two of them smoking pipes while the third cooked their supper for the evening. They had been told that the Indians in the area were fairly peaceful and hadn't caused any trouble for a good while, so they figured it was safe to have the fire. Even though the days were warm, the nights were still cool enough that the heat from the flames felt mighty good.

Not only that, the men were all too aware of the vast wilderness around them, and the light seemed to keep its threatening immensity at bay.

They weren't old men, but neither were they youngsters. All three had wives and children back east. Carl Pennington was from Ohio and had worked in a store there. Enos Mitchell had been a surveyor in Indiana. John Burton had come the farthest, all the way from New Jersey where he had been a clerk in a law firm. All three men had been dissatisfied with their lives and had headed west, striving to find something better, hoping to make their fortunes in the fur business and then go home. They had met in St. Louis and decided to partner up after hitting it off well.

The stocky, curly-haired Mitchell was the one frying up salt pork and cooking biscuits for their supper. Over the sizzling of fat in the pan, he said, "I have a feeling that all our traps are going to be full in the morning, boys."

"You keep that optimism, Enos." John Burton was a dour-faced, balding man who would never look comfortable in buckskins, no matter how long he wore them. On the other hand, the tight collars and the suits he had worn in the legal office had been even worse.

Carl Pennington puffed on his pipe. A red-faced bear of a man running to fat, his body was finally starting to toughen up after the soft life he had led in Ohio. He looked around at the darkness beyond the circle of flickering red light cast by the fire. "I always feel like there's something out there watching us."

"That's because there probably is," Mitchell said. "You've seen how much wildlife there is around here, Carl. There are probably plenty of animals watching us right now."

"Wolves," Burton said. "Bears."

"Maybe, but they won't bother us. The fire will keep them away."

"We can hope so," Pennington said.

Back in St. Louis, they had talked to as many fur trappers as they could before setting out for the Rockies, learning from the veteran mountain men how to go about setting their traps and luring the beaver into them. So far, it was a knack the three newcomers to the mountains hadn't really picked up. They hadn't been completely unsuccessful — they had about a dozen plews dried and packed away — but at this rate it would take them a long time to amass enough pelts to make their efforts worthwhile.

Mitchell took the skillet away from the

fire and set it on a rock near the flames. "All right, boys, help yourselves."

"Think you could have burned that salt pork any more than you did?" Burton asked.

Mitchell didn't seem offended by the question. "Tomorrow night'll be your turn to cook again, John. We'll see how you do."

Burton grunted and reached for one of the biscuits.

His hand stopped in mid-air as somewhere in the brush not far from the camp, a branch snapped with a sharp crack that sounded almost like a gunshot.

Jebediah Druke closed long, sausage-like fingers around the throat of the man next to him. He leaned over and whispered harshly into Sam Turner's ear, "I said be *quiet,* you damned fool, not go stompin' through the brush like a damned ox."

Turner made a little croaking sound. Druke knew the man couldn't breathe. If he hung on for a little longer, Turner would pass out. If Druke kept his tight grip on the man's neck for a few moments beyond that, Turner would die.

Druke didn't want that. He let him go. Turner might be a clumsy idiot at times, but he was still useful.

Turner rubbed his neck and tried not to

gasp too hard for breath. That would make noise, too.

They might as well get on with their business, Druke thought. Thanks to Turner, the three trappers by the fire already knew somebody was out in the brush. Druke had seen them react to the breaking branch. There was no longer any point in trying to be stealthy.

He straightened to his full height, which was considerable, cradled his rifle in his left arm, and stepped into the light. He knew his burly, broad-shouldered figure was impressive, even more so with the reddish firelight washing over it. To the men seated on the ground, he must have looked like a menacing giant.

It was exactly the way Druke wanted to look.

"Hello, the camp," he said in a mocking voice. "All right to come on in?"

He was already in, and they knew it. Their rifles were lying on the ground within easy reach.

Druke saw them glance at the weapons, then decide against reaching for the rifles as Turner and five other men had emerged from the brush behind him.

The three trappers quickly realized that they were badly outnumbered. They clung to the hope that the newcomers weren't looking for trouble.

Druke saw that in their eyes, as well.

The one who'd been doing the cooking swallowed hard. "Sure, come on in. Our supper's a mite skimpy, fellas, but you're welcome to share in it anyway."

"Mighty generous of you," Druke said without making a move to help himself to the food. "Maybe you'd be willing to share the pelts in those packs over there, too."

The skinny, sour-faced one said, "That's nearly a month's work for us, and pretty slim pickings, at that. Not worth your time to steal."

"Who said anything about stealing?" Druke thumbed back his hat on his bald, bullet-shaped head. "I thought we were all just bein' generous here and sharin'."

"What have you got to share?" the trapper snapped.

Druke abandoned his affable pose, since no one would have believed it, anyway. His mouth twisted in a sneer. "Powder and shot, mister. Powder and shot."

The sourpuss started to bluster, "You can't come in here and threaten us —"

"I'd say we're already doin' it," Druke cut in. He drew one of his pistols from behind his belt and thumbed back the hammer.

Behind him, he heard Turner and the other men cocking their weapons. "Tell you what I'm gonna do. I'll let you take your horses and ride out of here. The pelts you've taken and all your supplies stay with us. That includes your guns."

"You can't be serious," the fat trapper said. "We can't survive out here with no supplies and no guns."

"You'll make it," Druke said. "You might have to grub for food. But if you don't run into any redskins who want to lift your hair, you can get back to St. Louis alive." His voice hardened. "And if you do, you'll know never to come back to these mountains again. My name is Jebediah Druke, and King's Crown belongs to me!"

The sourpuss got to his feet and glared. "You're nothing but a common thief, Druke! Well, you don't frighten us, you hear? We have as much legal right to be here in this valley as you do."

The trapper who'd been doing the cooking paled. "John, don't. You can't —"

"I know the law," the sourpuss interrupted stubbornly. "I know our rights, by God!"

"So you know the law, do you?" Druke said. "Out here, there's only one law, mister . . . and you're lookin' right down the

35

barrel of it!"

He pulled the trigger.

CHAPTER 4

Will Gardner was already asleep when the light touch on his shoulder roused him. He woke up instantly, having picked up that frontiersman's trick in the year he'd been out west. He sat up, reached for the rifle lying on the ground next to his bedroll. "What is it?"

The shadowy figure next to him gestured and said in a whisper, "Men on the move."

"How many?"

"Six, seven."

"Druke and his bunch," Will breathed. "They're the only ones who wouldn't be settled down for the night already."

His companion didn't say anything, but Will took the silence for agreement.

"You were out scouting around again, weren't you?"

A silent shrug.

"Did you see them or just hear them?"

"I saw. Got back here as fast as I could."

Will came to his feet. He was tall and lean, with shaggy brown hair that fell down the back of his neck. He plucked a coonskin cap from the ground and settled it on his head, stuck a brace of loaded pistols behind his belt, and picked up the rifle. His buckskin-clad companion had a flintlock, too, along with a bow and a quiver of arrows slung over a shoulder.

"Druke's up to no good again." A grin flashed across Will's face in the starlight. "Let's go see if we can annoy him."

The two of them had had a fire to cook their supper, but they had put it out before darkness fell, making sure even the embers were no longer glowing so there wouldn't be anything to give away the location of their camp. They had clashed with the brutal Jebediah Druke in the past and knew the man would like to kill them.

They left their horses where they were, securely hidden in a thick grove of trees, and moved through the night on foot, their moccasin-shod feet making little or no sound as they trotted quickly through the shadows.

Three trappers had been in the valley called King's Crown for only a few weeks, Will recalled. Druke wouldn't have bothered them right away. It was Druke's habit to wait awhile, to let men he considered interlopers in his "kingdom" collect some pelts first, then move in, take the furs, and drive off the newcomers. Will had seen it happen several times in the past year.

From time to time, trappers simply disappeared. He was convinced that Druke's bunch had killed them and left the bodies for the wolves. He wouldn't put murder past Jebediah Druke, not for a second.

Will's companion held out a hand to stop him.

Will breathed in. "We're close?"

A silent nod.

"All right. Let's work our way in."

They went to hands and knees and crawled forward, being careful not to make any sound. Will smelled woodsmoke. Several nights in the past couple weeks, he'd thought that he'd spotted the glow of a campfire in the distance. That was just asking for trouble in King's Crown. Although to be fair, he had a hunch that the three trappers hadn't known about Jebediah Druke.

Angry voices could be heard through the dark. At least one of the trappers was in the mood to put up a fight. That wasn't good.

Will suspected that the men who had disappeared had challenged Druke's notion that he ruled the valley with an iron fist. Druke would likely kill anybody who dared to do that.

Reaching a rocky outcropping that rose so it overlooked the creek, Will and his companion went to their bellies and crawled up the slope. From the vantage point at the top, they looked down on the trapper's camp about twenty yards below. The firelight revealed a tense scene. Will could almost smell the impending violence in the air.

Jebediah Druke's massive figure was easy to pick out. Half a dozen of his followers were with him. At least twice that many men were in his gang. For a quick moment, Will wondered where the rest were.

Two of the three new trappers were still sitting beside the fire, clearly hoping that somehow this trouble would all go away.

Will knew that hope was futile. Druke wasn't going to back down, especially when the third man was on his feet, glaring defiantly at him and babbling something about the law and rights.

Like that meant a hill of beans to a renegade like Druke.

Will heard a whisper beside him, the sound an arrow made coming out of a soft buckskin quiver, then the faint creak of a bowstring. He smiled in the darkness, knowing what was coming next. His hands tightened on his rifle.

Down below in the camp, Druke thrust out the pistol in his hand and made some sort of dramatic pronouncement.

The next instant, several things occurred so close together they seemed to blend into one. The bowstring twanged, Druke's gun roared as the arrow skewered the fleshy part of his upper arm, knocking off his aim, the pistol ball plowed harmlessly into the ground, and Druke let out a howl of pain.

In the next heartbeat, Will Gardner rose up on his knees and snapped the flintlock to his shoulder. He drew a bead while Druke's men still stood around with their mouths hanging open in shock at what had happened to their leader. Will pressed the rifle's trigger. It boomed and belched fire and smoke, and down below, one of Druke's men cried out and fell as the ball tore through his right thigh.

Another arrow hummed through the air and embedded itself in a man's shoulder. He clawed at the shaft and screamed as he staggered to the side.

Not seeming to hurry but not wasting any time, either, Will set his empty rifle aside and drew the brace of pistols he carried behind his belt. He cocked them, aimed, and fired in two widely spaced directions as Druke's men began to scatter. One of the renegades pitched forward on his face as a ball hit him in the calf and knocked the leg out from under him. Another spun around from the impact of the shot that grazed his ribs.

"It's Gardner and that damned Indian!" Druke bellowed. "Get 'em!"

Will and his friend were already fading back into the shadows behind the rock. Will heard one of the men say urgently, "We gotta get out of here, Jebediah! Those two are like ghosts! We can't kill what we can't see!"

Will didn't expect Druke to agree with that, but for the first time in their skirmishes the big outlaw was wounded himself. It made him leery of continuing the fight, and after a second, Druke shouted, "Grab the wounded men! Let's go!"

"Do we allow them to flee?" The question was whispered into Will's ear.

"Seeing as how they still outgun us, I reckon we'd better."

"I'll make sure they really leave."

Before Will could argue, his companion was gone, vanishing into the night in the blink of an eye. Will knew he ought to be used to that by now, but the suddenness of it still startled him. He figured it probably always would.

Druke and his men made plenty of racket as they crashed through the brush. They would be easy to follow.

Will quickly reloaded his rifle and pistols, then circled to approach the camp.

The three trappers were all on their feet, holding their rifles and standing with their backs to the fire so they could peer out into the darkness and search for any more threats. Will could have killed all three of them before they even knew what was happening to them.

They would learn, he told himself.

They would either learn . . . or die.

He stayed in the shadows so that if they got trigger-happy and tried to shoot him, they wouldn't be able to see where he was. Raising his voice, he called, "Howdy. Take it easy now, boys. I'm a friend."

CHAPTER 5

The three trappers turned quickly toward him. In the firelight, their eyes were big and bright with fear. They searched the darkness, looking for somebody to shoot.

"Hold your fire," Will told them. "I mean you no harm."

Visibly shaken by Druke's attempt to shoot him, John Burton said gruffly, "Who are you? Show yourself!"

"I will if you promise to take your fingers off those triggers."

"I don't trust him." Carl Pennington shook his head. "It's probably a trick."

"It's not a trick," Will said, keeping his voice calm and level. "Tell you what I'll do. I'll step out where you can see me, and I'll have my hands in the air so you can see that I'm not trying to pull anything funny. Just don't shoot me, all right? I'd hate to have saved you from Jebediah Druke only to get ventilated in the process."

"So you know him." Burton looked like he'd just bitten into a lemon. "You know Druke?"

"I know who he is." Will slung his rifle over his shoulder and moved forward, keeping his empty hands raised to shoulder level. "I know he's the meanest renegade west of the Mississippi. I know he would have killed all three of you fellas if my partner hadn't put an arrow in his arm."

"I did see an arrow in Druke's arm," Mitchell, the third trapper said. "I think this young fella's telling the truth."

Will had reached the firelight's edge. They could see him, and visibly relaxed when they realized that he wasn't holding any weapons.

"My name's Will Gardner," he told them. "I'm a trapper, just like you boys."

Sour-faced, Burton said grudgingly, "I guess you can put your hands down. You must be the one who helped us."

"My partner and I," Will corrected.

"You're alone," Pennington said. "Where's this partner of yours?"

"Gone to make sure Druke and his bunch don't try to double back and cause more trouble."

"Who is he?" Mitchell asked. "Druke, I mean. The man looked as big as a bear."

"And twice as mean," Will said with a

smile. He lowered his hands. "You fellas might want to go ahead and eat your supper, then put that fire out. It'll get cold up here by morning, but better to be a little chilly than dead."

"We thought it was safe," Mitchell pointed out. "We were told the Indians weren't a threat around here."

"They're not. But there are worse things than Indians."

"There's some coffee in the pot. I'm Enos Mitchell, by the way." Mitchell introduced his companions.

"Pleased to meet you." Will hunkered next to the fire and took the tin cup that Mitchell handed to him. He filled it with coffee and sipped the strong, black brew while the three men ate. He kept his gaze away from the flames and looked all around the camp. Staring into a fire was the quickest way for a man to lose any night vision he might have.

"This man Druke is a brigand?" Burton asked.

"You could say that. I'd say that he's a no-good varmint. He showed up in King's Crown about eight months ago with three or four friends who were just about as bad as he is. The valley was full of trappers back then. Most of 'em got along pretty well, because this area is one of the richest for beaver in the mountains. Plenty to go around for everybody.

"But there were bad eggs already here, and they drifted into Druke's bunch as time went on. When he got enough men to back his play, he started trying to take over. He's run out probably half the men who were here to start with. Stolen their pelts, roughed 'em up, and sent 'em packing." Will took another sip of the coffee. "The ones who tried to fight back . . . well, they just sort of disappeared." He gave a meaningful nod. "Like you boys would have tonight, more than likely."

"If you and your friend hadn't saved us, you mean," Mitchell said. "How did you manage that, just the two of you against seven men?"

"We took them by surprise. Gray Otter and I decided we weren't going to knuckle under to Druke. We weren't going to run out, and we weren't going to let him kill us, either. We decided early on to take the fight to him, and we've learned the only way to do it is to hit him hard and fast when he's not expecting it, and then get out before he can do anything about it."

"And yet you're sitting here calmly drinking coffee," Burton said.

"We did more damage tonight than usual," Will explained. "Druke and his men will need to go off and lick their wounds before they coming hunting more trouble. Anyway, we're fixing to move, all of us, as soon as you finish eating. You need to put out this fire, pack up your possibles, and find yourselves another camp at least a mile from here."

"But this is a good campsite," Burton protested.

"And Druke knows where it is now," Will pointed out in a mild voice.

"Mr. Gardner's right. Finish up, boys, so we can get a move on." Mitchell turned to Will. "You say your partner is tracking Druke and his men?"

"That's what Gray Otter started out doing. Must've been obvious that Druke wasn't coming back tonight, though, because for the past couple minutes he's been standing over there behind you."

The trappers exclaimed in surprise as they looked around quickly and saw the slender, buckskin-clad figure standing in the shadows with an arrow nocked to bowstring.

"It's all right, Gray Otter," Will said as he made several elaborate gestures. "These gentlemen realize now that we're all friends here." He added to the trappers, "Sign

48

language. Gray Otter doesn't understand English."

That was a lie, of course, but one that came in handy at times.

Gray Otter signed back to Will, who told the trappers, "Druke and his bunch have some cabins about five miles from here, close to some of the mountains. That's where they've headed. They'll spend the rest of the night patching up their wounds and getting drunk, more than likely."

Burton asked, "What would have happened if your friend had come back here and found you in trouble?"

"Well" — Will smiled — "Gray Otter's pretty good at moving around without anybody knowing he's there. He was behind you, remember, with an arrow ready to fire."

Pennington shuddered. "I'm glad that you persuaded us that you're friendly and that we didn't do anything foolish."

"So am I, Mr. Pennington," Will said, still smiling. "So am I."

Jebediah Druke felt like he was on fire inside, not from any physical pain, but rather from anger. Pure, white-hot rage . . . although that hole in his arm where the redskin's arrow had skewered him hurt like hell.

It hadn't done any lasting damage, though.

The arrow's flint head had missed the bone and torn through skin and muscle. The first thing Druke had done once they were clear of the trappers' camp was to snap the shaft and pull it the rest of the way out of his arm.

Once they had gotten back to the collection of run-down cabins he had grandiloquently dubbed Fort Druke, he had soaked a rag in corn liquor and used a ramrod to run it through the hole. He had followed that with several healthy slugs of the whiskey down his gullet to dull the fiery agony.

"Bind it up tight," he told Sam Turner, who was tying a bandage around Druke's wounded arm. They sat at a rough-hewn table in Druke's cabin. A candle guttered and smoked in the middle of the table, next to the jug of whiskey. "I want to be able to use it just like it wasn't hurt."

"I don't know if you're gonna be able to do that, Jebediah," Turner said. "That arrow took out a pretty good chunk of meat."

Druke flexed his fingers and ignore the pain that caused in his arm. "It still works," he rasped. "That's all that matters. I can still hold a damned gun and pull the trigger."

"I reckon so," Turner admitted. He had come out of the fight at the trappers' camp uninjured, one of the few men in the group to do so.

Druke had thought about gathering up the rest of the men and returning to the camp right away to seek vengeance. Some of the men who'd been wounded were hurt pretty bad, though, and needed quite a bit of attention. It might be better to bide his time, he had decided.

But he wouldn't forget what had happened. No way in hell would he forget. Those three trappers would pay.

And so would Will Gardner and that damned redskin of his.

As if he'd been reading his leader's mind, Turner said, "You really think it was Gardner and Gray Otter who jumped us, Jebediah?"

"Who else? They're the only ones in King's Crown who've got the sand to try something like that. If I'd known how much trouble they were gonna be, I'd have killed them first, before we ever made a move on anybody else."

"Who could've figured it? A green kid and a half-pint Injun. Didn't seem like they'd be anything for us to worry about."

"But they've hit us a dozen times, damn their eyes." Druke moved his bound arm around a little to make sure it worked and

51

then nodded in satisfaction. He used that arm to reach for the jug again. "I'm tired of this. Those two got to die."

"Yeah, but they always slip away like they ain't even there. You know how many times we've tried to trail 'em, and they always throw us off the scent."

Druke took a swallow from the uncorked jug, thumped it down on the table again, and wiped the back of his other hand across his mouth. He glowered. "I know somebody who can find 'em. Find 'em and kill 'em."

Turner's eyes widened. His whiskery face went a little pale under its leathery, permanent tan. "Jebediah, you ain't talkin' about —"

"I sure am," Druke interrupted. "And you're gonna go find him and bring him to me, Sam."

Sheer terror twisted Turner's features.

Druke clenched his right hand into a fist, making pain radiate up his wounded arm. He reveled in it, drew strength from it. "Bring me Blood Eye."

CHAPTER 6

The trading post was called Voertmann's
and was run by a Dutchman, as many of
the frontier establishments were. The proprietor was known far and wide as Papa Voertmann. He was fat, jolly, and sported a bushy
white beard to go with his bald head. According to Preacher's friend Audie, who was
a well-educated man, having been a profes-
sor before he came west to take up fur trapping, Papa Voertmann was the spitting image of a character from Dutch folklore
called *Sinter Klaus,* the personification of
the spirit of Christmas.

But you couldn't always go by appear-
ances. Papa Voertmann would cut your
throat if he thought you were trying to cheat
him out of a nickel and laugh that booming
laugh of his while he was doing it. People
on the frontier had learned not to cross him.

Mama Voertmann, his skinny, prune-faced
wife, was even worse. Most mountain men,

after spending months in the Rockies, were hungry for the sight of a white woman, any white woman. A smile and a kind word from her would do wonders for their morale. They never got either of those things from Mama Voertmann. In fact, if they got on her bad side, they were liable to get a knife in the ribs.

Despite referring to each other as Papa and Mama, they had no children that anybody had ever heard anything about, although it was possible there were Voertmann offspring back in Europe that they never mentioned.

Papa kept several sawed-off, double-barreled shotguns stashed around the sprawling trading post, which was also part tavern, so that one of the weapons was almost always within reach. Any time a fight broke out, he didn't discriminate between the man who started it and the one who was defending himself. He just grabbed one of those shotguns and let loose with a double load of rock salt. The salt wouldn't kill a man, but it hurt like hell and generally put him on the ground.

That gave Mama time to break out her pistols, and if the combatants caused any more trouble, she would take more drastic action.

Because of that, things tended to stay pretty peaceful at Voertmann's. It was a good trading post, well-stocked, with fair prices, and hardly anybody ever went blind from drinking the busthead whiskey Papa brewed up.

Preacher reined Horse to a stop in front of the big log building. The pack horse trailing behind him obediently halted as well. Dog bounded up onto the porch while Preacher swung down from the saddle. "Stay," he told the big cur. "You know Mama and Papa don't allow no dogs in there. You try it and they're liable to skin you and cook you up."

Dog's pink tongue lolled out of his mouth. He didn't look impressed. He had taken on bears, wolves, catamounts, even an enraged bull moose, not to mention numerous men who had been trying to do harm to Preacher. He wasn't scared of a fat Dutchie and his harridan of a wife.

Preacher wasn't scared of the Voertmanns, either, but he respected their rules. As Audie had explained it once, barbarians and other men who lived far beyond the raw edge of civilization tended to be polite, because being rude could get them killed in a hurry.

Preacher looped the reins of both horses around a hitch rack. Several other horses were tied up there, which wasn't unusual. The Voertmanns did a pretty steady business. The trading post was located on the rolling plains at the confluence of two streams, and it was only about sixty miles away from the beaver-rich valley known as King's Crown, so a lot of trappers came through there.

A young man matching William Pendexter's description had been seen at Voertmann's by a trapper who was in St. Louis to sell his plews. The young man had been looking for a good place to do some trapping, and somebody had told him about King's Crown. Reportedly, he had headed in that direction when he left the trading post.

The problem was, that had been almost a year earlier. Anything might have happened to William since then, and probably had.

After their argument, Barnabas Pendexter's stiff-necked pride had kept him from looking for his son for a while. His delay had been a dreadful mistake.

Preacher had serious doubts that he would ever find William. The young man was probably dead. The wilderness tended to swallow up the unfortunate as if they had never been there.

Preacher stepped into the trading post's

dim interior, onto the puncheon floor. Shelves made of thick, rough-sawn planks were arranged haphazardly around the big room. With no ceiling, the massive beams that supported the roof were visible. Traps and tack hung from pegs on the walls, as did clothing and buffalo robes. Barrels of salt, flour, sugar, pickles, and crackers stood along the side wall to the right. At the rear of the room was a counter formed by planks lying across more barrels.

Papa Voertmann stood behind the counter. He held a slate in his hand and used a piece of charcoal to do some ciphering, obviously quite a chore for him. The tip of his tongue stuck out the left corner of his mouth and wiggled around as he frowned in thought. Several men stood in front of the counter, evidently waiting for him to finish his figuring.

The white-bearded Dutchman glanced up from the slate, looked between two of his customers, and spotted Preacher. He uttered an exclamation in Dutch and then said, "Preacher! *Ja!* You have come back."

It had been three or four years since Preacher had visited the trading post. Papa hadn't changed a bit in that time, and Preacher supposed he hadn't, either, since the fat old man had recognized him instantly. He grinned and nodded. "Howdy, Papa."

"You must go in the tavern and say hello to Mama." Voertmann pointed to the wide, arched doorway on the left, which led into the tavern area. "You know how fond she is of you."

To the best of Preacher's recollection, Mama Voertmann had never looked at him without wearing an expression like he was something she wanted to scrape off the bottom of her shoe, but she had never tried to stab, shoot, or poison him, either, so he supposed that might mean she was fond of him. He nodded again. "I'll do that before I leave, Papa."

One of the customers loudly tapped his fingertip on the counter. "You're supposed to be waitin' on us, old man, not gabbin' with your friends."

Good Lord, Preacher thought. That fella had to be a stranger in these parts, to talk like that to Papa Voertmann.

"*Och,* so? You are impatient for me to figure up your bill?"

"Just tell us what we owe you, so we can get on about our business. There's beaver out there just waitin' for us to trap and skin 'em."

Papa set the piece of charcoal aside and

picked up a rag. He began to wipe the slate clean. "You will trap these beaver without any assistance from me."

"What the hell does that mean?" demanded the disgruntled customer. He was ugly, with a patchy beard and a nose that had been broken and set badly sometime in the past. The three men with him were much the same sort, although not quite as rough-looking.

"It means," Papa Voertmann said, stiff with offended dignity, "that I will sell you no supplies. Your money is no good here. I will not take payment from louts."

Papa had taken payment from louts — and much worse — before, thought Preacher, but that was when those fellas had treated him with respect.

"Listen here, you damned Dutchie," the loudmouth said. "We need provisions, and there ain't no other place around here to buy 'em!"

Papa sniffed. "You should have thought of that before you spoke so rudely to me, *ja*?"

"I'll do a lot more than speak rude to you!"

The man lunged across the counter and grabbed Voertmann's apron, bunching his fingers up in the canvas. He drew back his other fist and poised it to punch the trading

59

post owner in the face.

Preacher didn't make a move. He knew Papa still had things under control.

As proof of that, the fat, jolly old Dutchman shoved both sawed-off barrels of the scattergun he took from under the counter into the belly of the man holding him and snarled curses in his native tongue. The man's fist stayed where it was, frozen where he had pulled it back for a punch that would never be thrown.

"This gun is loaded with rock salt," Papa went on in English, "but at this range it will blow a hole in your belly anyway, and you will die a slow, agonizing death. I will fire in two seconds if you do not release me."

Broken Nose let go of Papa's apron.

Preacher moved up to the counter, to one side of the four men, and casually leaned an elbow on the planks. He saw that Broken Nose's ugly face was as pale and washed out as could be.

Having the barrels of a scattergun shoved in your belly usually had that effect on a man, Preacher reflected wryly.

Broken Nose's companions had stiffened. One of them edged a hand toward the butt of a pistol. Preacher caught the man's eye, rested his hand on his hunting knife, and slowly shook his head.

The man moved his hand away from the gun.

"You got no call to treat us this way," Broken Nose said in a hollow voice. "We didn't do nothin' to you."

"You insulted me, and you insulted my friend," Papa responded.

"I didn't even say anything to him!"

"I was insulted anyway," Preacher drawled. "Bein' around stupid folks usually has that effect on me. Don't you know who this is?"

The nostrils in that crooked nose flared angrily. "Some Dutchman."

"This is Papa Voertmann. He may look like a friendly ol' soul, but he ain't. He's a touchy hombre who'll skin a man alive if the varmint looks at him sideways. Ain't that right, Papa?"

"Ja," Voertmann said.

"And his wife is even tougher," Preacher went on. "You boys are lucky that she must be busy over in the tavern. If she as in here when you talked to her husband like that, you'd be bleedin' already. Papa's inclined to let you turn around and walk out of here, though. You know why?"

Papa grinned. "I hate scrubbing blood-stains off the floor, *ja!*"

"All right. We'll go," Broken Nose said.

"But this ain't over."

Preacher had heard threats like that so many times they just made him tired. He sighed. "If you've got any sense, it better be."

The four men backed away from the counter, then turned and filed out of the trading post, but not without casting several hate-filled glances over their shoulders.

A few moments later, Preacher heard the drumming hoofbeats of their horses as they rode off. "You got to watch out for idiots like that, Papa. They might come back and try to make trouble."

"Idiots is right," Papa said. "One of them mentioned they were bound for King's Crown. I should have sold them supplies anyway and let them go. A dead man's gold spends as well as any other!"

A frown creased the mountain man's forehead. "What do you mean, a dead man's gold? What's wrong with King's Crown?"

"My friend, you have been away too long! You have not heard of Jebediah Druke?"

Preacher shook his head. "Tell me."

CHAPTER 7

Papa Voertmann told Preacher about Druke over buckets of beer at a table in the tavern while his wife hovered solicitiously nearby. Mama Voertmann might be pure poison to everybody else, but she doted on her big, magnificently bearded husband.

"This man Druke, I remember him stopping here on his way to the mountains," Papa said. "He caused no trouble, but I remember when I looked at him, a chill went through me. Something about his eyes, I think it was. They were cold and dead . . . like a snake's eyes. He frightened me. Me!"

Preacher agreed that that reaction was astonishing. Papa Voertmann might look fat and soft, but in reality he was one of the toughest men Preacher had ever known.

"*Ja,* me as well," Mama Voertmann put in, which was even more amazing. Preacher figured the feisty little woman would spit in the eye of Satan himself. If Jebediah Druke had scared her, he had to be really bad.

"The men with him were much the same," Voertmann went on. "But he was definitely the leader and they were followers. They stopped, bought a few supplies, had a few drinks in the tavern, and then moved on. I sighed a big sigh of relief when they rode away!"

Mama nodded solemnly to indicate that she had, too.

"They said they were headed for King's Crown?" Preacher asked.

"*Ja.* Druke mentioned that he had heard how plentiful the beaver were there. They planned to make a fortune trapping. In that respect, he and his friends were no different from hundreds of other men who have stopped here."

"What's happened since then?"

Voertmann lifted the bucket to his mouth, took a big swallow of beer, then wiped his mouth and beard with a corner of his apron. "About a month after that, a couple trappers came through here on their way back east. One of them had a broken arm. They had been in King's Crown, and they'd had some sort of trouble with Druke. He broke the man's arm in a fight. Then he and his friends pointed their guns at the trappers and told them that if they didn't leave the valley right away, they were dead men. They fled, leaving behind their traps, the pelts they had taken, and everything else. They were genuinely afraid for their lives, I could tell."

Preacher frowned. "Mountain men generally don't stand for things like that."

"Of course not. As Druke continued trying to run roughshod over the other men in the valley, some of them fought back." Voertmann paused. "Those men vanished as if they had fallen off the face of the earth. Each time that happened, the other trappers in the valley were less inclined to stand up to Druke and his heavy-handed tactics."

Preacher took a drink of beer and mulled over what Papa had just told him. For several reasons, he didn't like the sound of it. He didn't cotton to bullies, and that's what Jebediah Druke was, beyond a shadow of a doubt. Nor did he like it when folks allowed themselves to be bullied because they were scared. He could sympathize with them to a certain extent, he supposed, but he couldn't comprehend it.

There was no backup in his nature. When somebody struck at him, he hit back, harder and faster. That was just the way he had always been. "So this has been goin' on ever since?"

65

"*Ja,* some seven or eight months now. Some of the men in the valley Druke didn't run off. He must have been able to tell that they were kindred spirits, so he recruited them. Now he has more than a dozen men following him. One trapper told me they have built cabins and formed a little stronghold they call Fort Druke."

Preacher snorted. That sounded damned silly to him. He supposed it wasn't so silly to the honest trappers in the valley who were menaced by Druke and his cohorts.

"Druke says that King's Crown belongs to him now," Papa Voertmann went on. "He has made himself king, and the mountains are his crown."

"We'll just see about —" Preacher started to say.

When he stopped, Papa frowned in puzzlement. "What were you about to say, Preacher? Are you going to confront this evil man?"

That was Preacher's first impulse, all right. He would have liked to go into King's Crown, get the honest trappers together, and deal with the threat of Jebediah Druke once and for all. He had been forced to do such things before, to take action and stand up for what was right.

At the moment, though, he had another

job taking him to the valley known as King's Crown. He had taken Barnabas Pendexter's money to outfit himself for the journey, so the only honest thing for him to do was to carry out the mission he had been given.

Once that was done, though . . .

"Let me ask you about somebody else, Papa." Preacher described Pendexter's missing son. "He would have come through these parts a few months before Druke did. A young man in his early twenties. Tall, sort of good-looking, I suppose, with brown hair. He would have looked like a greenhorn, because that's exactly what he was. Oh, and he has a birthmark on the back of his neck, shaped like a half moon."

Voertmann's chair creaked a little under his great weight as he leaned back and spread his hands. "What can I tell you, Preacher? There might have been dozens of men who fit that description in this trading post in the past year. I cannot remember them all."

"What about you, Mama?" Preacher asked.

She pursed her lips and shook her head. "Like Papa says, there are too many trappers. Too many young men who think they will journey west and become rich. If they make no trouble, we take their money and they move on, and I have no memory of them."

Preacher sighed and nodded. "That's what I was afraid of, but I didn't figure it would hurt to ask."

Papa said, "This young man you seek, does he have a name?"

"William Pendexter."

Papa thought about it and shook his head again. "The name means nothing to me. Why are you searching for him?"

"His father hired me to look for him," Preacher said. That wasn't exactly true. Barnabas Pendexter had grubstaked him, rather than paying wages or promising a reward, but the end result was the same.

Papa smiled, "Ah, a boy who runs away from home seeking adventure! It was much like that with me, you know."

"Nope, I didn't."

"When I was young, I left my home and ran away to sea." A shudder went through Voertmann's big frame. "A horrible, horrible mistake. Such an existence a naïve young lad should never have to endure. But in the end it was worth it, I suppose. I left the ship in New York and met a beautiful young girl."

Preacher grinned. "Mama, I do believe you're blushin'."

She glared back at him. "Mind your tongue, *Arthur.*"

Preacher looked down at the table and muttered, "Yes'm." Hardly anybody west of Ohio ever used his real name anymore. Only a handful of folks even knew it. And only Mama Voertmann could make it sound so much like a threat.

"Her family had been there for many years," Papa went on. "New York was once called New Amsterdam, did you know that?"

"Seems like I recollect Audie sayin' something like that one time."

"Ah, the little man. Is he well?"

"Last time I saw him, he was fine and dandy. Him and Nighthawk both."

"And the Indian, as talkative as ever, I suppose?"

Preacher had to grin again. Nighthawk seldom said anything except "Umm," but that was enough for him and Audie to carry on long conversations.

"Yep, I reckon. I'll run into 'em again one of these days, I expect. Wouldn't mind havin' them with me when I go into King's Crown, but I don't reckon that's meant to be."

"You are going there?" Papa asked with a look of concern. "After everything I told you about Druke?"

"Somebody told William Pendexter's pa that the boy came through here on his way to King's Crown, so I reckon that's where I need to start lookin' for him."

Papa shook his head gloomily. "If this young man was still there when Druke and his minions arrived, there is a good chance he is dead now, Preacher. If he was as inexperienced as you say, he would have been no match for them. Even a man such as yourself —" Voertmann stopped short.

It was Preacher's turn to ask, "What were you about to say, Papa?"

Reluctantly, Voertmann answered. "I mean no offense, but even a man such as yourself may not be a match for a dozen or more killers led by a man like Jebediah Druke."

Preacher took another drink of beer and licked the foam from his mustache. "Reckon there's a good chance we might find out."

CHAPTER 8

Preacher spent most of the afternoon at the trading post. Late in the day, he loaded up the supplies he had bought, swung up into Horse's saddle, and rode west along the stream that led toward the mountains. He didn't go far before making camp in a grove of aspens about half a mile from the Voertmann place.

He could have spent the night at the trading post, but if the weather was good, he preferred to be out in the open rather than having a roof over his head.

After unsaddling Horse and picketing the stallion and the pack animal, he built a small fire to brew some coffee and cook his supper. Even though he didn't expect any trouble, he was in the habit of not having a fire after dark unless absolutely necessary, so he ate his supper and extinguished the flames while dusk was still settling down over the prairie.

He stretched out on his bedroll and watched through the branches of the aspens as the sky darkened and the stars began to appear overhead. There was no telling how many nights he had watched the same spectacular display without ever tiring of it. He was that rarest of creatures — a man utterly content with his life.

He was in no hurry to leave it, of course, and yet if it ended tonight, he knew he would die without any regrets, without mourning for things left undone. He had loved some good women. He had enjoyed the company of the best friends a man could ever have. He had lived his life on his own terms, doing the things he loved to do. He had stood in the high places and gazed out on breathtaking beauty, and he had breathed deeply of the clean mountain air. Nothing on earth lasts forever, he thought, but he had the satisfaction of knowing that none of his deeds had been done in vain. When he was gone, the world might soon forget him, but his life had meant something, if only to him.

He grinned in the gathering darkness, put the philosophical woolgathering aside, and rolled over to go to sleep with his head on his saddle.

He had barely closed his eyes when he

heard the shots.

Preacher sat up. Without even thinking about it, the two flintlock pistols he had placed beside his bedroll were in his hands, his thumbs looping over the hammers to pull them back. He listened intently for a couple seconds.

There had been two shots, but that was all. They came from the direction of the trading post. That didn't have to mean anything. Wolves roamed the plains sometimes. Papa Voertmann could have taken a couple potshots at some lobo skulking around the pens where the milk cow and her calves, the chickens, and the pigs were.

Preacher shook his head. The problem with that idea was that if a wolf came within a mile of where he was, Horse or Dog or both would have scented it and alerted him.

Dog had been out roaming the night, as usual. He padded up out of the darkness, stood tensely near Preacher, and growled deep in his throat. Preacher and the big cur had been trail partners for so long that the mountain man could understand Dog's growls almost as well as if they had been words.

It wasn't the sort of growl Dog would have let out if there was a wild animal that might be a threat somewhere nearby. The deep, rumbling noise warned of a different sort of predator.

Man.

Preacher let the hammers down on the pistols and came to his feet in a smooth, uncoiling motion. He picked up the belt to which his sheathed knife was attached and quickly tied it around his waist, then tucked the pistols and his tomahawk behind it. He picked up his rifle and his hat. He still wore his high-topped boot moccasins.

Horse and the pack animal would stay there. Preacher said quietly, "Come on, Dog," and headed toward the trading post in a ground-eating lope.

He could have gotten there quicker riding the stallion, of course, but running was quieter and instinct told him that stealth might be important.

Preacher was barely breathing hard as he approached the log building. Candles were burning inside; he could see the dancing yellow glow through the windows where the shutters were open. His keen eyes made out several large, dark shapes in front of the building that he recognized as horses tied up at the hitch rack.

It was unusual for travelers to stop at the trading post after dark, but not completely unheard of. That pair of shots put a whole

74

different face on things, though. It was barely possible that Papa Voertmann had gotten spooked for some reason and fired a couple warning shots when the riders came up, but Preacher didn't really believe that.

He believed it even less when the door opened and a man-shaped patch of darkness was visible for a second. The man stepped outside and pulled the door closed behind him, but didn't go to the horses, which meant he was lurking on the porch.

Standing watch, more than likely, Preacher thought.

Somebody was up to no good inside.

He could make out four horses, and that matched the number of men who had been there earlier. The possibility that Broken Nose and his friends had returned to the trading post to cause trouble for the Voertmanns came as no surprise. Preacher had been able to tell that they were sorry troublemakers just by looking at them.

He used the trees and bushes along the stream as cover and blended into the shadows. He was able to slip into a Blackfoot camp, cut the throats of several of his enemies, and get back out again without anybody knowing he had been there until the bodies were discovered the next morning. That had led the Indians to dub him

Ghost Killer.

Sneaking up on one white man who'd probably been drinking . . . well, that was something Preacher could have done in his sleep.

Minutes later, he crouched at the end of the porch as he looked along its length. The guard leaned against the rough log wall near the door, deep in the shadows underneath the thatched awning. Preacher's night vision was so good it was almost supernatural, so he didn't have any trouble seeing the man.

Loud, angry voices came from inside the building, clearly audible through the open windows. A voice he recognized as that of Broken Nose harshly ordered, "Shut up all the foreign jabberin'! If you want to cuss me, do it in English."

"*Ja,* I will curse you." Papa Voertmann's voice sounded like he was in pain. "And I will kill you if you harm Mama. I will strip the skin from you inch by inch, so that you take a long time dying, you —" He lapsed into cursing in his native language again.

Broken Nose laughed. "Don't worry, old man. We ain't gonna molest your wife. She's too ancient and ugly and dried up for that. We'll just cut her throat and kill her quick, but not until she's watched us beat you to

76

death. Hang on to him, both of you, while I see if I can put some blood in that white beard of his."

Papa Voertmann had to be wounded, Preacher thought. Otherwise even two men wouldn't be able to hold him. If he was at full strength he would have cracked those two varmints' heads together and busted their skulls, then broken the other man's back to go with his busted nose.

Preacher heard the thud of bone against flesh and Mama scream. He didn't know which of the Voertmanns Broken Nose had just hit, but it didn't matter. It had gone on long enough.

He slid the tomahawk from behind his belt, pulled back his arm, and let fly. The weapon made a faint noise as it whirled through the air, then a soggy thud sounded as the sharp stone head embedded itself in the guard's skull.

The man grunted, folded up, and died without another sound. His friends inside the trading post would have no idea that he was dead.

Preacher bounded lithely onto the porch. He leaned the long-barreled flintlock rifle against the wall and drew his pistols. A couple long-legged steps took him to the door. He stepped over the dead man and

77

raised the latch. The door swung open, its leather hinges creaking faintly.

Broken Nose heard the sound and paused with his fist drawn back, much as he had that afternoon when Papa had stuck the shotgun in his belly. Some of the blows had already fallen. The man's knuckles were smeared with blood, and Preacher saw crimson splattered through the snowy expanse of Papa's beard.

"Snyder, I told you to keep an eye out," Broken Nose snapped as he turned his head to look over his shoulder at the door. "What are you —" He stopped short and his eyes widened in surprise and sudden fear as he saw the tall, grim-faced mountain man standing there, a cocked pistol in each hand.

Preacher waited a second, just long enough for Broken Nose to realize what was about to happen and who was going to do it.

Then he pulled the right-hand gun's trigger.

CHAPTER 9

The pistol's boom echoed against the low ceiling as smoke and flame gushed from the muzzle. One of the balls struck Broken Nose about an inch and a half above that prominent feature, in the center of his forehead. It shattered bone and bored on through into his brain. The other ball ripped into his throat, severed an artery, and caused blood to spurt in a bright red stream that arced out several feet in front of his body.

Already dead, the man stood there for a second as wildly spasming nerves and muscles made him jitter grotesquely before he collapsed.

Preacher pointed the left-hand pistol at the two men who held Papa Voertmann's arms. Papa wore a nightshirt, an indication that he had already turned in when the intruders arrived. A large bloodstain soaked the front.

Mama Voertmann, also in her night-clothes, sat on the floor a few feet away, propped up against a barrel. Her wrists and ankles were tied with strips of rawhide pulled so tight they cut cruelly into her flesh.

The two men holding Papa stared in shock at Preacher, who told them, "You boys help him sit down. He's hurt."

The man on Papa's left swallowed hard and said to his companion, "His other gun's empty now. He can't shoot both of us."

"That's true, I can't," Preacher agreed in a mocking drawl. "But I can sure kill one of you. When you fellas figure out which one it's gonna be, you let me know, hear?"

The man on the right raised his chin. "He can't risk a shot, not with us bein' so close to this big whale."

A laugh rumbled out of Papa Voertmann. "Do you know who this is? This is Preacher! The best shot on the frontier, or anywhere else! He can kill you in the blink of an eye. Go ahead, Preacher. Shoot one of them, and I will break the other in half!"

"Just as soon not kill anybody else tonight if I don't have to," Preacher said. "There's already enough blood on the floor to clean up."

That was true. A large puddle of the red stuff surrounded Broken Nose's head as he lay motionless on the puncheons.

Preacher went on. "I reckon there'll be a mess on the front porch, too. Fella out there's got his head stove in with a tomahawk, so there's probably some brains mixed in with the blood. Sorry about the extra work, Papa."

A grin curved Voertmann's lips where the crimson-spattered beard wreathed them, but Preacher could tell that the big man was weakening. Judging by the stain on Papa's nightshirt, he had lost quite a bit of blood from his wound.

"Perhaps we should let these two live and force them to clean it up, *ja*?"

The one on his left growled, "You go to hell, old man!" and leaped to the side. He clawed at the pistol behind his belt as he tried to reach the cover of a nearby barrel.

Preacher turned slightly to track the man with his pistol, but it wasn't that difficult a shot. The gun boomed and both balls slammed into the man's torso and spun him off his feet. He crashed into the sturdy barrel and bounced off, then sprawled on his back on the floor as blood welled from the wounds.

The last man tried to duck behind Papa and use the big Dutchman as a human shield while he dragged out his pistol. That

81

proved to be a mistake. Papa threw himself backward and his weight drove the man against one of the shelves. They went down with a huge crash and clatter and landed in the welter of pots and pans that spilled off the shelves.

Preacher stepped over to the trapper quickly, bent down, and wrenched the pistol out of the man's hand. Papa rolled over, used his bulk to keep the man pinned to the floor, and locked hamlike hands around his throat. He didn't waste time choking the man to death. He just heaved and snapped the luckless varmint's neck. The man twitched a few times and then went still.

Preacher tucked his pistols away and pulled his hunting knife from its sheath. Carefully, he worked the point under the rawhide strips around Mama Voertmann's wrists and ankles and sawed through the bonds. She cursed up a storm in her native tongue as blood flowed back into her extremities.

Preacher then knelt beside Papa Voertmann. "How bad are you hurt, Papa?"

"I don't know." Papa's shoulders slumped wearily. "The one with the broken nose shot me."

"I figured as much. Let's get you to your bed."

Mama Voertmann appeared at her husband's side. She packed a surprising amount of strength in her wiry little body, so she was able to help Preacher lift Papa to his feet and steer him toward the canvas-curtained door that led into their living quarters. The mountain man still had to do most of the work, but he was grateful for Mama's help.

Papa settled onto the corn-shuck mattress on the massive four-poster bed he had built himself. He groaned. "I will get blood on your sheets, Mama."

"Don't trouble yourself about that, old man," she told him. She lifted his nightshirt. "We must see how badly you are hurt."

"Mama . . . have you no decency?"

"Oh, shush. The wound doesn't look too deep. Preacher, go in the tavern and fetch back a jug."

"Yes, ma'am."

They spent the next fifteen minutes cleaning and bandaging the hole where a pistol ball had ripped through Papa's side. Preacher could tell by the angle that the ball hadn't penetrated deeply enough to do any significant damage. The worst thing had been the blood that Papa had lost, and he would recover from that. Mama would see to it that the wound didn't fester.

When Preacher was convinced that the woman had things under control, he went back out into the trading post's main room and commenced to dragging out the corpses. He considered throwing them into the hog pen but decided against it. He wouldn't want to accidentally poison the hogs.

He had planned on getting an early start the next morning, but he supposed he could tarry at the trading post long enough to dig a shallow mass grave.

William Pendexter had been missing for a year already. The likelihood of a few more hours making a difference was pretty small.

Before Preacher buried the four men the next morning, he went through their possibles in an attempt to find out who they were. A couple had letters from back east among their belongings. Preacher gave them to Mama Voertmann, who promised that she would have Papa write to the families and let them know that their relatives had been killed out on the frontier. It wouldn't be necessary to go into detail about those deaths. Papa could afford to be generous and spare the families' feelings since he ended up with the dead men's horses and belongings to sell.

As for the other two, if they had any kinfolk, they would just have to wonder what had happened to the men when they never came back.

After the burying was done, Preacher and Mama stood on the trading post's porch. The woman sighed. "It is hard to believe that such terrible men have loved ones who cared for them. But I suppose everyone has a family at one time, *ja*?"

"I reckon. Don't lose any sleep over them bein' dead, Mama. It was their own choice to turn around and come back. They could've just kept ridin'. And don't forget they planned to kill you and Papa."

"Oh, I will lose no sleep, I assure you, Preacher. I would have gladly killed them myself, had I the opportunity." Her stern face softened slightly, the first time Preacher had ever seen that happen when she spoke to anybody other than Papa. "You saved our lives. We can never repay you. You are like a son to us now."

Preacher wasn't sure he could stand the sight of Mama Voertmann getting sentimental. "I count that as an honor, Mama. But now I got to be ridin' on. Say so long to Papa for me, would you?"

Voertmann was still in bed as he recuperated from his injury. Preacher had looked in

85

on him earlier and seen that while Papa looked stronger, it would be a while before he was up and around again. Preacher would have offered to stay and help run the trading post until Papa was on his feet again, but he had that job to do for Barnabas Pendexter.

"I will tell him," Mama promised. "You will stop here if you come back this way?"

"Sure. I always do when I'm in these parts."

"You never stay in one place for long, though, do you?"

"Not if I can help it," Preacher replied with a grin.

He had fetched Horse and the pack animal back to the trading post the night before, and they were both ready to go. Preacher swung up into the saddle, and Dog bounded off along the river, eager to be on the trail again.

"Preacher . . ." Mama Voertmann's voice trailed off.

"What is it?"

"You are still going to King's Crown in search of that young man?"

"I said I'd do it, so I've got it to do."

"Those men" — she gestured at the mound of freshly turned dirt about fifty yards away — "were bad. But they were nothing compared to Jebediah Druke. You hear me, Preacher? You be careful in that valley."

"I will, Mama."

As he turned the stallion toward the mountains, he thought that anybody who could strike fear into the heart of Mama Voertmann had to be more monster than man.

CHAPTER 10

The three novice trappers, Mitchell, Pennington, and Burton, moved their camp on the night of their encounter with Jebediah Druke, as Will Gardner had suggested. For the next couple days, Will stayed with them and helped them run their trap lines, although Gray Otter was seldom seen.

"Don't you have your own traps to tend to?" Mitchell asked Will as the four men walked along a stream, rifles over their shoulders. It was a glorious day in the high country.

"Gray Otter will take care of them," Will explained. "We don't do as much trapping as some, just enough to get by. You see, we're not trying to get rich."

Burton grunted. "Then why in God's name would you come to this Godforsaken wilderness in the first place? The possibility of getting rich is the only reason I can think of for enduring such hardship."

"It's a hardship to spend your days in some of the most beautiful country on earth?" Will responded with a smile. "Take a look around, Mr. Burton. Majestic, snow-capped peaks, tall pine trees, wildflowers blooming in the meadows, sunlight spar-kling on the river, the clearest air you'll ever breathe . . . what could be more lovely than these surroundings?"

"You sound like an educated man, Will," Pennington said. "Surely you miss civiliza-tion."

Will shook his head. "Why should I? I have everything I need, right here in King's Crown."

Burton shook his head, obviously unable to comprehend how anyone could feel that way. Will didn't mind. He was used to traveling his own path and having people not understand why he would do so.

"What do you think we should do about Druke?" Mitchell asked. "He and his men are bound to show up again one of these days. If he's determined to take over the entire valley, he can't let people get away with standing up to him."

"We didn't stand up to him," Burton pointed out. "This young man and his Indian friend did."

"But we're still alive and we've still got

89

our pelts," Pennington said. "That's got to annoy Druke."

"More important, he'll worry that it makes him look weak in the eyes of his men, and in the eyes of the other trappers still here in King's Crown," Will said. "To be honest, the smartest thing for you gentlemen to do is get out while you still can. Take the pelts you have and head back east."

"That's not enough for us to break even on the trip," Burton protested. "If we go back now, we'll be failures."

"You'll be alive," Will said. "I think that will mean more to your families than anything else."

Burton shook his head stubbornly. "You don't know my wife. We're not abandoning what we set out to do. Isn't that right, men?" He looked at Pennington and Mitchell.

Pennington's doubtful expression said that maybe he thought Will's idea of leaving King's Crown was a good one.

But Mitchell said, "I reckon we can stay around a while longer and see how things go."

Pennington didn't argue with that sentiment.

"If that's the way you feel, it's your decision to make," Will said. "In that case, I can give you some advice. Somebody needs to be standing guard all the time. I mean around the clock. If you're working on your trap line, then two men handle the traps while the third watches for any trouble. The same thing goes for sleeping. One man should always be awake and alert. Don't have a fire at night —"

"I think we learned that lesson," Mitchell put in.

"And don't camp out in the open," Will went on. "Find some rocks or trees that will give you cover if you have to fort up. Any place you consider as a possible campsite, ask yourself how well it can be defended."

Burton said, "We haven't been standing guard all the time since the run-in with Druke."

"Somebody has been, either me or Gray Otter. You just didn't realize it."

Mitchell chuckled. "Let me guess. Gray Otter is watching us right now *and* keeping an eye out for Druke. We just can't see him. Is that right?"

Will smiled. "That's about the size of it."

Pennington asked, "We can't talk the two of you into throwing in with us permanently, can we?"

"I'm afraid not. We have our own things we need to do. We'll be somewhere here in the valley, but King's Crown is a big place. Chances are we won't be close enough to help if you run into Druke and his men again."

"It's a chance we'll have to take," Burton said with grim determination.

"So be it."

Later that day, Will took his leave of the trappers. He shook hands with each of them and wished them luck before he rode off. He didn't know if he would ever see them again.

He wished he didn't believe that possibility was quite as doubtful as he did.

An hour or so after riding off, Will reined in as another figure on horseback emerged from a thick stand of trees and came toward him. A smile spread across his face as he recognized the slim, buckskin-clad rider. "I thought I'd run into you around here. You kept an eye on those three for a while after I left them, didn't you?"

Gray Otter didn't answer that directly, but replied, "No sign of Druke or any of his men. They're lying low after what happened to them."

"But it won't stay that way."

"No," Gray Otter agreed. "It won't."

"We've done what we can for now. I think we ought to head for the cave and lie low for a while ourselves."

Gray Otter nodded.

The cave Will mentioned was as close to a home as they had in King's Crown. It was fairly high on the slope of one of the mountains and hard to spot. As far as they knew, they were the only ones who were aware of its existence. It made a good hiding place from Druke.

They heeled their horses into motion and rode toward the cave. Will couldn't help but smile as he thought about what was waiting for them there.

Sam Turner hadn't prayed since he was a kid and his ma had dragged him to services in the little country church not far from the Turner farm back in Virginia. He had never seen much evidence of God in their ramshackle cabin, nor in the beatings he'd received from his drunken, no-account father, even though the old man always claimed that he was trying to beat the Devil out of young Sam.

After he'd finally had enough of it, stuck a pitchfork in the drunkard's belly one night, and ran away from home, he didn't see any point in asking for help from somebody he figured wasn't there to hear him in the first place. Even if God was up there somewhere in Heaven, the hard-hearted ol' skinflint didn't listen to prayers from the likes of Sam Turner.

It was only after Druke had sent him out alone to look for Blood Eye that Turner realized maybe God had given him the courage and strength to kill his pa and leave. He'd started praying for courage again, and for God to watch over him so that damned heathen didn't kill him.

Turner hadn't slept a wink the night before, he was sure of that. His eyes wouldn't close. They'd stared into the darkness as he'd searched for any movement.

Exhaustion gripped him in the morning, but he forced himself to keep going. Nobody knew where Blood Eye could be found at any particular time, of course; the renegade Crow was like a phantom, able to turn up anywhere without warning.

According to Druke, Blood Eye's home, if he had one, was up the narrow canyon that cut into the mountains forming King's Crown. Just ride up the canyon, Druke had told Turner, and sooner or later Blood Eye would find him.

What Druke hadn't said, but what Turner knew, was that the loco redskin might kill him on a whim. Nobody knew why Blood Eye spared some people and others he strung up and put through hell itself before he finally killed them.

Some connection existed between Druke and Blood Eye, but Turner didn't know what it was. He suspected the two of them had worked together in the past, before Turner became part of Druke's gang. All Turner knew for sure was that Blood Eye had shown up in King's Crown not long after Druke and had come out of the canyon from time to time to help the gang get rid of some particularly stubborn opposition.

Blood Eye probably murdered other trappers from time to time, whether Druke told him to or not. It wouldn't surprise Turner to find out that Blood Eye even *ate* his victims, like some sort of wild animal.

He moaned as that thought went through his head. He imagined himself winding up in Blood Eye's belly. Would the renegade cook him, or just tear his flesh from his bones and gobble it down raw?

He rode past one of the big slabs of rock that littered the canyon floor as that ghastly image haunted his mind. With no warning, something slammed into his back and side and knocked him off the horse. Turner hit the ground so hard it knocked all the breath out of his body and stunned him.

He couldn't put up a fight or even squeal

in terror as his attacker rolled him onto his back and put a knife at his throat. Turner knew he was about to die, but couldn't do a blasted thing about it.

His eyes widened as he gazed up at the figure looming over him. He had seen Blood Eye before, so the Indian's appearance didn't come as a complete shock to him. It was the first time he had ever been so close, though.

Blood Eye wore a single feather that stuck up at an angle from his thick black hair. His high-cheekboned, heavily pitted face looked like it might have been hacked out of red sandstone. His nose seemed as sharp as an ax blade. His thin-lipped mouth drew a grim line across the lower part of his face.

Turner found himself staring at the feature that gave the renegade his name. The white man couldn't tear his own eyes away from it.

The Indian's right eye had been injured in battle when he was a young warrior, causing the eyeball to turn red. The dead black pupil was surrounded by crimson. Blood Eye couldn't see anything out of that blind orb, but the other eye worked just fine. He saw plenty well enough to kill.

Turner realized that he had stopped breathing. Afraid to move even a fraction of an inch, he knew if he did, Blood Eye's knife would slash his throat and it would all be over.

Instead, Blood Eye lifted the knife away from Turner's skin and grunted. "Druke's man."

Involuntarily, Turner gasped for air.

When he trusted himself to talk, he said, "That . . . that's right. Druke sent me. He . . . he wanted me to find you . . . or rather, for you to find me . . . so I can take you back to him."

"I know where Druke is." Blood Eye spoke passable English, although his voice was so guttural he was difficult to understand. "I know where everything and everyone is in this valley."

"Yeah, I . . . I don't doubt it."

Blood Eye put his left hand on Turner's chest and pushed himself to his feet. With his right hand, he slid the knife back into its sheath.

Turner knew better than to ask the renegade for a hand up. Blood Eye might cut it off, instead. Turner rolled onto his side and clambered upright. His horse had dashed away about fifty yards along the canyon floor, he saw.

"What does Druke want with me?" Blood Eye asked.

Turner's pulse still raced. Blood pounded in his head. Just being close to the renegade caused that. He swallowed. "I reckon he wants you to kill somebody."

"Who?"

"A trapper named Will Gardner, and Gardner's friend, an Injun called Gray Otter. You know them?"

Blood Eye really surprised Turner then.

He smiled.

"I know who they are," Blood Eye said. "They move like the night wind through the trees. You see the proof that they are there, but you cannot see them."

Turner figured Blood Eye meant you knew when Gardner and Gray Otter were around because men got hurt, but you never saw where the arrows and the rifle balls came from. That described it pretty well, all right.

"They're causin' more and more trouble," Turner said. "You reckon you could, uh, get rid of 'em for us?"

"Why would I do that?"

"Because you and Druke are . . . I dunno. Friends?"

Blood Eye shook his head. "I have no friends. But I will come and talk to Druke about this. I would not mind killing this Gardner."

Turner knew he might be pushing his luck, but he was scared of Jebediah Druke, too, and wanted everything to work out to the boss's satisfaction. "What about Gray Otter?"

Blood Eye's smile widened, but that didn't make Turner feel any better. A harsh laugh came from the renegade. "I have plans of my own for Gray Otter."

Turner had no idea what Blood Eye meant by that, but he was absolutely certain of one thing.

He wouldn't have wanted to be Gray Otter, not for all the beaver pelts west of the Mississippi.

CHAPTER 11

Jebediah Druke's wounded arm still throbbed a little every time he moved it, a frequent reminder of just how much he hated Will Gardner and Gray Otter and wanted to settle the score with them. Sam Turner had been gone for a couple days. Druke waited impatiently for his lieutenant to return, although he knew there was no way of telling how long it might take him to find Blood Eye.

That damned renegade was everywhere . . . and nowhere, Druke mused as he sat in his cabin and drank from a jug of whiskey. Nobody found Blood Eye unless the Crow wanted to be found.

Druke hoped Blood Eye wouldn't take the notion to kill Turner. It might happen that way, and Druke knew it. So did Turner. That was probably why Turner looked so walleyed when he left the crude little settlement.

The door, slightly askew on its leather hinges, stood partially open. Druke heard footsteps approaching the cabin. He lowered the jug he had raised to his mouth and set it to one side on the table. He rested his hand on the loaded pistol in front of him as a shadow appeared in the doorway.

Vargas paused in the opening. A Spaniard, he had already been in King's Crown when Druke arrived and had volunteered to join up as soon as he saw the handwriting on the wall. Druke recognized that Vargas was tough and didn't have an ounce of mercy in him, so he'd agreed to take the Spaniard into the gang.

"Creighton just rode back in, boss." Vargas spoke good English having spent more than ten years in America, most of it as a fur trapper out on the frontier.

"Did he find anything?" Druke had sent Creighton, as well as several other men, out to look for Will Gardner and Gray Otter. He wanted to know where to find them when the time came to strike back.

"Says he did," Vargas drawled.

Druke scowled and reached for the jug again. "Well, don't just stand there," he snapped. "Go get him and bring him here."

"Just wanted to make sure you weren't resting before I disturbed you, boss. What

101

with you being hurt and all, you know."

Druke growled. "Get Creighton."

Vargas disappeared from the doorway, returning a minute later with a tall, lean figure in buckskins. Matthew Creighton had a long, thin face made to seem even longer by the pointed goatee he wore. He had been a lawyer somewhere back east before he came west.

A crooked lawyer, Druke suspected, but he never pressed any of his men for details about their past. That was their business.

Druke pushed the jug across the table toward the newcomer. "Have a drink first, then tell me what you found, Creighton."

The outlaw picked up the jug, tipped it to his mouth, and took a swallow. The busthead burned like fire as it went down, but Creighton never showed any sign of discomfort. "Gardner and the Indian are holed up in a cave in the side of a mountain about ten miles from here."

"Can you find the place again?"

"Of course." Creighton paused. "But there's no guarantee they'll still be there when you decide to make a move against them, Jebediah."

"Let me worry about that." Druke growled.

"That's not all," Creighton said. "They

have a woman with them."

Druke leaned forward in sudden interest. Vargas had stopped in the doorway and casually leaned a shoulder against the jamb, but he stood up straight when he heard Creighton's words.

"A woman," Druke repeated.

"Well . . . a squaw. But a very attractive one. I spotted her when she came out of the cave to fetch water this morning, wearing only a loin cloth. That left no doubt as to her gender, although I wasn't close enough to make out any other details, even with the spyglass I was using. I couldn't afford to get too close to them because I didn't want Gray Otter to realize they were being followed."

"Where'd the woman come from?" Druke asked.

"She must have been waiting there for Gardner and Gray Otter. I followed them to the cave yesterday evening, just as it was getting dark. I waited overnight to make sure they weren't going to pull out early this morning, but I didn't see either of them, just the woman. When it seemed likely that they weren't leaving the place today, I got back here as fast as I could."

Druke nodded slowly as he considered Creighton's report. He wasn't confident that his enemies would stay at that cave for more than a day or two. Gardner and Gray Otter probably had similar hideouts scattered all over King's Crown.

But the knowledge that they had a woman with them was new, and it might turn out to be important. A woman represented a potential weakness, and Druke made a habit of using every possible weakness against his adversaries.

"Good work," he told Creighton, then looked past the scout at Vargas. "When Turner gets back with Blood Eye, you bring them straight here to me, no matter what time of day or night it is or what I'm doing, you understand that?"

"Sure, boss," Vargas agreed. He looked a little uncomfortable at the mention of Blood Eye, as did Creighton.

Druke didn't really blame them for feeling that way. He had never seen anybody scarier than that damned renegade.

Unless maybe it was himself.

When Creighton was gone, Vargas lingered. "There's something else we need to talk about, boss."

"What's that?" Druke had had enough whiskey, and his arm hurt enough, that he was starting to get surly again.

"Those three trappers we tried to run out

a few days ago, they're still here in the valley."

Druke frowned. "They didn't light out when they had the chance?"

"No, they're still running their trap lines. Having Gardner and Gray Otter save their bacon must've made them bold."

"Well, that was a damned mistake." Druke thought about handling the situation himself, then decided it would probably be a good idea to let his arm heal some more before he used it for anything too strenuous. "Take some men, Vargas, and show them how wrong they were."

"You mean —"

"I mean kill them," Druke said. "No warnings this time. Just kill them and fetch their load of pelts back here."

He reached for the jug of whiskey as Vargas nodded and left the cabin. Things were looking a little better. As soon as Will Gardner and Gray Otter were taken care of, there wouldn't be anything standing in the way of him ruling over King's Crown as he was destined to do.

Enos Mitchell, John Burton, and Carl Pennington had taken Will Gardner's advice to heart ever since the young man had parted company with them the day before. One of

105

them had been on guard the whole time. They took turns studying the landscape around them as they held a rifle ready to fire if need be.

At the moment, Burton was the sentry while Mitchell and Pennington worked a beaver carcass loose from one of the traps they had set up at the edge of a fast-flowing stream. The former law clerk turned his head from side to side as he stood on the bank with his long-barreled flintlock rifle slanted across his chest. Through narrowed eyes, he searched the wooded hills around them for any sign of movement.

"This is the fourth beaver we've gotten today," Pennington said. "I think we're gettin' better at this, fellas."

"Another month or so and we ought to have a decent load of pelts to sell," Mitchell said. "Should we take 'em all the way back to St. Louis or try to sell them at one of the fur company outposts?"

Burton said, "The prices are better in St. Louis."

"But it's a long way," Mitchell said. "And once we're there, it'd be mighty tempting not to come back."

Pennington said, "I'm not sure there's anything wrong with that. This whole trip has been a lot harder than I expected it to be. More dangerous, too."

Burton snorted. "There's a reason it's called the frontier, Carl. You can't expect all the comforts of civilization out here."

"Maybe not, but you expected that varmint Druke to follow the rule of law," Mitchell pointed out.

"Someday there'll be law and order out here," Burton insisted. "You can count on that. It's inevitable."

"Can't be soon enough to suit me," Pennington said as he stepped up onto the bank. "I —"

His sentence went unfinished as a rifle blasted somewhere in the trees. Pennington jerked back as a dark, red-rimmed hole suddenly appeared in the center of his forehead. With his arms flung out to the sides, he toppled over backward into the stream with a huge splash that sent glittering drops of water sailing high into the air.

CHAPTER 12

Preacher heard the sudden outburst of gunfire and stiffened in the saddle. It wasn't unusual to hear shots out on the frontier, but that many of them so close together nearly always meant trouble.

He had ridden into King's Crown early that morning through a pass in the ring of mountains that formed the valley. Since then, he hadn't seen anybody, but the gunshots were proof positive that someone was nearby . . . and probably in trouble.

He dropped the pack horse's reins. He could always retrieve the animal later. His heels prodded Horse's flanks and sent the stallion loping forward. They were in a little saddle between two hills, and below them about half a mile away lay one of the streams that twisted through the valley. The thick growth of cottonwoods and aspen along its banks clearly marked its course. The gunfire continued as Preacher approached. He took to the trees as soon as he could. There was a good chance that once he sized up the fight, he would side with one bunch or the other, and when he took cards in this game, he wanted it to be a surprise.

Eager to get in on the action, Dog bounded ahead, but Preacher called him back. Preacher trusted Dog's instincts, but he wanted to see what was going on for himself before he turned the big cur loose.

He hauled back on the reins and slowed Horse as he swung out of the saddle while the stallion was still moving. Preacher landed with his rifle in his hands and glided through the brush until he reached the creek's edge.

He dropped to one knee and peered through a screen of leaves. The creek was about twenty yards wide and ran a couple feet deep over a gravel and sand bed. A man lay in the water near the opposite bank. The current moved him a little, but his feet dragged in the bed and kept him from floating away.

Preacher could tell that he was dead.

He saw two more men who were alive. Both of them lay in the stream and hunkered up as close to the bank as they could. They were using the bank for protection, Preacher realized. The shots came from the trees on the other side of the creek. Dirt flew in the air just above the heads of the two men as rifle balls struck the ground.

They had ducked behind the highest part of the bank, Preacher noted as he looked up and down the stream. If they tried to move, they would be exposed to the rifle fire. But they couldn't stay where they were. Sooner or later, the men who had bushwhacked them would try to flank them.

In fact, one of the killers was already making an attempt to do that. A man darted from the trees and ran at an angle toward a deadfall that lay with its base on the bank and its branches in the water. If he reached the cover of that log, he would have a better shot at the men hiding under the bank.

Right away, Preacher had noticed the beaver trap in the water near the two men as well as the bag lying on the bank with several objects — dead beaver, no doubt — stuffed into it. Those three had been working a trap line when they were ambushed.

Maybe they were poachers. Maybe the riflemen hiding in the trees were in the right. Preacher's gut told him that wasn't the case, but as he lifted his rifle to his shoulder there was just enough doubt in his mind to make him drop his aim a little and drill the man running toward the deadfall through the leg instead of killing him.

The man cried out in pain, dropped his rifle, and spilled off his feet. He clapped his hands to his wounded leg, struggled to his feet, and hobbled forward to throw himself behind the log just in case somebody else wanted to take a shot at him. Preacher heard him moaning.

He had drawn the attention of the other men in the trees when he shot the would-be flanker. More shots boomed, clouds of powder smoke spurted from the shadows under the trees, and rifle balls hummed and whickered through the brush around Preacher as he sprawled out on his belly.

Somebody on the other side of the stream yelled, "It must be Gardner again!"

Preacher had no idea who Gardner was, but obviously the bushwhackers didn't like him.

Dog belly-crawled up next to Preacher and growled. The mountain man looked over at the big cur. "All right. I reckon those varmints have proven they ain't friends of ours. Hunt!"

Dog backed off and vanished into the brush. A minute later, from the corner of his eye Preacher saw Dog bound across the creek about fifty yards upstream. He was gone in a flash, and even if the bushwhackers had noticed him, they wouldn't have had time to draw a bead on him.

Dog would be drawing a bead on them, though, thought Preacher with a grim smile.

The men on the other side of the stream continued to blaze away at Preacher and also at the two men hunkered under the bank. Even at the warmest time of year mountain streams ran cold from snowmelt, so Preacher figured those two hombres were pretty chilled.

Having reloaded his rifle while lying on the ground, he pulled back the hammer, nestled his whiskery cheek against the smooth, hand-carved stock, and watched over the barrel for a muzzle flash. When he saw one, he lined up the shot and pressed the trigger in a fraction of a second, then rolled swiftly to one side to avoid return fire from anyone aiming at *his* muzzle flash.

The ambushers were so well-hidden that he couldn't tell if he had scored with his shot, but after a moment he heard a high-pitched, agonized wail and figured he had found his target. Somebody over there was hurting, that was for sure.

Preacher shimmied behind a thick bush and reloaded again. He noticed that the two men under attack glanced back in his direction from time to time, as if they wondered who had pitched in to lend them a hand. Introductions could come later, Preacher thought. With any luck, maybe those men could give him a lead to William Pendexter.

A terrified scream suddenly erupted from the trees, followed by savage growls and snarls. Dog had gone to work, Preacher thought with a grin. A pistol boomed, but the screaming went on for several seconds before it died away in a grotesque gurgle.

One of the bushwhackers had just gotten his throat torn out.

Several startled yells came from that direction. A man stepped out from behind a tree trunk. A heartbeat later, the man collapsed as a ball from Preacher's rifle smashed into his chest.

"Come on!" somebody shouted. "Let's get the hell out of here!"

That was all it took to set off a frenzied retreat. Preacher heard brush crackle as men stampeded through the undergrowth. More growling and snapping punctuated the racket as Dog hurried the ambushers on their way. Preacher let out a shrill whistle to call the big cur back, otherwise he might chase them to kingdom come.

The two men hidden under the bank looked like they were about to stand up.

Preacher called, "Hey!" and motioned for them to stay down. One or more of the bushwhackers might try to double back. That was a pretty unlikely possibility, but he couldn't rule it out.

He hadn't forgotten about the wounded man who had crawled behind the deadfall, either. The man had dropped his rifle when Preacher shot him, but he might have a pistol or two on him. No shots had come from that direction during the fight, so Preacher hoped that meant the man had either passed out or else wanted no more part in the conflict.

He waited until he heard hoofbeats pounding away from the area before he came to his feet in a crouch. He ran along the bank until he could see behind the fallen log. The man lay there clutching his wounded leg. He was conscious, but didn't seem to be any threat at the moment.

Preacher kept the man covered anyway as he waded across the stream. Dog trotted up. The big cur's muzzle was smeared with blood. Preacher pointed at the wounded man and ordered, "Watch." Dog planted himself stiff-legged a few feet away and snarled. He looked utterly ferocious. The captive lay motionless, with wide, terrified eyes.

Confident that nobody would try any tricks with Dog watching over them, Preacher turned his back and went toward the two men they had rescued. One was a little below medium height and stocky, with a round, friendly face. The other was taller, slimmer, and a lot more dour. Both, however, looked very relieved as they stood up with creek water streaming off their buckskins.

"Th-thanks, m-mister," the smaller one said as his teeth chattered from the chill of being submerged in the water for so long. "You sure s-saved our b-bacon."

"You fellas can climb out of there now," Preacher told them. "Build a big fire, get out of those wet clothes, and dry off. I'll take a look around and make sure that bunch is gone." Preacher inclined his head toward the body lying in the creek. He could see the wound in the man's forehead and knew there was no way the unlucky fella could have survived. "Friend of yours?"

"Carl Pennington," the sour-faced man said. "Yes, he was a friend and a partner."

"I hope he didn't suffer too much," the other man said.

"Reckon he never knew what hit him," Preacher said.

He trotted off into the woods and cast

back and forth for a good fifteen minutes without seeing anyone. Convinced that the bushwhackers were well and truly gone, he returned to the creek bank.

The two men had built a blazing fire, as Preacher had suggested, and stripped down to their long underwear. Those garments were soaked, too.

Preacher said, "Take 'em off. You need to get dry down to the skin, or else you're liable to catch the grippe. You sure don't want that."

The men complied. Their skin was fish-belly white and they looked a little ridiculous, but Preacher didn't say anything because he knew he looked the same way except for the dark, permanent tan on his hands, face, and neck.

The two men had also lifted their friend's corpse from the creek and stretched it out on the bank. A blanket from their gear covered the man's face and upper body.

Since things were under control, Preacher walked over to the wounded man, who looked up at him and said in a weak voice, "Mister, you got to get this wolf away from me."

Dog growled.

"He ain't a wolf. He's a dog."

"Whatever he is, I think he . . . he's going

to eat me."

"Not unless I tell him to." Preacher frowned in thought. The man looked to be a Spaniard — someone he didn't run into every day so far north of Mexico. "What's your name?"

The prisoner hesitated, and for a moment Preacher thought he wasn't going to answer. Then he said sullenly, "Vargas."

"Well, Señor Vargas, you better tell me what's goin' on here, otherwise I'm liable to let Dog gnaw on you for a spell. I reckon I could probably stop him before he killed you, but I wouldn't want to take the chance if I was you."

"I . . . I can't tell you anything," Vargas stammered. "I don't dare!"

"Well, then, I reckon you have to ask yourself who you're more scared of right now. Jebediah Druke" — Preacher grinned and drawled — "or me and Dog?"

CHAPTER 13

Vargas looked surprised that Preacher knew Druke's name. That might have been what convinced him to talk, but he wasn't going to be completely cooperative. "First you have to call off that beast."

Preacher had already spotted the pistol behind Vargas's belt. He reached down and pulled it free, then said, "Back up, Dog. Sit. Guard."

The big cur did as he was told. He backed away, sat down, and watched Vargas with a hungry gleam in his eyes.

"You're safe now, as long as you don't make any sudden moves," Preacher told the Spaniard.

Vargas took one hand off his wounded leg, grabbed hold of the log, and pulled himself into a sitting position propped against it. "I am going to bleed to death," he complained.

"Maybe. Looks to me like you've got a ways to go, though. I can hurry the process along by shootin' you in the other leg if you want."

"Who are you?" Vargas asked through gritted teeth as he shifted his injured limb slightly.

"They call me Preacher."

Vargas took a sharply indrawn breath. Obviously, he had heard of him. "What are you doing here in King's Crown?"

"I thought I was supposed to be askin' the questions. Suppose you tell me what *you're* doin' in King's Crown."

With a sullen frown on his face, Vargas answered, "I work for Jebediah Druke, as you seem to know already."

"I wasn't sure, but I appreciate you confirmin' it." Preacher jerked a thumb toward the two men drying out by the fire. "What's Druke's grudge against those fellas?"

"They're trapping here without his permission. He told them they would have to leave, but they defied his orders."

"So you shot one of 'em down in cold blood?" Preacher's voice was sharp and angry as he asked the question.

Vargas grimaced and looked away. "We were just following orders. Señor Druke is the one who decides what happens in this valley."

"What gives him that right? Druke don't

own this land. Nobody does."

"The right of possession," Vargas answered as his mouth twisted in a faint sneer. "The right that belongs to any man who is stronger than another man."

"Seems like this country fought a couple wars against the Englanders to prove that don't always hold true."

Preacher had, in fact, fought in one of those wars as a stripling youth, at the Battle of New Orleans. The War of 1812 was over at the time, but no one on either side knew it while the cannons were booming and the bullets were flying.

"Where's Druke now?" Preacher went on. "Was he with the bunch that lit a shuck out of here?"

"I don't have to talk to you." A stubborn look appeared on Vargas's face again.

"Dog . . ." Preacher said.

The big cur leaned forward and bared his fangs.

"Druke wasn't here," Vargas said quickly. "Those two can tell you he was wounded in our last encounter with them. We were attacked from ambush."

"Sort of like today, eh, only the other way around. Who jumped you?"

"Will Gardner and his redskin friend."

That explained who the mysterious Gardner was, Preacher supposed, if not in any great detail.

"Where's Druke now?"

Vargas shook his head. "I'm not going to tell you that. You can kill me if you want, but I'm not going to say anything else."

Preacher nodded. "I reckon I can find somebody else to tell me how to find that so-called Fort Druke." He shook his head as surprise appeared again in Vargas's dark eyes. "Damned silly name, if you ask me."

Vargas just glared at him.

"Tell you what I'm gonna do," Preacher went on. "I'll patch up that hole in your leg and let you go, on a couple conditions."

Vargas frowned, clearly suspicious of the offer. "What conditions?"

Preacher held up a finger. "One, you go back to Druke and give him a message for me. Tell him that things are gonna change around here. He ain't the big skookum he-wolf in these parts no more."

"If I tell him that, he'll come after you and kill you."

"He can try," Preacher said. "Here's the second condition. You answer a question for me that don't have anything to do with Druke."

"What sort of question?"

"I'm lookin' for a young fella name of Wil-

121

liam Pendexter. Good-lookin' hombre in his twenties with brown hair and a half-moon-shaped birthmark on the back of his neck."

Vargas stared at Preacher in obvious stupefaction. The mountain man could tell that the name and the description meant nothing to him.

"You don't remember runnin' somebody like that out of King's Crown . . . or killin' him?"

Vargas said, "I accept both of your conditions. I know nothing of this man Pendexter."

"All right. Let's have a look at that leg." Preacher leaned his rifle against the log, well out of Vargas's reach, and hunkered on his heels next to the wounded man. Vargas took his hand away from the bloody injury. Preacher leaned forward to rip the man's trousers back so he could see the extent of the damage.

Some instinct made him glance up just as a canny gleam appeared in Vargas's eyes. It was enough warning so that the man's sudden move didn't take him completely by surprise. Vargas's other hand darted out from behind his back, clutching a dagger hidden under his buckskin shirt. The blade glinted in the sun as it slashed at Preacher's throat.

Preacher's left hand flashed up faster than the eye could follow and caught hold of Vargas's wrist. A sudden twist and a hard shove, and Preacher drove the dagger deep into Vargas's chest. The outlaw gasped and his head dropped. He stared down in shock at the weapon's handle. His own fingers were still wrapped around it.

"Tryin' to kill me sort of trumps them other conditions," Preacher said.

Vargas gasped a couple more times and then his head slumped forward as a thread of blood drooled from the corner of his mouth. His final breath rattled in his throat.

Preacher stood and picked up his rifle "Come on, Dog."

Leaving the dead man where he was, they went to join the two men by the fire, neither of whom appeared to have noticed what had happened, the action had been so quick and subtle.

The trappers weren't shivering anymore. They had propped up sticks near the fire and hung their clothes on them so the garments would dry quicker.

The sour-faced man nodded toward the deadfall. "What about Druke's man? You were talking to him for a long time."

"I was tryin' to make a deal with him," Preacher said. "I wanted him to go back to Druke and tell him things are gonna be different here in King's Crown. His day is done."

"Are you crazy?" the smaller trapper said. "That would just make Druke even more determined to come after you and kill you."

"You're probably right about that," Preacher admitted. "And I've got another chore to take care of here before I tangle with Druke. Either of you fellas know a youngster named William Pendexter?"

The two men looked at each other, frowned in thought, and then shook their heads.

"Never heard of him," said the smaller man. "But my name is Enos Mitchell, and my partner here is John Burton. We already told you poor Carl's name."

"They call me Preacher."

Burton had been keeping a nervous eye on Dog. "Is that wolf tame?"

"He's a dog, not a wolf. And I wouldn't say he's exactly tame. But he won't hurt you unless I tell him to, or unless you try to hurt me."

"After you saved our lives, that won't be happening," Mitchell said. "What about Druke's man? What are you going to do with him?"

"Bury him, I suppose. He got cocky and tried to plant a dagger in my throat when he thought I wasn't lookin'."

Both men looked shocked.

Burton said, "Wait a minute. You killed him right over there, no more than twenty yards away from us, and we didn't even notice?"

"That's the thing about dyin'," Preacher said. "A lot of the time it sort of sneaks up on you."

CHAPTER 14

After retrieving Horse and his pack animal, Preacher rejoined Mitchell and Burton on the creek bank. The two trappers took turns digging a grave for their friend at the edge of the trees. Preacher did likewise for Vargas, although Druke's man was planted with no ceremony.

As the three men stood beside Carl Pennington's grave after lowering the blanket-wrapped figure inside it, Burton took off his hat and said, "This is all my fault. I was supposed to be standing guard. I was right there on the bank looking at the trees when one of those outlaws shot Carl. I never even saw where the shot came from."

"I reckon those fellas had considerable experience at skulkin' around in the woods," Preacher pointed out. "Anyway, seems to me like the blame goes to the varmint who pulled the trigger, and to Jebediah Druke for sendin' those men after you."

"We can talk about Druke later," Mitchell said. "Right now, I want to say a prayer for Carl's soul."

"Thank you, Enos," Burton said quietly.

Preacher and Mitchell took their hats off, too, and bowed their heads as Mitchell asked God to have mercy on Carl Pennington's soul.

"I know he would have preferred it to be different," Mitchell concluded, "but this is a beautiful place to spend eternity. Amen."

"Amen," Preacher echoed.

They filled in the grave, then started back to the horses.

The mountain man said, "Those fellas who got away know where they found you. It'd be smart if you boys moved on and found yourselves a good place to camp somewhere else."

"Will you come with us?" Mitchell asked.

Preacher considered the invitation. "For the night, I reckon. I don't know how far it is back to Druke's place. We can't rule out him sendin' some more men after you right away. He's got a grudge against you because you didn't turn tail and run when he tried to scare you off the first time. Can't have folks standin' up to him. That makes him look bad."

"We're not going to let him scare us off,"

Burton said.

Mitchell grunted. "Speak for yourself."

"If we leave now, Carl will have died for nothing," Burton insisted. "Besides, I think that a third of whatever we make from our pelts should go to his family, and I want it to be as much as possible."

"Well, I sure can't argue with that," Mitchell said with a nod. "I'd feel a mite better about things if you'd throw in with us, Preacher. I've heard about you. I think Jebediah Druke might have met his match in you."

"Under normal circumstances I might be tempted to do that, but I'm lookin' for that young fella I mentioned, William Pendexter, and I promised his pa I'd do my best to find him." Preacher paused. "Of course, that don't mean I won't take a hand in a ruckus like the one here today, any time I come across one. I figure just in the natural course o' things, there's a good chance I'll tangle with Druke and his men."

"Be careful," Burton warned. "They're ruthless." He glanced toward Carl Pennington's grave. "We've seen plenty proof of that."

Following Preacher's suggestion, they moved along the stream the rest of that day and traveled several miles before they stopped to make camp. When they did, they chose an area at the base of a bluff where several boulders had come to rest in ages past, a choice that Preacher would have agreed with if they had asked him. The rocks provided good cover for men and horses alike.

Preacher added some jerky to their supper. They ate and then put out the fire as shadows of evening began to settle down over the valley.

As they sat there beside the dead embers, Preacher commented, "You fellas seem to know what you're doin'. You must've learned something from that other run-in with Druke's bunch."

"We learned from Will Gardner," Mitchell said. "He gave us plenty of good advice."

"Unfortunately, it wasn't enough to save Carl's life," Burton added with a touch of bitterness in his voice.

"Tell me about Gardner," Preacher said.

Mitchell said, "There's not much to tell. He's just a young trapper. He struck me as being pretty experienced, though, despite his youth."

"And he acted like he's declared war on Druke for some reason," Burton added. "He and Druke's men had fought before. That night he helped us wasn't the first time they clashed."

"What about the Indian who was with him?" Preacher asked.

"Gray Otter? If anything, he was even more dangerous than Gardner. I never saw a man who could move so quietly or strike so swiftly."

"What tribe is he from?"

"I have no idea," Burton said. "I don't think that subject was ever brought up, was it, Enos?"

"No, now that you mention it, I don't believe it was. That's a little odd, isn't it? I thought most Indians were proud of their tribe. But Gray Otter never talked much, and even then he didn't really . . . talk. He and Gardner used sign language because Gray Otter doesn't speak English."

It wasn't that unusual for a white man and an Indian to befriend each other and travel together, Preacher mused. Audie and Nighthawk were perfect examples. "You have any idea where I could find those fellas?" he asked Burton and Mitchell.

"None at all," Burton said. "They seemed to appear out of thin air and vanished the same way, once Gardner was ready to move on."

"Why do you want to find them, Preacher?" Mitchell asked.

Preacher scratched at his beard. "Well, from the sound of it they've been around these parts for a while. I was thinkin' they might be able to help me find William Pendexter."

"That's a good idea," Mitchell agreed. "I wish we could be of more help. You saved our lives, and we haven't done anything to repay you."

"Shared your fire and your coffee with me," Preacher said with a grin. "That's enough for now. Maybe someday you'll have a chance to do somethin' else."

"If you ever need us, all you have to do is call on us," Burton said solemnly. "We owe you a debt, and we'll pay it."

"I'll remember that," Preacher promised.

As he rolled up in his blankets a short time later, he thought that it was much more likely Will Gardner would be able to help him rather than these two novice trappers, but Burton and Mitchell meant well. If Gardner was as savvy as they made him sound and had been around King's Crown for a while, he might be Preacher's best lead to William Pendexter.

Another thought danced momentarily around the back of Preacher's mind, but it never really came clear. Sooner or later it would, he knew, so he didn't worry about it as he dozed off.

By evening, Jebediah Druke was snockered, but as he liked to boast, whiskey didn't muddle his mind any. At least he didn't think so, although being drunk, it was hard to say for sure.

The important thing was, he had guzzled enough of the busthead so that his wounded arm didn't hurt anymore. A warm, pleasant glow enveloped his entire body as he sat on a log near the big cook fire and ate stew from a wooden bowl. A jug of whiskey sat on the ground next to him. From time to time he reached down, picked it up, and washed down the food with a slug of the fiery liquor.

Several more men were enjoying their supper as well. Druke didn't worry about having the big fire burning after dark, because he didn't think anybody could ever harm him in his sanctum. Guards were posted all around the place and would warn him in case of any trouble.

One of those guards hurried up just as Druke was finishing the stew." A couple riders comin', boss. Looks like it's Sam Turner . . . and that Indian."

The lookout's tone was a little nervous as he referred to Turner's companion, so

Druke knew it had to be Blood Eye. The renegade Crow could give even the most hardened killer the fantods.

Druke got to his feet. The warm glow that had surrounded him abruptly vanished. He threw off the whiskey's effects and was sober again. "Bring them here," he snapped, then realized that the order wasn't necessary. Turner would come straight to him. It was damned well about time, too.

Druke wouldn't admit it, but he had started to get a little worried about Turner. It was impossible to predict what Blood Eye would do in any given situation. He might well have killed Turner on sight, rather than waiting for the man to explain why he was there. Druke had known that when he sent Turner to look for Blood Eye.

Luckily, from the sound of it, nothing like that had happened. Still, Druke was relieved when the two men rode into the big circle of light cast by the fire and he could see with his own eyes that Turner was hale and hearty.

Blood Eye looked the same as he always did — downright scary. The Indian was coldly expressionless as he slipped down from his pony's back.

Turner dismounted, too, and took the reins of Blood Eye's horse from the Crow.

"Here he is, boss, just like you wanted."

Druke jerked his head in a curt nod. He didn't believe in praising his men for doing their job. Granted, Turner's current chore hadn't been an easy one, but that didn't matter.

Druke turned to the Indian. "Blood Eye, my friend. It's good to see you again, as always."

Blood Eye just grunted. He didn't seem to believe Druke, nor did he care.

"I asked Turner to bring you here because I have a job for you." Druke hadn't actually asked Turner. It hadn't been a request, it had been an order . . . but the result was the same.

"There are a couple men I want you to hunt down and take care of for me."

"Will Gardner," Blood Eye said. "Gray Otter."

Druke nodded. "That's right. What do you think? Can you do it?"

For a second, an angry fire flared in the Crow's good eye, as if Druke had offended him by asking such a question.

Druke saw the reaction and wondered if he could pull the pistol from behind his belt, cock it, and fire before Blood Eye brained him with the tomahawk at his waist. It would be a near thing.

But it didn't come to that. Blood Eye's gaze turned stony again. "I will kill Gardner."

"What about Gray Otter?"

"The one you call Gray Otter will never trouble you again," Blood Eye said.

"That's good enough for me."

Druke was about to bend down for the jug and suggest that they seal the bargain with a drink when he heard hoofbeats. Several more riders approached the cabins at a fairly fast clip. Druke stiffened and barked, "Get your guns ready. This could be trouble!"

The hoofbeats slowed and a familiar voice called, "Hello, the fort!"

The voice belonged to Frank Helton, one of the men who had gone with Vargas to wipe out those three defiant trappers.

"Come on in, Helton!" Druke shouted. He kept his hand on his gun anyway, just in case somebody was trying to cook up some sort of trick.

Five men rode up to the campfire and wearily dismounted. They were leading two more horses with bodies lashed facedown over the saddles.

Druke didn't see Vargas and wondered if the Spaniard might be one of the dead men. "What the devil is all this, Helton?" he demanded. "Where's Vargas?"

"We had to leave him behind. He was wounded and we couldn't get to him. We'd already lost two men and had more wounded."

Druke saw the bloodstains on the clothes of several men. Anger boiled up inside him. "What the hell are you talking about? Those three greenhorns couldn't have put up that much of a fight!"

"We killed one of 'em," Helton said. "Vargas nailed him with his first shot. But then the other two had help."

"Gardner and Gray Otter," Druke breathed out.

Helton shook his head. "I don't know, boss. We never really got a look at whoever it was pitched in on their side. Seemed like there was only one man, though . . . and a wolf."

Druke frowned. "A wolf?"

"Or else a damned big dog, I ain't sure which." Helton inclined his head toward the corpses tied to the two horses. "Creature tore Stallings's throat out, the poor guy, and chewed up Reynolds pretty good."

That didn't really sound like the work of Gardner and his Indian friend, thought Druke, but it didn't matter. One of those trappers was dead. The other two had to

136

die, and the sooner the better.

Druke turned to look at Blood Eye. "I still want you to go after Gardner and Gray Otter, but I've got another job for you first."

An expression that might have been a smile if it hadn't been so ugly stretched the renegade Crow's thin lips. "Who do you want me to kill now?"

CHAPTER 15

Preacher took his leave of Burton and Mitchell early the next morning. Part of him felt like he was abandoning them, but he had the search for William Pendexter to carry out. Also, he was curious about Will Gardner and Gray Otter and wanted to see if maybe he could find them, too.

It wouldn't be easy. King's Crown was a good twenty miles across, which meant it covered a lot of ground. It wasn't easily searched, either, as the terrain was pretty rugged in places. Preacher could cover all of it, but the chore might take him a couple weeks.

To get started, he rode toward the center of the valley. He intended to circle out from there in an ever-widening pattern that would eventually cover all of King's Crown. He hadn't gone very far when he began to get the feeling that he was being watched.

He didn't stop and look around or let on

in any way that he was suspicious. He kept Horse moving at an easy lope. Dog ranged out ahead of him and investigated every bit of brush for small animals, so there was a chance the cur might flush out whoever was spying on him. Preacher turned his head enough to scan the landscape on both sides of him, but he didn't see anything out of place.

Whoever was watching him had to be pretty stealthy to escape his keen-eyed scrutiny. Preacher didn't even consider the notion that he might be imagining the sensation. He trusted his instincts far more than that.

Then, suddenly, the feeling was gone. It could mean only one thing.

The watcher had departed.

That knowledge didn't make Preacher relax. Until he knew who it had been, the question would nag at him.

Around mid-morning as he traveled along one of the streams, a group of riders emerged from a thick stand of trees in front of him and plodded toward him on horseback. He counted eight men, all of them in homespun and buckskin and all riding with rifles balanced across their saddles. They led more than a dozen pack horses and mules.

The strangers didn't look threatening, but Preacher reined in and unslung his own rifle from its lashings on the saddle, anyway. He waited for the men to come to him, and as they approached he noticed that several of them had shifted their rifles so that the weapons pointed more toward him. Even with that, they still struck Preacher as more wary than menacing.

One man moved his horse slightly ahead of the others. He was short and squat; Preacher could tell that even though the man was still in the saddle. He wore a buckskin jacket decorated with bear claws and a flat-brimmed, round-crowned black hat with a hammered silver band.

A hat band like that would reflect sunlight from a long way off and give away its wearer's location to an enemy. Preacher wouldn't be caught dead wearing such a flashy thing.

The other riders slowed and stopped while the short man rode on toward Preacher. He had a round face and a short, grizzled red beard. When he was about twenty feet away he brought his horse to a stop and lifted a hand in greeting. "Good day to you, sir. I don't believe I've had the pleasure."

"That's a big assumption," Preacher drawled.

The man looked vaguely puzzled. "What is?"

"That meetin' me would be a pleasure."

Before the man could figure out whether or not he ought to take that as an insult, one of the other riders called, "Hey, Monkton, I know this fella. That's Preacher!"

The mountain man looked at the one who had spoken and felt a moment of recognition. It took him a few seconds to come up with the man's name, but when he did, he grinned. "Howdy, Karnes. Ain't seen you since the rendezvous a couple years ago."

"That's right." Karnes was a rawboned man with a pleasantly ugly face and a thatch of straw-colored hair under his pushed-back coonskin cap. He heeled his mount forward.

Preacher's nerves eased. Karnes was a trapper, a decent sort he had met half a dozen times over the years. The other men looked to be much the same sort. Preacher figured they had been working in King's Crown for a while and that the packs on the animals they led were stuffed full of beaver plews.

Karnes rode up close enough to reach out and shake hands with Preacher.

Monkton said, "Preacher, eh? I've heard of you, sir. You're something of a legend in

141

these mountains."

"I don't know about that." Preacher scanned the faces of the other men and saw several he recognized. He nodded to them and lifted a hand in greeting. "From the looks of it, you fellas have been runnin' trap lines here in the valley."

"That's right," Karnes said. "Most of us came up here on our own, but we sort of threw in together a while back." The trapper's grin disappeared and his long face grew solemn. "You may not know it, Preacher, but there's trouble afoot here in King's Crown."

"You talkin' about Jebediah Druke?" Preacher asked.

"So you *have* heard of him." Monkton's voice hardened. "You and he aren't allies, are you?"

Before Preacher could answer, Karnes said, "Cap'n, you couldn't be more wrong about that. The only thing Preacher would have to do with a polecat like Druke would be to go after him and skin him alive, like the worthless critter he is."

Monkton shrugged. "I meant no offense."

"None taken," Preacher said. "Why don't one of you tell me what's goin' on here?"

"As Mr. Karnes mentioned, we've banded together for protection. One man alone, or even two or three, are helpless targets in King's Crown these days. We all know men who have been killed or run out of the valley by Druke and his cohorts."

"We figured that if we tried to get our pelts out of the valley by ourselves, Druke'd stop us," Karnes added. "Even if he let us live, he'd steal the pelts we worked so hard for. But we thought if we rode out together, maybe Druke wouldn't bother us. Even though his bunch still outnumbers us, we could put up a good stiff fight." Karnes nodded toward Monkton. "That's why we elected Mr. Monkton here our cap'n. He's had military experience."

"I served under Colonel Andrew Jackson in Alabama during the Creek Wars," Monkton said with a note of pride in his voice.

"I was with Old Hickory at New Orleans," Preacher said. "Chased the British all the way back down the Mississipp' to the Gulf of Mexico."

"Perhaps we should have accompanied him to Washington to serve in his presidential administration, eh?" Monkton suggested with a smile.

Preacher's eyes widened as he exclaimed, "Good Lord! I've been tied up by Blackfeet so they could burn me at the stake. Reckon

I'd rather take my chances with that again than go to Washington City and get mixed up in *politics.*" He made it sound like he'd said *buffalo dung* instead of *politics.*

Karnes changed the subject. "Did you come to King's Crown to try your hand at trappin', Preacher? I see you've got an outfit with you."

Preacher shook his head. "I've already taken one load of pelts back downriver this season, from up along the Yellowstone. Thought I might try for another, but I got mixed up in somethin' else first. A fella asked me to try to find his son. Name of William Pendexter."

"Is that the person you're looking for, or the person who made the request of you?" Monkton asked.

"That's the fella I'm lookin' for." Preacher reeled off young Pendexter's description, including the half-moon birthmark on the back of his neck. "Any of you boys know him?"

Karnes frowned in thought and shook his head. "Can't say as I do."

"I haven't encountered the young man, either," Monkton put in. "Are you sure he's here in King's Crown?"

"I'm not sure of anything," Preacher admitted honestly. "He was supposed to be

144

headed in this direction last time anybody saw hide or hair of him. That's really all I know."

None of the other men knew William Pendexter, either. Preacher was disappointed, but he didn't let it show. He had realized from the start that the job likely wouldn't be an easy one.

He tried another tack. "Do any of you know Will Gardner?"

"Ah, Druke's nemesis," Monkton said. "A very fine young man."

The others nodded in agreement with that assessment.

"Know where I might be able to find him?" Preacher asked.

"No idea. I haven't seen him for several weeks. He's something of a will-o'-the-wisp, he and his little Indian friend."

Karnes said, "If we run into him on our way out of the valley, we can tell him you're lookin' for him, Preacher. What's his relation to that fella Pendexter?"

"No relation, as far as I know. I just thought he might be able to give me a lead to Pendexter."

"Gardner always seems to know what's going on in King's Crown, that's true," Monkton said. "He might be able to help you."

Karnes shook his head. "It's a shame you just got here instead of bein' on your way out of the valley, Preacher. It'd sure please me if you was to throw in with us."

Everybody wanted him to join up with them, Preacher thought, but he still had his job to do. "I'd like that, too, if things were different, Karnes. I'd better let you fellas be on your way. I expect you're anxious to get out of here."

"Indeed," Monkton said. "I'd like to put King's Crown behind us before nightfall. That's the only way we'll be safe from Druke and his men."

"Good luck to you, then," Preacher said as he moved Horse to the side.

"Good luck to you," Karnes said as he shook hands with Preacher again. "You're the one who's stayin' here in this hellhole, so you're the one who's likely to need it."

CHAPTER 16

It seemed odd to Preacher for anyone to refer to a place as beautiful as King's Crown as a hellhole, but he knew what Karnes meant. Any place, no matter how pretty, could seem like hell if your life was in danger all the time.

The group of trappers resumed the trek out of the valley, and Preacher rode toward the center of it again. He gnawed some jerky from his saddlebags at midday without stopping for an actual meal and washed the stuff down with creek water.

Not long after, he reined in and lifted his head to listen. Shots popped in the distance behind him. His jaw tightened as the gunfire continued. It had to be quite a fight.

Two possibilities suggested themselves to him. Druke's men could have come after Enos Mitchell and John Burton again, or Karnes, Monkton, and the other trappers could have run into the renegades.

Either way, it was likely that good men were dying, and that knowledge gnawed at Preacher's gut.

He was pragmatic enough to know that he couldn't be everywhere at once, couldn't prevent every injustice that occurred on the frontier. Good men died every day out there, often under the most unfair conditions. Might as well rage against the sun coming up every morning.

Besides, he had given his word to Barnabas Pendexter, and Preacher was nothing if not a man of his word.

Those shots were several miles away. Chances were, even if he turned around and galloped toward them, the battle would be long over by the time he could get there, and he knew it.

The only sensible thing to do was keep going.

That resolve lasted all of five seconds before Preacher hauled the stallion around, called, "Come on, Dog!" and heeled Horse into a run.

His sense of direction was uncanny, and once he had the sounds of gunfire located, he had no trouble riding right toward them. He had to backtrack once to avoid a deep ravine and had to go around a ridge too steep for Horse to climb. Those delays chafed at him. When he paused to listen again, he no longer heard the gunfire.

That wasn't good.

He put Horse into a run again. The pack animal struggled to keep up, but Preacher couldn't do anything about that. He wasn't going to leave his outfit behind.

He came to a wide, parklike meadow between two wooded ridges and reined in as he spotted something odd in the trees at the base of the opposite ridge. It took only a second for the grim realization to hit him.

He was looking at two men, each tied to the trunk of a pine. Their heads hung forward.

"Damn it," Preacher said softly.

Just as he had feared, he was too late. He rode hard across the meadow anyway, just in case either of the men might be clinging to life.

When he came closer he saw the blood-soaked buckskins and knew they had been tortured. The clothes were in bloody shreds, and so was the flesh under them. Preacher hauled back on the reins, swung down from the saddle, and ran to the trees.

Even with their bodies mutilated, he recognized Mitchell and Burton and could tell which was which. Blood still dripped from Burton's chin as Preacher took hold

149

of it and lifted the man's head.

He had seen too much violent death out on the frontier to ever be truly shocked again, but the sight of what had been done to Burton's face etched grim trenches in Preacher's cheeks.

The eyes had been gouged out, the tongue hacked from the mouth, the nose sliced off. Preacher lowered Burton's head and rested his hand on the man's gore-streaked chest to search for a heartbeat.

He didn't expect to find one, and that assumption proved correct. Burton was dead. And a merciful death it must have been, after the torment he had endured.

Mitchell groaned.

Preacher stepped over to him and carefully lifted his head. Mitchell's eyes were gone, too, but his nose and tongue had been left for some reason. At Preacher's touch, he gasped and choked out, "No! No . . . more . . . please, God . . ."

"Mitchell," Preacher said, his voice firm and sharp enough to cut through the man's agony. "Mitchell, it's me, Preacher."

"P-Preacher! Thank God! Help . . . John . . ."

"It's too late for that," Preacher said, his words gentle. "He's gone. But maybe I can do something for you."

A hollow laugh came from Mitchell. "You can . . . kill me. Put me . . . out of my misery."

Preacher glanced down at the ground. A big puddle of blood had formed at Mitchell's feet and was soaking darkly into the ground. It was a wonder the man had held on to life as long as he had. Preacher knew Mitchell had only minutes left, if that.

"Druke did this?"

"Druke . . . and an Indian . . . ugliest Indian . . . I ever saw. One eye . . . red . . . like it was . . . filled with blood. He's the one who . . . did most of this."

Preacher frowned. He had never crossed trails with a renegade who looked like that, but he was confident that he would know the man from Mitchell's description. "I'll settle the score for you and Burton, Enos," Preacher vowed. "Druke and his bunch won't get away with this."

"What about . . ."

Mitchell couldn't finish the question, but Preacher knew what the man was asking.

"I don't care about Pendexter right now. Druke's a mad dog, and it sounds like the red-eyed varmint he's got with him is even worse. They got to be put down, and the sooner the better."

"You can't fight them . . . alone."

151

"You let me worry about that."

Already, the wheels of Preacher's brain were turning over rapidly. Now he had another reason for finding Will Gardner and Gray Otter. If that mysterious twosome were carrying on a crusade against Jebediah Druke, then Preacher wanted to join forces with them. They would whittle down the odds until they got to Druke himself, and then there would be a reckoning.

"I'm sorry, Enos," Preacher went on. "Reckon I should've stayed with you and Burton for a while after all."

"You didn't know . . . It was up to us . . . to protect ourselves . . . We failed Carl . . . failed each other . . . Never should've let them . . . take us by surprise . . ." Mitchell groaned again. "God . . . it hurts . . ."

"Are you a married man, Enos?"

"Y-yeah . . . Got a wife . . . couple sons . . . a little girl . . ."

"You remember what they look like?" Preacher asked as he slid one of his pistols from behind his belt.

"Sure, I . . . remember."

"You put their picture in your mind right now." Preacher cocked the pistol, being quiet about it. "It'll help, I promise. You see 'em?"

Mitchell's bloody lips curved slightly in a

smile. "Yeah," he whispered as Preacher raised the pistol. "I may not have . . . eyes anymore . . . but I see 'em . . . plain as day . . . They're beautiful . . ."

Preacher held the muzzle a couple inches from Mitchell's forehead and pulled the trigger.

Later, when he rode away from the two fresh graves he had dug under the trees at the edge of the slope, he thought about Jebediah Druke and that Indian with the bloody eye. He remembered a verse from the Good Book that Audie had quoted around a campfire more than once, about how vengeance was the Lord's.

That was all well and good, thought Preacher, but when it came to Druke and that Indian, the Lord was just gonna have to wait His turn.

CHAPTER 17

Druke's arm ached, but he felt pretty well satisfied with himself, anyway. Those other two trappers were dead, and the way Blood Eye had left them tied to those trees, whoever found them was bound to get the message that it wasn't smart to mess with Jebediah Druke.

Some of Druke's men had turned away muttering while Blood Eye worked on Burton and Mitchell. A couple had even ducked into the bushes to upchuck.

Druke had watched the whole thing. Not that he took any real pleasure from the torture, not like Blood Eye did, anyway, but to him it was a vivid demonstration of something he firmly believed.

The world was a terrible place, to Druke's way of thinking, and the only real way to survive it was to be more terrible. Some people might consider that evil, but to Druke it was just a matter of being stronger and molding the world to his will, rather than the other way around.

Blood Eye was an instrument of Jebediah Druke's will, a tool to be used, nothing more or less.

Druke's former master, the one who had bought him as an indentured servant when Druke was only a boy, had beat him relentlessly for years. He would sure as hell be surprised to see Druke now.

As Druke rode along with the screams of the two trappers still echoing in his ears, he wondered if the brutal old man was still alive. He would have given a lot to introduce him to Blood Eye.

Sam Turner moved his horse up alongside Druke's. "Are we headin' back to the fort, Jebediah?"

"That's right," Druke said.

"What about sendin' Blood Eye after Gardner and that other redskin?"

"I'm still going to do that, but I reckon he's done enough work for one day. He might want to rest up a mite before he goes after those other two."

A little shudder went through Turner as he glanced over at Blood Eye, who rode by himself to one side of the group, traveling with them but definitely not a part of them. A man like Blood Eye rode alone no matter how many men might be around him.

"I ain't sure he counts killin' as work," Turner said to Druke. He kept his voice quiet enough that Blood Eye couldn't hear him. "Seemed to me like he was enjoyin' it."

"Just let it alone," Druke snapped.

"You bet, boss," Turner said quickly. "I didn't mean anything by — What's that, now?" He stood up a little in the saddle and pointed.

Druke saw the same thing. Coming toward them was a man who had just ridden around a big rock in front of them. What looked like a heavily laden pack mule followed him at the end of a lead rope.

The stranger spotted the large group of riders at the same time. He reined in sharply and turned his horse.

"Get him!" Druke ordered. He had no idea who the man was, but it didn't matter. He wasn't one of them, so he was the enemy.

Turner and several of the other men kicked their horses into motion and galloped after the fleeing man. Blood Eye merely reined in his pony and sat waiting expressionlessly to see what was going to happen. His specialty was killing, not chasing. Anybody could chase down prey.

It took special talent like his to elevate

killing to an art form.

The lone man dropped the lead rope and abandoned his pack mule. One of Druke's men stopped to take charge of the animal, but the others raced around the rock to continue the chase. A couple minutes later, they returned with the captive riding along in the center of the little group. Terror twisted the man's bearded face into grotesque lines.

Druke regarded the man solemnly. "Do I know you?"

"N-no, sir. My name's Ned Harris. But I know who you are. You're Jebediah Druke!"

Even though the man was terrified of him, Druke was gratified to hear that Harris knew who he was. In the back of his mind was the idea that he would make himself a very rich man by taking over the valley and all the fur trade in it, and once he had amassed a big enough fortune he would return to the East in triumph. Everybody would know his name once he was one of the wealthiest men in the country. He'd be as famous as John Jacob Astor himself!

But Druke never let himself dwell on those thoughts for very long. He couldn't achieve his goals unless he kept all his attention on the job at hand, and that was to make sure King's Crown was under his complete control.

"That's right," he said to Ned Harris. "I'm Jebediah Druke. This is my valley, and those are my furs you've got in your packs, Harris. You were trying to sneak out of here with them, weren't you?"

"I . . . I really need the money, Mr. Druke," Harris said. "And when I missed joinin' up with them others —" He stopped short and looked even more horrified, as he realized that he had said too much.

Druke's interest quickened as he leaned forward in the saddle. "What others?" he asked harshly.

"I . . . I can tell you," Harris said, "if you'll promise not to kill me —"

"Are you trying to bargain with me?" Druke roared. "I'm not haggling with you, Harris!" He jerked one of his pistols from his belt and pointed it at the cringing trapper as he eared back the hammer. "Tell me what you're talking about, or I'll blow you right out of the saddle." He had no doubt that Harris wasn't brave enough to defy the ruthless men who had captured him.

He wasn't surprised when the trapper babbled, "I'll tell you everything, Mr. Druke, everything!"

Druke lowered the pistol and gave him a curt nod. "Go ahead."

"Some of the other fellas who've been trappin' here in the valley had the idea of gettin' together to take their pelts out . . ."

The story poured from Harris's mouth. According to the terrified trapper, eight men had banded together so they could put up a fight if Druke tried to stop them from leaving King's Crown with their pelts. The one called Karnes had approached Harris about joining them and Harris had agreed to do so, but his saddle horse had had a loose shoe and that had delayed him and made him miss the rendezvous. So he had set out alone in the hope that maybe he could catch up to the others before they left the valley.

Instead, he had run smack-dab into Druke and his men. That was bad luck for Harris, Druke reflected wryly when Harris's voice trailed off nervously.

He recognized a few of the names Harris mentioned — Monkton, Karnes, Cassidy, Summerville. "You say they were riding out of the valley today?"

"Yes, sir, that's right." Harris glanced up at the sun. "I'd say there's a good chance they ain't reached the pass yet, so they're probably still in King's Crown."

Harris had just betrayed his friends and put them in danger. Busy with Burton and Mitchell, Druke might not have known about the other men trying to slip out of the valley. He could tell Harris hoped that treachery would buy him his life.

"Take the pelts," Druke told Turner. "We'll take them with us."

"We're goin' after Monkton's bunch?" Turner asked.

"Damn right we are. I'm not going to let them get away with that."

Turner nodded toward Harris. "What about this one?"

Druke laughed and called, "Blood Eye."

The renegade Crow rode over to them, not getting in any hurry. Harris saw him coming, and when he got a good look at Blood Eye, he tried to jerk his horse around and flee again, but one of Druke's men had a firm grip on the mount's headstall.

Since he couldn't get away, Harris started to scream.

Will Gardner had a deer carcass draped over his shoulders so he could carry it back to the camp he shared with Gray Otter. They needed fresh meat. Gray Otter had downed it with an arrow a short time earlier.

It was how they did most of their hunting. Using an arrow saved powder and shot, and it was silent so it wouldn't give away their position. Such caution had become a deeply ingrained habit.

Will knew how badly Jebediah Druke wanted both of them dead. They were the only ones who had stood up successfully to Druke's would-be reign of terror.

Gray Otter had vanished after bringing down the deer. Will didn't worry any more than he always did whenever his companion was out of his sight. He knew how skilled Gray Otter was at moving silently, undetected, through the woods. He had seen plenty of demonstrations of prowess with the bow and arrow, too.

But a certain amount of concern nibbled at the back of his brain. Strokes of bad luck couldn't always be guarded against. Fate sometimes caught up to people no matter what they did.

He and Gray Otter certainly had plenty that could catch up to them, Will mused.

He had just gotten back to their camp, well hidden in a thick grove of pines that backed up against a hill, and lowered the carcass to the ground when Gray Otter suddenly appeared, as silently as ever.

"Druke and all of his men are close by."

Will stiffened in alarm at that news. "Are they hunting for us?"

"No. Eight trappers are trying to leave the valley with their pelts. I got a good look at them. Karnes, Monkton, and several others we know."

"That's actually pretty smart," Will said. "There's strength in numbers."

"It would have been smart . . . if Druke hadn't gotten wind of it somehow. Now he's closing in on them."

"And his force outnumbers them," Will said grimly.

"By quite a bit."

Will glanced at the carcass. There wasn't going to be time to dress it out after all. He unslung the rifle from his back. "I reckon we'd better get moving, then, hadn't we?"

CHAPTER 18

The pass still loomed high above Captain Monkton's group of trappers, but as Pete Karnes looked up at it, he figured there was a pretty good chance he and his companions would reach it before nightfall. It would be a hard climb up the twisting trail, but they could make it.

Once they were through the pass, they could start down the eastern slope toward the plains and find a place to camp somewhere on the way down. It probably wouldn't matter how far they went. The odds of Jebediah Druke leaving King's Crown to come after them seemed pretty small. Over the past months, Druke had confined his reign of terror to the circular valley.

Of course, there was no guarantee that would continue, Karnes mused. Druke was ruthless, and he didn't like being challenged. He might pursue anyone who defied him out of the valley.

But in order to do that Druke would have to know what was going on, and so far Karnes hadn't seen any signs that was the case. He had been keeping a close eye on their back trail, and he was starting to hope that Druke didn't even know they were leaving King's Crown with a big load of pelts.

Zach Summerville moved his horse up alongside Karnes and grinned. "Looks like we're gonna make it."

Even though he had just been thinking the same thing, Karnes quickly said, "Don't go talkin' like that, Zach. You don't want to jinx us."

"I ain't superstitious enough to believe in things like jinxes," Summerville scoffed. "I've always thought a fella makes his own luck."

Karnes didn't disagree with that, but at the same time he knew there were always things a man couldn't control. In the end, you prepared for trouble the best you could and hoped for the best.

"Just keep your eyes open," he warned Summerville. "We've still got a ways to go."

Up ahead, Captain Monkton was riding in the lead. He reined in suddenly, turned in the saddle, and called, "Karnes."

"I better go see what the cap'n wants,"

Karnes told Summerville. He heeled his horse into a trot.

When he came up to Monkton a moment later, he saw the worried frown on the man's bearded face. "Somethin' wrong, Cap'n?"

"Nothing I can put my finger on," Monkton replied, "but it just doesn't feel right. I wouldn't go so far as to say that we're being watched, but . . ."

Now that the captain mentioned it, Karnes experienced a little of the same sensation. Monkton had served in the army under Old Hickory Jackson and fought the Creek Indians; Karnes had served in no army but his own and fought Blackfeet, Arikara, Crow, and Cheyenne. The way he saw it, that put them on roughly equal footing, although he hadn't minded deferring to Monkton's orders. The group had elected him captain fair and square.

The two of them were in agreement. Karnes raised a hand and signaled for the others to stop. As they did so, Summerville called, "What's wrong?"

Karnes looked around quickly. The trail they followed led past a wooded bluff before curving up the lower slopes of the mountain toward the pass. It suddenly struck Karnes that it might be a good idea to circle wide around that bluff. If Druke and his men had somehow gotten ahead of them . . .

"Who's that?" Monkton nodded toward the trail ahead.

Karnes looked up and saw that one man had appeared on the trail. The stranger rode slowly toward them. He was a big man; Karnes could tell that even at a distance. And there was something ominously familiar about him.

"Good Lord!" Karnes exclaimed suddenly. "That's Druke!"

"You're sure?" Monkton asked.

"Yeah, that's him, all right. I got a look at him once."

"Is there anyone with him?"

"Not that I can see. But I don't reckon Druke would try to face us down alone. His men are around here somewhere. They have to be!"

Karnes glanced again toward the trees on top of the bluff next to the trail. Did he see movement up there, he asked himself, or was it just a trick of his eyes?

No trick, something definitely moved. An instant later, he saw the afternoon sun reflect off metal.

Karnes realized that the other men who had been strung out along the trail had ridden up to him and Monkton before stopping, so now they were all in a bunch. "Scatter!" he yelled. "It's a trap!"

He had just lifted his horse's reins when a rattle of rifle fire came from the bluff. Powder smoke spurted from under the trees.

Karnes felt something smash into him and drive him out of his saddle. He had just enough time to gasp in pain and surprise before he hit the ground.

Druke had ridden out into the open as a diversion, Karnes realized as he tried to catch his breath. Druke had drawn their attention while his men moved into position on the bluff.

Rifle balls thudded into flesh. Men cried out in pain. The horses, spooked by the shots and the smell of blood, danced around skittishly in the trail.

Even though a hot poker seemed to be jammed into Karnes's side, he rolled over and got his hands and knees under him and scrambled toward some rocks and brush at the side of the trail. He was almost stepped on by the horses a couple times, but he reached the scanty cover and flattened out behind it.

Twisting around so that he could look back toward the trail, he saw three more men lying there. Two of them writhed in agony from their wounds, but one of them — Zach Summerville, Karnes realized —

lay motionless. Summerville wouldn't ever move again, at least not under his own power. A rifle ball had blown away a good-sized chunk of his head.

So much for not believing in jinxes.

The other four members of the group were still mounted. Monkton struggled to control his horse with one hand while at the same time he lifted a pistol in his other hand and fired toward the bluff. That wasn't going to do any good, Karnes thought. The range was too far.

A second later, Monkton doubled over and dropped his gun as he was hit. He managed to stay in the saddle as his horse dashed off along the trail. Karnes lost sight of him.

Karnes had dropped his rifle when he was shot out of the saddle. He had a pistol behind his belt, but it was useless in that situation. All he could do was lie low behind the rocks and wait.

And maybe pray for a miracle.

Will and Gray Otter heard the shots before they came in sight of the ambush. Given the distance and the direction of the sounds, Will had a hunch that Druke's men were firing from the top of Badger Bluff. That position overlooked the trail and was perfect for an ambush.

Gray Otter reached the same conclusion. "We should circle to the north and see if we can get behind them!"

Will nodded in agreement and turned his horse in that direction. "If Druke has all his men with him, we'll have to take them by surprise. Otherwise we won't have a chance."

"Neither will those trappers."

That was a grim truth, Will thought as he put his horse up a slope. They weaved around rocks and clumps of trees as they worked their way higher and circled around the sounds of battle.

A moment later, they reached a wide, upward-sloping ledge that allowed them to ride faster as they climbed. The ledge came out on a bluff that was even higher than the one overlooking the trail out of King's Crown. Will galloped along it with Gray Otter right behind him.

When the shooting was close, Will hauled back on his horse's reins and slid out of the saddle. He took his rifle with him as he ran toward the edge of the bluff. He knelt there and looked down at Badger Bluff, so called because some trappers had discovered a den of the feisty creatures there a while back.

The badgers, not wanting to be bothered

by humans, had moved on, but polecats had replaced them.

Two-legged polecats.

Hiding behind rocks and trees, more than a dozen men ranged along the top of the lower bluff, blazing away at the trail below them.

From where he was, Will couldn't see the trail, so he didn't know for sure who was down there, but he felt confident Druke's men were firing at the group of trappers who had tried to leave the valley with their pelts. He didn't see Druke, but that didn't mean anything. The outlaw had to be around somewhere close by.

Gray Otter came up and knelt beside Will. "Are we going to fight them?"

"We can't stand by and let them massacre those men," Will said.

"As long as the shooting has been going on, there's a good chance most of the trappers are dead already," Gray Otter pointed out.

Will couldn't argue with that. They'd come to the party late. If he and his companion took cards in the game, they would be risking their lives and probably wouldn't be much help to the men who'd been ambushed.

But as long as there was a slim chance

170

they might be able to save some of the trappers, Will couldn't turn his back and walk
away. He had never been able to abandon
someone who was in trouble, and Gray Otter knew that better than anybody else.

With a faint smile, Gray Otter pulled an
arrow from the quiver and nocked it. "I
thought that would be your answer."

"I didn't say anything," Will protested.

"You said plenty, for someone who knows
how to listen."

With that, Gray Otter pulled back the bow
and loosed the arrow, which flew swift and
straight to drive its flint head deep into the
back of one of the men reloading his rifle
for another shot at the hapless victims below.

CHAPTER 19

The bushwhacker screamed, dropped his rifle, threw his hands in the air, and slumped forward over the rock he had been using for cover.

An instant after Gray Otter loosed the arrow, Will fired his rifle and another man collapsed as the heavy lead ball blasted a path through his body.

Shooting people from behind went against the grain for Will, but under the circumstances he and Gray Otter didn't have any choice.

Gray Otter had sent three more arrows lashing down into the ambushers by the time Will had his rifle reloaded. Each of the shafts found its target. Three more of Druke's men were on the ground, either writhing in pain or lying motionless in death.

Will added to that total with another lethally accurate shot from his rifle.

In less than a minute, they had killed or badly wounded five of the renegades.

But the element of surprise was gone. Druke's men knew they were under attack from the upper ridge, and they twisted around to send rifle shots whistling up at Will and Gray Otter. The barrage forced them to draw back.

"Maybe if any of those trappers are still alive, they'll have a chance to get away while Druke's ruffians are occupied with us," Will said.

Gray Otter nocked another arrow. "That's what I hoped —"

Will spotted a figure behind Gray Otter and called out a warning, but it was too late.

A war club thrown with strength and precise accuracy whirled through the air and slammed into Gray Otter's back with stunning force.

"No!" Will cried as he saw his companion collapse. He whipped his reloaded rifle to his shoulder and fired as the buckskin-clad shape hurtled over Gray Otter and bounded toward him.

Will hurried his shot too much. He didn't know where the rifle ball went, but his attacker never slowed down.

In that brief moment of time, Will got a good look at the man. He saw the eagle feather, the thick raven hair, the coarse, pockmarked face, and most of all the red, staring, sightless right eye.

He had heard rumors that Jebediah Druke had a renegade Crow called Blood Eye working for him, or with him. Will hadn't had any idea why the man was called by that grotesque name.

But now he knew, although he barely had time for the thought to flash through his mind before Blood Eye crashed into him and drove him over backward.

Will clung desperately to his rifle and slashed at his attacker with the stock. Blood Eye squirmed like an eel and avoided the blow. His hand sought Will's throat.

Will tried to twist away, but the Crow's fingers closed around his throat and clamped down hard on his windpipe. Will gasped for air that could no longer reach his lungs.

The quarters were too close for the rifle to be any good as a club. Will dropped it and hammered at Blood Eye's head with a fist, using his other hand to claw at the Indian's good eye.

Blood Eye jerked his head back to avoid both of Will's attempts at self-defense. He got hold of Will's throat with his other hand and lifted the young man's upper body off the ground.

Then he slammed it back down so that Will's head smashed hard against the rocky earth. Combined with the lack of air, the blow left Will half-senseless and unable to muster much of a fight.

Blood Eye followed that up by ramming his knee into Will's belly. A ball of sickness swelled and exploded to fill Will's entire body.

No matter how much courage and resolve Will possessed, no matter much he hated Blood Eye or how much he was worried about Gray Otter, there was nothing he could do. Blood Eye's fierce, relentless attack had overwhelmed him, and a black tide of oblivion rose in Will's brain.

The darkness swallowed him whole, and he knew nothing else.

Pete Karnes had passed out with the sounds of slaughter filling his ears. As awareness seeped back into his brain, he realized that he didn't hear any more gunshots or screams.

Not everything was quiet, though. Men called out to each other, and from time to time he heard hoofbeats as horses moved around.

The wounded man pried his eyes open.

He couldn't see anything except the brush all around him.

Karnes felt bad about that. While his friends were under attack and fighting for their lives, he had attempted to hide. It was shameful.

The pain in his side, along with the hot, sticky flow of blood from the wound, had told him that he was badly hurt. He'd be so dizzy if he'd tried to stand up, he would have fallen down again. He knew his chances to help the other trappers had been mighty damned small, but the knowledge didn't make him feel any better.

He remembered creeping backward on his belly until the ground seemed to drop out from under his legs. He'd slid down into what seemed like a gully. It was so thickly choked with brush that if he hadn't been flat on the ground he never would have gotten into it.

Even that much effort had been too much for him and he'd passed out cold.

A part of him was surprised that he hadn't just gone ahead and died.

A spark of life remained, though, and time had allowed it to grow a little stronger. He had regained consciousness but with no idea how much time had passed since he blacked out.

Somebody was still around, that was for sure. He could hear them.

Carefully, Karnes moved a hand to his side. His buckskin shirt was stiff with drying blood that was still a bit tacky. He didn't try to probe under the shirt for the wound. It was there, no doubt about that, but as long as he didn't know exactly how bad it was, maybe he could ignore it.

He lifted his head, dug his elbows into the ground, and pulled himself forward a few inches. The gully's slope wasn't steep. He could climb out if he worked at it hard enough.

Not sure why he wanted to do that, it seemed like he ought to stay right where he was, hidden from Druke's men. They hadn't found him so far. Maybe they weren't even looking for him.

Something drove him on. Guilt, maybe. He hadn't even tried to help his friends. He felt around his waist and discovered that his pistol was still there. He could put up a fight if he had to.

That thought made a grin stretch across his rawboned face. Or maybe it was just a grimace.

He could make out some of the words he heard. A heavy voice ordered, "Don't leave any of those pelts behind."

Druke. Karnes would have bet on it. He had never actually heard the man speak, but the tone of command was obvious.

Another man asked, "What about our men who were killed?"

"We'll take them back to the fort and bury them, of course," Druke replied.

It was definitely a savage grin that curved Karnes's lips. So some of Druke's men had been killed during the ambush, he thought. That was good. He wasn't quite sure how it had happened, but it was good to know, anyway.

"And the prisoners?"

"Blood Eye will take care of them."

Karnes stopped right where he was. He had heard of Blood Eye; most everybody in King's Crown had. The renegade Crow had a fearsome reputation, so bad, in fact, that it was almost tempting to doubt if he existed. Blood Eye was like a made-up monster that parents used to scare their kids into behaving.

Karnes realized that Blood Eye was real and worked for Jebediah Druke, just like the rumors said. And he had prisoners. Some of the trappers who had tried to slip out of the valley? Karnes wondered. He didn't see how it could be anybody else, but he was surprised Druke hadn't just killed them outright, instead of taking them prisoner.

Curiosity impelled the wounded trapper to crawl a few more feet. He reached the top of the slope and peered out through a narrow gap in the brush. He stayed back far enough that he didn't think he would be noticed.

The rocks where he had taken cover earlier blocked some of his view, but he could see enough of the trail to tell what was going on. Druke and his men were mopping up after the ambush. A couple of them had gathered up the pack animals that were loaded with pelts.

Bloody corpses were scattered everywhere. Karnes bit back a sorrowful groan at the sight of his dead friends.

The earlier mention of prisoners made him search for them. He spotted a couple saddled horses with men slung over their backs and lashed into place. The prisoners didn't move any, so Karnes figured they were unconscious.

An Indian on a pony sat next to the two horses and held their reins. That would be Blood Eye, Karnes thought. He couldn't get a good look at the renegade Crow from where he was, but what he saw was enough to make a chill go through him.

Or maybe that was just the loss of blood. Karnes didn't think so, though.

He stiffened as he caught sight of Druke. The big man rode slowly on the trail with arrogance fairly radiating from him.

A smaller, bearded man rode beside him and asked, "How about them trappers? We buryin' all of them, too?"

"Leave them for the wolves and the buzzards," Druke snapped. "That ought to be a lesson for the others still in this valley. They'll know they can't defy me anymore."

A self-satisfied smile creased Druke's brutal face as he went on. "This has been quite a day, Sam. Close to a dozen enemies wiped out, and now Gardner and his pet redskin are in my hands, too. He's the one who's been keeping the other trappers stirred up against me. Once Blood Eye is through with them, that'll be the end of it. King's Crown will be completely mine from now on."

"You're right, Jebediah," Druke's lieutenant said instantly. "Too bad Blood Eye didn't grab those two before they managed to kill some good men."

"Their deaths will be avenged." Druke's voice began to fade as he and his companion rode away from the ambush site. "Blood Eye will make Gardner and Gray Otter pay . . ."

Weariness caught up to Karnes. He saw Druke's men ride by with the pack animals behind them, and then he closed his eyes and lowered his head. His strength had deserted him and taken with it any thought of taking a shot at Druke.

That opportunity had already passed him by.

For an unknowable amount of time, Karnes drifted in and out of consciousness. When full awareness finally came over him again, shadows had settled down over the land. Night would fall soon.

Karnes heard the steady *clip-clop* of hoofbeats as someone else rode along the trail. One of Druke's men had come back for something, he thought. Maybe even Druke himself.

Karnes closed his fingers around the pistol butt at his waist and summoned every bit of strength he had left in his body. He could tell from the sound of the horse that only one rider was out there.

If he could take the man by surprise and get off one shot, maybe he could redeem the honor he had lost by failing his friends earlier.

One shot, that was all he asked.

CHAPTER 20

Earlier in the afternoon, Preacher had heard shots coming from this direction, enough shots that he knew they meant real trouble, but he was too far away to reach the place quickly.

Even though the shooting had stopped, he still wanted to investigate, so he'd turned around and ridden back toward the pass. He hoped that he wouldn't come upon the scene of a massacre, but that seemed like a distinct possibility.

He couldn't help but remember the group of trappers he had encountered earlier. They had hoped to slip out of the valley without Druke finding out about it, and at the time it had seemed like they might get away with it.

But Druke was on the prowl in King's Crown. The grisly fates of Enos Mitchell and John Burton were proof enough of that. Druke could have gotten wind of Monkton's party somehow and moved to intercept them.

Given the number of shots he'd heard, Preacher figured that was the most likely explanation.

He hadn't found the location of the battle yet when dusk began to settle in. Soon he would need to find a place to camp. But he could search a little more first, he told himself.

It was a few minutes later when Preacher saw the huddled shapes sprawled in the trail up ahead. He muttered a curse. The grim sight was exactly what he'd expected to see . . . and hoped that he wouldn't. He heeled Horse into a little faster pace.

Suddenly, a man burst out of the brush to the right of the trail and waved a pistol at him. "You lowdown mongrel!" the man shouted hoarsely.

Before he could pull the trigger, before Preacher could even swing his rifle in that direction, a gray streak flashed through the air. Dog slammed into the man and knocked him down. The pistol discharged, but the ball went harmlessly into the air.

A moment later, the big cur would have torn out the man's throat, but Preacher yelled, "Dog, no!" before the slashing fangs could do their bloody work. In the fading light, he had caught enough of a glimpse of the man's face to recognize him as Pete Karnes.

As he swung down quickly from the saddle, the mountain man called, "Dog, guard!"

Dog backed off a couple feet and stood there with his hackles raised. He growled, but didn't make another move to attack Karnes.

Preacher ran to the fallen man and dropped to a knee beside him. The left side of Karnes's shirt was dark with blood.

Dog hadn't done that, which meant that Karnes had been wounded earlier in the battle Preacher had heard. He slipped a hand under Karnes's head and lifted it a little. "Pete, can you hear me? Pete?"

Karnes's face was drawn and haggard. His eyes were closed. Judging by the gory stain in his shirt, he had lost enough blood that it could have killed him. He clung to life, though, his chest rising and falling shallowly.

After a moment, Karnes's eyelids fluttered and then lifted. He couldn't seem to focus very well, but he rasped, "P-Preacher?"

"That's right, pard. You hang on. I'll take care of you, and you'll be all right."

"I . . . I'm shot."

"I can see that. I reckon Druke ambushed you."

"Y-yeah. Everybody's . . . dead . . . except for . . . Gardner . . . and that Indian."

"Gardner and Gray Otter?"

That was news to Preacher. He hadn't known that Gardner and Gray Otter were in the vicinity, let alone with Monkton's bunch.

But he could sort that out later, he told himself. At that moment Karnes needed help.

Preacher got his arms around the wounded man and lifted him with a grunt of effort. Preacher's rangy body held a lot of strength, but Karnes wasn't a small man, and semiconscious, he was dead weight.

Still, Preacher didn't struggle too much in carrying him to a grassy area not far from the trail. He lowered Karnes carefully to the ground, then fetched a blanket from his outfit, folded it to make a pillow, and slipped it under Karnes's head.

With that done, Preacher gathered some sticks for a fire. Even though having a fire at night could be dangerous, the light in the sky was fading fast and he had to be able to see in order to tend to the trapper's wound.

When he had the flames crackling and leaping, he tried to lift Karnes's shirt so he

185

could see how bad the injury was. The blood had dried and the shirt was stuck to the wound. Preacher fetched his canteen, poured water on the shirt, and soaked it for a while before he carefully worked the shirt loose.

He saw where the rifle ball had gone into Karnes's side, but he didn't find an exit wound. That wasn't good. It meant the ball was still inside Karnes's body. The chances of him surviving dropped even more. Most men would have been dead already.

Preacher had dug rifle balls out of men in the past, but not from their vitals. If he went to rooting around in there, he would do more harm than good.

There was really nothing he could do for Karnes except keep him comfortable. He lifted Karnes's head again and dribbled a little water into his mouth.

Karnes roused from his stupor. He blinked his eyes and peered up at Preacher with what seemed like a little more comprehension than he had displayed earlier. "Preacher?" he whispered.

"I'm right here, Pete," the mountain man said.

"I'm hurt . . . pretty bad . . . aren't I?"

"Bad enough," Preacher admitted. "Wish I had some whiskey to give you to help with the pain, but I don't."

"That's . . . all right. To tell you . . . the truth . . . it don't really hurt . . . that much. Just feels . . . cold."

"I'll get a blanket for you."

"Wouldn't do . . . any good," Karnes insisted. "Chill's comin' . . . from inside."

Preacher supposed that was right. A time or two in the past, he had been badly hurt and lost quite a bit of blood. He remembered how it felt.

In the time that Karnes had left, Preacher wanted to find out as much as he could about what had happened. He knew that was callous of him, but since there wasn't anything he could do for Karnes anyway, it made sense to find out what he could.

"Listen, Pete, I need to talk to you. Did Will Gardner and Gray Otter join up with your bunch?"

"No, we . . . we never saw 'em." Karnes's voice was weak, but he struggled to go on. "They must've . . . heard the shootin' . . . and come to see . . . what Druke was doin'. Those two . . . have been devilin' Druke . . . for months now."

"How did Druke capture them?"

"Don't know . . . Must've happened . . . while I was passed out. After I . . . got shot off my horse . . . I hunted cover . . . and

187

wound up in . . . a gully. I heard Druke and his men . . . talkin' . . . while they were gettin' . . . all those pelts. Druke said . . . Blood Eye would take care of . . . Gardner and Gray Otter."

"Could you tell if they were hurt?"

Karnes's head moved slightly from side to side. "They were tied onto . . . a couple horses. . . . Looked like they were . . . out cold . . . but I don't know if . . . they were hurt worse'n that."

"Looks like I'm gonna have to find Fort Druke and see if I can give 'em a hand."

"Thought you were . . . lookin' for somebody else."

"I was," Preacher said. "I reckon I still am, but that job will have to wait. You boys aren't the first ones Druke and his bunch jumped today. They killed a couple trappers named Mitchell and Burton."

"Don't reckon I . . . know 'em."

"Blood Eye tortured them," Preacher said bluntly, "but Mitchell was still alive when I found them. I promised him I'd go after Druke and Blood Eye and settle the score." He paused. "Now there's an even bigger one to settle. I figure Gardner and that Indian pard of his will make good allies when I set out to do that."

"You plan on . . . puttin' Druke outta

business?"

"You're damned right I do. I figure I'll put him under the ground while I'm at it. Somebody needs to bring justice back to King's Crown."

Karnes managed to chuckle. "Now that's the best news . . . I've heard all . . ." His voice trailed off and his head sagged. A sigh came from him.

Preacher knew that sound.

Karnes was dead.

Even though the trapper could no longer hear him, Preacher said, "Don't worry, Pete, I'll see to it that you're laid to rest proper, and Monkton and the others, too. King's Crown won't be a bad place to spend eternity, once I've sent Druke and Blood Eye and the rest of those varmints to hell where they belong."

He closed Karnes's sightlessly staring eyes and stood up. Digging graves for all the trappers would take quite awhile and wouldn't be that easy by firelight, so Preacher figured he'd better get started. He couldn't leave the bodies lying out overnight for scavengers.

He hoped Barnabas Pendexter would understand why the search for his missing son had to be postponed. Druke's reign of terror couldn't be allowed to continue unchecked. Someone had to stop him. It seemed to Preacher like he'd been elected for the job.

With some help from Will Gardner and Gray Otter, he thought, if he could get those two out of Druke's hands.

CHAPTER 21

Will's head pounded. Each beat of his heart made it feel like his brain might swell to the point that it would explode and blow his skull apart. At the same time, sickness roiled his stomach. It was all he could do to control the feeling and keep from throwing up his guts all the way down to his boots.

All that misery was a direct result of being thrown facedown over a saddle, tied into place, and forced to travel that way for miles and miles.

Gray Otter was in the same position. When Will had regained consciousness, he had been able to lift his head enough to catch a glimpse of buckskin-clad legs dangling next to the side of another horse being led along a trail. They had to belong to Gray Otter, who had to be alive.

Will wasn't going to allow himself to consider any other option.

The last thing he remembered was Blood

191

Eye choking him and banging his head on the ground. He was more than a little surprised that the Crow hadn't gone ahead and killed him.

He figured Blood Eye had spared his life and that of Gray Otter because he wanted to torture them to death. It was a chilling realization, but Will knew there was a good chance it was true.

The grisly idea would appeal to Jebediah Druke, too. The would-be ruler of King's Crown held a powerful grudge against the two of them. Surely he would enjoy watching them be killed inch by agonizing inch. Druke might even make an entertainment out of it for his men, like the ancient Romans with their arenas where prisoners suffered bloody deaths to the delight of the decadent crowds.

There was no use speculating about such things, Will told himself. For the moment, he was helpless and couldn't do anything to help himself or Gray Otter, no matter what gruesome fate Druke and Blood Eye had planned for them.

That might not always be the case, though. Will had to be patient, wait for an opening, no matter how small. . . .

Night had fallen and the riders were still

moving. They seemed to know the route quite well and didn't need light to see where they were going. That told Will they were on their way to Fort Druke.

More than once, he and Gray Otter had spied on the ragtag collection of cabins that Druke fancied to be a fort. They had talked about sneaking around and setting fire to the buildings, but Will knew that wouldn't have done any good in the long run. Druke's men would just chop down some of the trees that covered the valley and build more cabins.

After what seemed like an eternity, the group finally came to a stop.

Druke ordered, "Cut those two loose and get them off the horses."

Some of Druke's men started to follow the command, but a harsh voice instantly responded, "Stay away. I will take care of them."

"You've done enough work for one day, Blood Eye," Druke said. "Somebody else can handle the prisoners for a while."

"No!" The Crow was adamant. "They are my captives, Druke, not yours."

"All right, all right," Druke grumbled. "Do whatever you please."

"I always do," Blood Eye said coldly.

A moment later, Will felt a hard hand grip

his shirt. Blood Eye used a knife to saw through the rawhide lashings that held the young man on the horse.

Will slid off, with Blood Eye giving him a shove so that he landed on his rear end instead of his head. The jolt went all the way through him.

Will's hands and feet were still tied. Blood Eye took hold of his ankles and dragged him away from the horses. Somebody lit a lantern, and its flickering light revealed a pole corral where Druke and his men kept their horses.

A couple thick posts made from the trunks of saplings had been hammered into the ground near the corral. Blood Eye dragged Will over to one of them, leaned his back against the post, and tied him to it.

While Blood Eye returned to the horses to fetch Gray Otter, Will tested his bonds and found them to be so tight and so skillfully tied the chances of him being able to work loose were practically nonexistent.

He tried to keep his spirits up, but it wasn't easy.

Gray Otter didn't seem to have regained consciousness. Blood Eye hoisted the buckskin-clad figure over his shoulder and carried it to the other post. He set Gray Otter on the ground, then repeated the same sort of tying job he had done on Will.

There was one difference, however. When Blood Eye was finished, he cupped a hand over Gray Otter's cheek.

The gesture was a fleeting one and lasted only a second, but Will saw it and felt his heart sink even more. Blood Eye's touch, plus the fact that the Crow wouldn't let any of the rest of Druke's men get too close to the prisoners, told Will all he needed to know.

Somehow, Blood Eye had discovered the truth.

Druke's eyes narrowed as he watched Blood Eye tying the two prisoners to the posts near the corral. The Crow wasn't being any too gentle with them, but compared to what would come later, his treatment of them was nothing to complain about.

When Druke thought about how much trouble those two had caused him since his arrival in King's Crown, he looked forward to watching and listening as they died. He figured he could count on Blood Eye to make it last a long, agonizing time.

Blood Eye bent over to finish tightening Gray Otter's bonds. When he was finished, he reached up toward Gray Otter's face.

"I wouldn't trade places with those two

195

for ten thousand dollars."

The comment came from beside Druke and distracted him enough that he turned his head and looked over at Sam Turner.

"Of course not," Druke said. "They'll be dead in less than a day. Money wouldn't do you any good if you were in their place." He laughed. "Anyway, I didn't know you could count as high as ten thousand, Sam."

"I can count money," Turner said. "That's the only kind of cipherin' I'm any good at."

When Druke turned back to look at the prisoners, Blood Eye had left them tied to the posts and moved over to his pony. He took the mount's reins and led it away. He didn't keep his pony with the other horses, just another example of how he didn't associate with Druke's men any more than he had to.

To be honest, Druke thought, his men were probably glad about that. They didn't want to be around the Crow any more than was necessary, either.

It appeared that Gray Otter was still unconscious. Gardner was awake, though. Druke walked toward him, prompted by the urge to make some pointed comments about the torment Gardner would soon be forced to endure.

Blood Eye appeared as if out of nowhere.

He planted himself between Druke and Gardner and shook his head. "I take care of the prisoners."

Druke scowled. "I just wanted to let Gardner know what he's in for."

"No one comes near the prisoners but me."

Blood Eye's high-handed attitude got under Druke's skin. Without thinking, he said, "I think you've forgotten who's the boss here, Blood Eye. You work for me, remember?"

Behind Druke, Sam Turner took a sharply indrawn breath, as if he expected to see sudden violence and bloodshed erupt any second.

Blood Eye just smiled — or what passed for a smile on his hideous face, anyway. "We are allies, Druke. We work together. You are not my master. No man is."

Druke reined in his temper. He didn't need Blood Eye at the moment, since Gardner and Gray Otter were already his prisoners. The Crow hadn't even had to track them down; the two troublemakers had deposited themselves right into Druke's hands.

But there was no telling when he might need help from Blood Eye in the future. The smart thing to do was to stay on the renegade's good side as much as possible.

Realizing that, Druke forced himself to say, "You're right, of course, Blood Eye. I meant no insult. If you want to be in charge of the prisoners, that's fine. Just let me know when you're ready to start working on them. I want to see that."

Blood Eye grunted.

Druke didn't know what he meant by that, but it was better to assume that they were in agreement. If things turned out to be different, he would deal with the problem then.

To keep the peace, Druke turned to Turner. "Pass the word, Sam. Everybody is to steer well clear of the prisoners. Blood Eye is the only one who goes near them. Got it?"

"Got it, boss," Turner agreed. He hurried off to do Druke's bidding.

None of it really mattered, Druke told himself. What was important was that the last real threat to his reign was just about done for. Once Gardner and Gray Otter were dead, nobody would be left in King's Crown who would dare stand up to him.

Nobody.

CHAPTER 22

Preacher had only the vaguest idea where Fort Druke was. Under different circumstances, he might have waited until morning before he started his search for the place, but as long as Will Gardner and Gray Otter were Druke's prisoners, he didn't have that luxury. If he waited, the two of them might well be dead before he found Druke's stronghold.

He knew the cabins were somewhere close to the mountains that ringed the valley. It made sense to follow their great curving circle, since he was fairly close to those mountains when he'd finished burying Pete Karnes and the other trappers who'd been ambushed by Druke's men.

Sooner or later he was bound to come to Fort Druke.

He didn't say any words over the graves, just mounted up and rode away. Words sometimes made a difference, he supposed, at least for the folks left behind when somebody died, but in this case they wouldn't.

Any loved ones the trappers had were hundreds of miles away. The best thing Preacher could do for them, whether they ever knew it or not, was to see that justice was done.

With darkness cloaking the valley, the going was maddeningly slow. The floor of the broad depression that formed King's Crown wasn't flat and level. Hills, ridges, gullies, and ravines blocked Preacher's path from time to time and forced him to detour.

In addition, weariness settled into his bones. The day had been a long one, and he wasn't as young as he'd once been. He was far from being old, but he wasn't a wild young hellion anymore.

The stars wheeled through the ebony skies overhead as Preacher searched for Fort Druke. Hours passed.

It might take him until morning to locate Druke's hideout, he mused. He was keenly aware that Blood Eye might be torturing the prisoners while he searched.

He couldn't do anything about that except keep going, Preacher told himself.

Dog ranged far ahead of him. Most of the time, Preacher didn't know where the big cur was. But long after midnight — judging by the stars — Dog came bounding up to him and barked.

Preached hauled back on Horse's reins and brought the stallion to a halt. Dog sat down on his haunches and whined.

"You find something, Dog?" If Preacher had had something belonging to Gardner or Gray Otter, he could have given Dog the scent and told him to hunt. If Dog had been searching for the fort, it was because he had picked up on what Preacher wanted. At times it seemed that Dog and Horse were connected to him in an almost supernatural way.

Dog barked again in answer to Preacher's question.

Preacher swung down from the saddle. "All right, let's go take a look."

He tied Horse and the pack animal to a tree, took his rifle, and set off on foot after Dog. The big, wolf like creature stayed close enough for Preacher to follow, instead of vanishing into the darkness.

Preacher figured they had gone about half a mile when he caught a whiff of wood smoke. Out on the frontier that could mean one of only two things. Either a forest fire, which Preacher ruled out because the smoke would have been stronger, he would have seen the orange glow of flames in the sky, and would have been able to hear the crackling.

Or a campfire, which was much more likely.

Didn't have to be Fort Druke even if the smoke was coming from a campfire, he reminded himself. The fire might belong to some innocent trapper who hadn't run afoul of Druke's bunch yet.

But it had to be checked out. Preacher advanced cautiously through the pine trees and undergrowth, coming to a large open area at least half a mile wide. Mountains rose on the other side of it. Between the woods where Preacher stood and those slopes on the far side, a large fire burned in the middle of a straggling group of cabins.

It wasn't much of a fort, Preacher reflected wryly, but he was pretty sure he had found what he was looking for.

Dog pressed against Preacher's leg and growled. He wanted to charge in there and see what he could rip up.

Preacher scratched the big cur's head. "Not just yet, varmint," he said quietly. "We gotta get the lay of the land first. Find out what's what."

His keen eyes studied the so-called fort. He didn't see anyone moving around, but he figured Druke had guards posted out of sight. He couldn't just waltz in without somebody sounding the alarm.

His gaze came to rest on a couple posts not far from the corral. He could think of only one reason why somebody had stripped those tree trunks and then pounded them into the ground. They were there so prisoners could be tied to them and tortured.

Sure enough, two buckskin-clad figures were bound to the posts. They were sitting with their backs to the posts and their arms behind them. Their heads drooped forward.

The prisoners were either dead or asleep, their hands lashed behind the poles, Preacher thought. Since he couldn't see any blood on their clothes, he figured they were asleep.

He hoped that was the case, anyway.

The captives were several hundred yards away, so he couldn't make out any details, but he was convinced he was looking at Will Gardner and Gray Otter.

Seeing them tied to the posts brought back some vivid memories for him. When he was much younger, Blackfoot warriors had captured him and taken him back to their village. There he was tied to a similar post, and the Blackfeet, who hated and feared him, planned to heap branches around his feet and burn him alive the next morning.

Preacher had had something to say about that. In fact, he'd had a lot to say. He remembered a street preacher he had seen in St. Louis and had started to imitate the man. He let the words flow from him in a seemingly endless stream. It didn't really matter what he said as long as he kept talking.

Curious, the Blackfeet had gathered around to listen to him, even though most of them had no idea what he was saying. He talked all night and on into the next day, and as the hours passed and the Indians hadn't killed him, he began to realize that his plan was working.

They believed he was loco, and the Blackfeet, like most tribes, would not harm someone they considered to be touched in the head. To do so was to invite the wrath of the spirits. Madness made even their most hated enemy immune from their vengeance.

The ploy had saved his life. Once the story had gotten around among the other mountain men, the young trapper called Art had been dubbed "Preacher," and the name had stuck ever since.

As he looked at Gardner and Gray Otter,

he wondered if Blood Eye planned to burn them at the stake. It didn't seem likely.

From what he had seen of Blood Eye's work, the renegade Crow seemed to prefer using a knife.

As late as the hour was, Preacher thought that maybe Blood Eye planned to wait until daybreak to start torturing the prisoners. He was skillful enough at it to make the gruesome spectacle last all day.

Preacher gave serious consideration. He might have until dawn to free the two captives . . . but he couldn't afford to waste any time.

The open area around the cabins was going to make it difficult to approach them without being seen. What he needed was a distraction.

He thought he could circle the cabins and come at them from the direction of the mountains. He would be less likely to be spotted that way, with the dark backdrop of the peaks behind him.

If he could reach one of the cabins, he could set it on fire and free Gardner and Gray Otter while Druke and the others were occupied with fighting the blaze.

The corral was close by, and that was good. Once Gardner and Gray Otter were free, they could jump on three of the horses and scatter the others to slow down pursuit.

The one he'd really have to watch out for was Blood Eye. He wasn't sure the renegade Crow would be fooled by the fire.

Preacher considered the plan from every angle and decided that it stood a good chance of working. He couldn't come up with anything better, and there was no point in waiting. It was the time of night when most men slept the soundest.

"All right, Dog. Let's go." Preacher didn't waste any time. They worked their way through the trees and circled toward the looming peaks.

Within an hour they had gotten around to the other side of the fort. Preacher used every bit of shadow to cover their approach, and when they were within two hundred yards of the closest cabin, he stopped and whispered to Dog, "Stay."

Dog whined quietly, deep in his throat.

"I know you want to be in the big middle of it, old son, but you got to stay here," Preacher told the cur. "When hell starts to pop, I'll whistle for you."

Confident that Dog would follow his commands, Preacher went to his belly and began to crawl toward the cabin.

He didn't get in any hurry. Moving too fast would draw attention to him. To any sentry who happened to glance in his direction, he wanted to be nothing more than a slowly shifting patch of shadow on the ground.

Finally he reached the cabin's rear wall. Gaps between some of the logs where they hadn't been chinked very well allowed him to hear what sounded like several men snoring inside.

Preacher took out his knife and used the razor-sharp blade to carve quite a few strips of wood from the bottom log to serve as kindling. When he had a nice-sized pile, he poured powder from his powder horn around and on top of the pile. He didn't want to waste a lot of time getting the blaze started good.

With that done, he poured a thin train of powder as he backed away from the cabin. After about ten feet, he stopped and took out flint and steel from the possibles pouch at his waist.

One spark would do the job.

He was about to strike it when he caught a faint scent and recognized it as a mixture of bear grease and unwashed human flesh.

It was all the warning he needed to make him twist around, grab his rifle, and lunge up from the ground as Blood Eye hurtled out of the darkness at him.

CHAPTER 23

Preacher didn't know how Blood Eye had spotted him, but he didn't have time to worry about that. Nor could he be sure that his attacker was the renegade Crow, even though all his instincts told him that was the case.

Again, it didn't matter.

What was important was the tomahawk descending toward his head at blinding speed.

The mountain man jerked his rifle up and blocked the blow with the barrel. The tomahawk's handle hit the rifle with such force it almost drove the weapon out of Preacher's hands.

He hung on to it and pivoted at the waist as he rammed the stock at Blood Eye's head. Blood Eye darted aside just in time to avoid the blow and whipped the tomahawk at Preacher again, in a back-handed slash.

Preacher swayed away from it. If the

tomahawk had come any closer to his chin it would have given him a shave. But the miss threw Blood Eye off balance for a second, and that opening allowed Preacher to raise a knee into the Crow's belly.

Blood Eye doubled over, trying to turn that to his advantage by charging forward with his head lowered. He butted Preacher in the chest and sent the mountain man staggering backward.

Preacher figured Blood Eye would start raising a racket at any second, but instead the Crow fought in grim silence. Too proud to yell for help, Preacher decided.

That was fine with him. They would settle this man to man.

Preacher could have raised the rifle and shot Blood Eye as the Crow charged in again, slashing with the tomahawk and the knife he had pulled from its sheath. But a gunshot would have alerted Druke and his men more than a shout, and Preacher didn't want that. He whipped the rifle back and forth to parry the blows. Steel rang against steel, loud enough to risk alerting the guards without any shots being fired.

Blood Eye suddenly changed tacks. Close enough to kick Preacher in the right knee, he knocked Preacher's leg out from under him. He fell but caught himself on his left knee.

Blood Eye bulled into him and drove him over backward. That tactic backfired as Preacher planted his left foot in the Indian's belly and levered him up and over. Blood Eye sailed through the air and crashed down on his back.

Preacher rolled over swiftly and pushed up off the ground. His knee hurt where he'd been kicked, but the leg supported his weight. As Blood Eye started to get up, Preacher smashed the rifle stock into his jaw again. The blow stretched the renegade on the ground, out cold.

For a second, Preacher considered drawing his knife and cutting Blood Eye's throat. Some people would consider that cold-blooded murder, but to Preacher's mind it was more a case of justified execution.

Besides that, it would keep Blood Eye from getting on his trail later and seeking revenge.

But before Preacher could do that or anything else, he heard voices behind him.

"I tell you, I heard something movin' around back here."

"It was probably just an animal. I promise you, since we got Gardner and that Injun tied up, there ain't nobody else in this valley brave enough — or stupid enough — to come sneakin' up to the fort."

By the time the two men walked around the cabin's rear corner, Preacher had leaned the rifle against the wall and pulled both pistols from behind his belt. As the men stepped into view, he moved like a shadow behind them and slammed the guns down on their heads. The two men dropped like sacks of flour.

Irritated at the time he'd already been forced to waste, Preacher tucked the pistols away and hurried to find the end of the powder trail he had laid a few minutes earlier.

He dropped to one knee beside the line of powder, leaned over and used flint and steel to strike sparks. Several of them fell on the powder and ignited it. With a menacing hiss, fire crawled toward the pile of powder and twigs he had built against the rear wall of the cabin.

Blood Eye and the other two men he had knocked out were still unconscious. He had no time to deal with them. As the makeshift fuse sputtered and sparked behind him, he turned and started circling toward the corral and the posts where the prisoners were tied.

The rest of the so-called fort was quiet.

Evidently the two men who had walked behind the cabin were the only ones who had heard his struggle with Blood Eye.

The mountain man reached the cabin closest to the corral and crouched in the deep shadows next to it. From where he was, he could watch the cabin where he had set the fire.

He couldn't see any sign of flames. Had the little pyre failed to ignite? Had it not caught the cabin on fire after all?

Then he spotted a faint glow above the cabin's roof, and a moment later little orange tongues of flame licked into view. They grew rapidly and set the shake roof on fire. The dry wood went up with a *whoosh!*

Yelling came from inside the cabin, the smoke having roused the occupants from sleep. The door burst open and men dashed outside. Their shouts were louder as they called for help and bellowed, "Fire! Fire!"

More men appeared and ran toward the burning cabin. When several men emerged from the cabin beside which Preacher waited and dashed toward the blaze, he figured it was safe to make his move.

With his rifle in his left hand and his knife in his right, he ran toward the prisoners.

Will Gardner and Gray Otter lifted their

heads as he approached. Preacher called softly to them, "It's all right! I'm a friend!"

He ran behind the post where Gray Otter was tied. "Pull your hands up as far as you can and hold them apart."

When Gray Otter had done so, the mountain man leaned down and slashed the rawhide bonds. Gray Otter sagged forward.

"See if you can untie your feet while I cut Gardner's hands loose." Preacher moved over to the other post.

As Gardner lifted his hands and held them apart as much as he could, he asked, "Who are you, mister?"

"They call me Preacher. I've got a grudge against Druke, too."

"I've heard of you. I reckon you started that fire."

"Seemed like the thing to do at the time," Preacher replied dryly.

He was worried that some of Druke's men would discover Blood Eye and the other two men he had knocked out. That would warn them that something else was going on besides just a simple fire.

Gray Otter was still working at the ankle bonds.

Preacher hurried back over there. "I'll get 'em." He slid the blade between Gray Otter's ankles and sawed through the rawhide.

213

The strips were tough but no match for the razor-keen edge of Preacher's knife.

"I've got mine." Gardner pushed himself to his feet, then staggered a little. "Feet are a little numb from being tied for so long."

He stepped over to Gray Otter, clasped his friend's upraised hand, and hauled back. Gray Otter came upright.

"Can you run?" Gardner asked tensely.

Gray Otter nodded.

The cabin that Preacher had set on fire was completely engulfed by flames. Men ran around it, yelling and using buckets filled with water from the nearby stream in an attempt to put out the conflagration. They weren't going to be able to save the cabin, but they might keep the fire from spreading.

The hellish red light from the blaze stretched across the compound toward the corral. If any of Druke's men looked in that direction, they would know the prisoners were no longer tied to those posts.

"Let's go," Preacher said. "We don't have much time."

He led the former captives at a trot toward the corral. The horses had smelled the smoke from the burning cabin and were skittish in the way that animals always instinctively fear fire.

Preacher ducked between the poles. Gardner and Gray Otter followed him. The mountain man went to one of the horses that appeared to be the least spooked, a big, dark animal that stood facing him as he approached.

He held out a hand, let the horse smell him, and then scratched the horse's nose. When he was confident that the horse wouldn't dance away from him, a bound put him on its back.

He looked over and saw that his two companions had chosen mounts as well and gotten up on them. Preacher heeled his horse forward and rode over to the gate. He lifted the rope latch holding it closed.

At that moment, renewed shouting from the direction of the burning cabin caught his attention. Several men were running toward the corral. Flame bloomed in the darkness as they fired pistols.

Preacher swung the gate wide and shouted to Gardner and Gray Otter, "Scatter 'em!"

The former prisoners yelled and drove their mounts against the other horses. Already spooked, that was all it took to make the horses stampede wildly through the open gate and run away from the fire.

Preacher, Gardner, and Gray Otter were right behind them. They used the stampeding horses for cover and leaned over the necks of their own mounts to make themselves smaller targets.

With a hand gripping his mount's mane, Preacher guided the horse toward the trees. He let out a shrill whistle, a summons for Dog to follow them.

With chaos and commotion behind them, muzzle flashes spurting redly in the night, and rifle balls humming through the air, Preacher, Will Gardner, and Gray Otter lit a shuck away from Fort Druke.

CHAPTER 24

Preacher led the way toward the spot where he had left Horse and the pack animal. The horse he was on seemed to be a good sturdy one with decent speed, but he wanted his usual mount under him while they tried to get away from Blood Eye, Druke, and the rest of the killers.

If Preacher was sure of one thing, it was that Blood Eye would come after them.

If things had worked out differently, he would have killed the renegade Crow and considered it a good job well done.

Preacher had never been one to mope over things and wish they were different, but rather deal with life the way it was. That made his goals rather simple: put some distance between themselves and Fort Druke; give the slip to any pursuit; find a place to hole up; and then figure out things from there.

Even though they had been in the valley

for months, Gardner and Gray Otter seemed content to let Preacher take the lead. A few minutes later, he rode up to Horse and transferred from one mount to the other without touching the ground in between.

"You fellas have been dodgin' Druke for quite a while," he said to his two companions. "Is there a particular place you want to head for?"

"There's a cave we've been using as a hideout," Gardner replied. "I don't think Druke knows about it. If he did, he would have come after us there before now."

"Can you find it in the dark?"

Gardner laughed. "We can. You want me to lead the way?"

Preacher had untied Horse and the pack animal. "Go right ahead. I'll bring up the rear."

"I think I should warn you. It's kind of crazy, but I think I saw a wolf following us a few minutes ago."

It was Preacher's turn to laugh. "That was no wolf. That was Dog."

"A friend of yours, I take it."

"That's right."

"Well, I didn't get a very good look at him, but good enough to know that I'm glad he's on our side!"

Gardner heeled his horse into motion again. Gray Otter fell in behind him. Preacher was last in line, leading the pack animal. The horse he had ridden away from Druke's stronghold followed along, although Preacher had no way to lead it.

Gardner seemed to know where he was going. Preacher had to give him credit for that. The young man set a fairly fast pace despite the darkness.

Preacher listened for sounds of pursuit behind them, but didn't hear any. He thought they had a pretty good lead on Druke's men, and the way the horses had scattered, it was going to take awhile to round them up.

Gardner led the small party toward the mountains about halfway between the pass that opened in King's Crown from the east and Fort Druke, which lay toward the northwestern peaks. He found a trail that ran back and forth through the foothills and ascended gradually.

When Preacher glanced back after a while, he saw that they had climbed quite a bit without it being obvious. The valley floor lay a couple hundred feet below them.

The pines thickened until the riders had to proceed single file. A thick carpet of fallen needles muffled the thuds of the horses' hooves. After a time, they came out of the trees and found themselves facing a sheer sandstone bluff that rose another hundred feet.

Gardner rode toward the bluff, as if expecting his horse to climb up it like a fly.

Preacher was curious, but he didn't ask any questions. He figured he would find out what Gardner's intentions were in good time.

As they reached the bluff, Preacher finally saw what Gardner and Gray Otter had known was there all along. A narrow ledge, almost invisible from a distance, zigzagged back and forth up the sandstone face.

"I wish we had our own ponies," Gardner said as he paused at the base of the trail. "They're sure-footed, and they're used to this route. I don't know about these horses."

"Take it slow and easy," Preacher advised. "I don't reckon we need to rush. I don't think Druke and his bunch are anywhere close to us."

"Let's hope you're right." Gardner hitched his mount forward and started up the back-and-forth trail at a deliberate pace.

Gray Otter went along behind him, following closely, but not too close. It was never a good idea to crowd a person on a mountain trail. That had a way of leading to disaster.

Preacher came next, then the pack animal. The extra horse stopped at the base of the trail, seemed to study it for a moment, then turned and trotted away.

Preacher let the animal go. He could have rigged some sort of lead rope, but had chosen not to. In the fairly close confines of King's Crown, with mountains all around them, it was highly doubtful that their survival would depend on an extra horse.

The darkness and the narrow trail made for a nerve-wracking climb, but at least it didn't last very long. When they reached the top Preacher saw that they were on a bench about a quarter mile wide, dotted with trees and brush.

A rocky slope rose on the far side of the bench, but it wasn't nearly as steep as the bluff. When they reached the slope, Gardner dismounted and led his horse up. Gray Otter and Preacher followed suit. The angle was steep enough that Preacher was winded after a while.

What he had taken for a patch of shadow on the mountainside was actually the mouth of a cave. He called to Gardner, "That's your hideout?"

"That's right. Nobody but us knows that it's up here. And now you, of course."

"I don't figure on spreadin' the news. You ought to have a good view of the whole valley from up here."

"We do," Gardner agreed. "That helps us keep track of what deviltry Druke is up to."

"How'd you wind up declarin' war on him and his bunch, anyway?"

Gardner paused. "We saw what he was doing to the other trappers in the valley. Somebody had to stand up to him and try to put a stop to it." The young man shrugged his shoulders. "I have this . . . flaw in my character, I suppose you could say. I can't stand to see someone else being mistreated. Do whatever you want to me and I might put up with it, but try to hurt or take advantage of someone else, especially someone innocent, and I'll do my best to oppose you."

"I don't reckon anybody could call that a flaw," Preacher said. "Sounds like a mighty good quality to me."

"Well, sometimes it gets me into trouble." Gardner glanced at Gray Otter. "I'm sorry to say that sometimes it gets those I care about into trouble, too."

Gray Otter appeared to pay no attention to him. Preacher had a hunch the Indian wanted to fight Jebediah Druke just as much as Gardner did.

222

They reached the cave a few minutes later. The opening was big enough that the horses could be led through it one at a time. Once they were inside, the echoes told Preacher that the cave opened up into a fairly large chamber.

He heard the faint metallic ring of flint and steel, and light suddenly flared up. Preacher's eyes adjusted to the glare, then he saw that Gardner had lit a torch fashioned from pitch-coated rags wrapped around a branch that was stuffed into a crack in the cave wall.

Gray Otter untied a rawhide thong that held back a blanket hung over the entrance. The blanket fell so that it draped the entrance and blocked the light from the torch.

That was smart and told Preacher that the two of them had devoted some thought to making the hideout secure.

He looked around. The cave was about forty feet deep and maybe thirty feet wide. Big enough so that horses could stay on one side and people on the other.

In fact, a crude fence of plaited rawhide lay on the stone floor. Once the horses were led into the left side of the cave, that fence could be pulled up and fastened to keep them there.

Water filled a basin in the rock. Preacher couldn't tell if it was natural or if someone had hollowed it out. But either way it served to provide water for the horses.

The other part of the cave was furnished with rough shelves on the walls to hold supplies, a fire pit located under a natural chimney that would carry the smoke out, and a pile of thick buffalo robes on the floor.

"Not exactly all the comforts of home," Gardner said with a grin, "but we like it. We don't actually spend much time here. We prefer being out in the open."

"Can't blame you for that," Preacher said. "I'm the same way."

Gray Otter went to a pile of firewood in the corner, selected several branches, and returned to the fire pit to start building a fire. Gardner took the torch from the wall and lit the branches when Gray Otter had them ready.

When the fire was going, Gardner took a package wrapped in oilcloth from one of the shelves. "We still have a little salt pork, Preacher. We'd be glad to share it with you."

"I don't want to cause your supplies to run short."

"If it weren't for you, we'd still be tied to those posts facing death in a few hours. I think we can spare some salt pork."

"Well, in that case I'm much obliged. I'll throw in the makin's for some biscuits. We'll have us a feast."

"Might as well. And then after we've eaten" — Gardner's face and voice became grim — "we'll figure out how we're going to stop Jebediah Druke and that murderous Indian of his from hunting us down and killing us."

CHAPTER 25

The red haze of fury that seemed to hang in front of Jebediah Druke's eyes made the light from the burning cabin more garish. He waved his arms at his men still throwing buckets of water on the blaze in a vain attempt to quell it, and shouted, "Forget the damned cabin! Let it burn! Round up the horses, *now*!"

Sam Turner hurried up to Druke. "There's something around back here you need to see, Jebediah."

"What is it now? More proof of how incompetent all the rest of you are?"

Turner didn't answer that. He just hurried around the burning cabin.

Druke followed his second in command, still seething with anger.

The flickering light from the flames washed over three dark shapes on the ground. Two men had sat up already; the third still lay senseless on the ground.

One of the men who had regained consciousness was Blood Eye. He stood up sharply as Druke and Turner approached.

For one of the first times in Druke's memory, the renegade Crow wasn't stoic and expressionless. Lines of rage were etched into his leathery face. His good eye burned with a killing passion.

"Where is he?" Blood Eye demanded.

"Who?" Druke asked.

"The man who did this!"

"He got away," Druke said. "And that's not all. He freed the prisoners and took them with him."

"Gray Otter? Gone?"

"Yeah, and Gardner, too."

It struck Druke as a little odd that Blood Eye seemed more concerned with Gray Otter getting away than he did about Will Gardner's escape, but he pushed that thought aside. He had more important things to worry about. Somebody else had challenged him, had defied his rule in King's Crown, and that couldn't be allowed to stand.

"They scattered the horses, too," Druke went on, "but I've got the men rounding them up. We'll be able to get on their trail soon."

"My horse was not with the others,"

Blood Eye muttered. "I will go after them now." He started to turn away.

Druke took hold of his arm and stopped him.

Blood Eye's head snapped around as he glared a warning at Druke for touching him. Druke returned the glare, and his gaze was just as steady and angry as Blood Eye's. They were two very dangerous men. After the stalemate continued for a few tense seconds, Blood Eye looked away.

Druke knew better than to take that gesture as surrender. He knew Blood Eye didn't want to waste time arguing.

"Did you see who did this?" Druke asked.

"A tall man in buckskins."

"One of the other trappers from the valley?"

Blood Eye shook his head. "None of them are brave enough to invade your stronghold. Even if such a man existed, I would have killed him when we fought. This man is one we have not seen before."

"As fast and strong as you, huh?"

"Almost," Blood Eye replied.

It seemed to Druke that since Blood Eye was the one who'd wound up on the ground, unconscious, there wasn't really any "almost" about it. It wouldn't serve any purpose for him to point that out, however, so he kept the thought to himself.

Blood Eye started to turn away again when Druke stopped him by saying, "I know where they might be headed."

"Tell me," Blood Eye snapped.

"One of my men was doing some scouting a few days ago and saw Gardner and Gray Otter going into a cave in the mountains about ten miles from here, back around the valley to the southeast. You know it?"

Blood Eye didn't say anything.

Druke had a hunch that the renegade Crow was unaware of the cave's existence, but didn't want to admit it.

"Whoever it was that helped 'em escape, chances are they'll head for the hideout Gardner and Gray Otter have been using," Druke continued. "That's where we're going to start looking for them."

"I go alone."

"No, I'm coming with you," Druke insisted. "My men will start bringing in the horses any minute now, and I'm claiming the first one." He looked over at Turner. "Sam, fetch my rifle and plenty of powder and shot."

"You bet, Jebediah." Turner scurried away to obey the order.

"I go alone," Blood Eye said again, stubbornly.

"Not this time," Druke said. "When we find Gardner, Gray Otter, and the one who helped them get away, I'm going to be there to take care of them myself."

Most of the night was gone by the time Preacher rolled himself in one of the buffalo robes on the floor of the cave and went to sleep. Gardner had said that he and Gray Otter would take turns standing guard in the hours of darkness that were left.

Weariness quickly caught up with Preacher. He had the frontiersman's knack of being able to drop off to sleep whenever he had the chance. He slept deeply, although a small part of him remained alert for trouble, allowing him to wake up instantly whenever he needed to.

Dog hadn't come into the cave, but Preacher knew the big cur was somewhere in the vicinity. He was the best sentry of all, but Preacher didn't say that to Gardner and Gray Otter. No need to hurt their feelings.

A change in the light woke Preacher. He opened his eyes to slits so they would adjust quickly. The fire was out, and sunlight slanted into the cave through the tiny gaps around the blanket that closed off the entrance. Preacher knew the sunlight was what had roused him from sleep.

He heard someone moving around. Gray Otter's slight figure knelt beside a little pool on the same side of the cave.

A few feet away, Gardner snored lightly in his robe.

Gray Otter's back was turned toward Preacher. As the mountain man watched, Gray Otter grasped the bottom of the buckskin shirt and peeled it off, baring a smooth, golden-skinned back. The reddish hue Preacher expected to see was missing.

Not only that, but a wide band of white cloth was wrapped around the upper part of Gray Otter's torso, just under the arms. Preacher didn't see the point of that unless the Indian had been wounded and the cloth was a bandage.

Gray Otter leaned forward, lowered cupped hands into the water, and lifted them to wash.

Something about watching those ablutions made Preacher uncomfortable. The whole thing felt too intimate somehow. He closed his eyes and decided he would just pretend to be asleep for a while yet, until Gray Otter finished.

The sound of someone else moving around made him change his mind. He opened his eyes again, but just barely.

Gardner's snoring had stopped. The young man crawled out of his blankets, stood up, and stretched. He went over to the pool and dropped down on his knees next to Gray Otter.

Gardner took off his shirt like his friend had, although unlike Gray Otter, once he did he was bare from the waist up. He splashed water on his face and chest and then leaned forward to plunge his whole head into the pool.

When he came back up he laughed softly. For a second, his wet hair hung forward, rather than dropping down over the back of his neck the way it usually did.

The light in the cave was actually rather dim, but it was bright enough for Preacher to catch a glimpse of something on the back of Will Gardner's neck. He stiffened and his eyes opened wider as he realized what he had just seen.

Gardner had a birthmark on his neck shaped like a half moon.

Just like William Pendexter was supposed to.

Preacher closed his eyes for a moment and cursed himself as ten different kinds of fool. He should have suspected long ago that Will Gardner was actually the young man he had come to King's Crown to find.

And yet there was no solid reason for him to have done so, he mused, other than the similarity in names . . . and there were a hell of a lot of fellas named William or Will to be found west of the Mississippi, and everywhere else, for that matter. True, Gardner and Pendexter had shown up in this part of the country about the same time, but that didn't mean anything, either.

At least he no longer had to feel guilty about the job he had promised Barnabas Pendexter he would do. He had carried out his mission, even without meaning to.

The discovery he had just made didn't have any effect on their immediate problems. Druke and Blood Eye would still come after them, and Preacher and his new friends had to deal with that threat somehow.

Preacher sensed as much as heard more movement and opened his eyes again. He wished he hadn't as soon as he realized what he was looking at.

Will Gardner had drawn Gray Otter into his arms. The two of them kissed passionately as they knelt next to the pool. As Gardner embraced Gray Otter, he pulled the band of white cloth down his friend's back.

Preacher didn't much care what folks did in their own bedrolls, but he didn't particularly want to see what he was seeing. Pretending to be asleep was going to be a mite more difficult, he thought as he squeezed his eyes shut.

"No, Will, we can't, not with —"

Even though the words were whispered, Preacher realized the voice belonged to a woman. Surprise snapped his eyes open and he pushed himself up on one elbow. "What the hell!" he exclaimed.

A few yards away, Gray Otter gasped and jerked around toward him. That motion revealed small breasts tipped with coral and unmistakably those of a woman. She wailed, "Oh, no!"

Will Gardner moved quickly in front of her to shield her.

As for Preacher, he realized that he'd been wrong earlier when he thought he was ten different kinds of fool.

Twenty kinds was more like it.

CHAPTER 26

"We didn't really mean to lie to anybody," Will Gardner said a short time later after he and "Gray Otter" were fully dressed again. "It's just that it was easier — and safer — to let everybody think that Charlotte was a man."

"Masquerading as an Indian was my idea," she said. "I thought it would make people look less closely at me. My hair and skin are dark enough, and Will concocted a dye from some berries that made my hands and face appear slightly more reddish."

The three of them were sitting on the buffalo robes in the cave, Gardner and Charlotte side by side and Preacher facing them. So far Preacher hadn't mentioned the birthmark on the back of Gardner's neck or the fact that he knew the young man was really William Pendexter.

It was enough for the moment to deal with "Gray Otter" being a young woman.

"You're not angry with us, are you, Preacher?" Will asked.

Preacher scratched at his beard. "No, I reckon I ain't exactly mad. It ain't really any of my business, to start with, and last night we had our hands full gettin' away from Druke and his bunch. Wasn't much of a chance to sit down and explain that Gray Otter here is really a gal." He chuckled. "And to tell you the truth, I was a mite relieved to find that out, instead of what I was thinkin' for a minute there."

Charlotte's face was plenty red as she looked down at the floor of the cave. "We thought you were sound asleep," she said quietly.

"It was my fault," Will added. "I got carried away —"

Preacher lifted a hand to stop him. "Don't worry about it. I ain't one to go pokin' around in other folks' private business. Right now, we need to figure out what we're gonna do about Druke and that red-eyed varmint he's got workin' for him." Any revelations about Will's true identity could wait until later, he thought, as well as an explanation of who Charlotte really was and what she was doing all the way out on the frontier. From the sound of her accent, Preacher figured she was from back east

236

somewhere, like Will.

Maybe they had known each other in Philadelphia, and that was the real reason William Pendexter had run away to the mountains. It could be that her father had forbidden the two of them to be together.

"Do you really think they'll come after us?" Charlotte asked. "We've been bedeviling Druke and his men for months now. I'm not sure how what happened last night is any different."

"Blood Eye wasn't involved then," Will said. "You didn't get as good a look at him as I did. The man's insane. Once he sets his sights on something, I don't think anything would stop him except death."

The young man paused, then went on. "There's something else to consider, Charlotte. I'm not sure how he figured it out, but I believe there's a good chance he knows that you're a woman."

"You mean —"

"I think maybe he wants you for himself," Will said grimly.

Now that Preacher knew the truth, it seemed obvious to him that Charlotte was female. But in the slightly baggy buckskins, with her breasts bound and her hair braided Indian-fashion, with her hands and face dyed to a more reddish tint, if she stayed in the shadows and never spoke, he could see how it was possible she had pulled off the masquerade. It wouldn't stand up to close scrutiny, but she had done everything she could to avoid that.

"Druke's bound to be pretty fed up with you two interferin' with his plans, too. That's another reason for him to come after you again. But you said they don't know about this cave, so that gives us a little leeway. I think maybe what we should do is turn the tables on 'em."

"An ambush, you mean?" Will asked.

"That's right. Blood Eye's probably a pretty good tracker, and we were in a hurry last night, so we weren't takin' the time to cover our trail. But with the horses scattered and it bein' dark to boot, chances are he didn't get on our trail until this mornin'. We ought to have time to backtrack a little and get ready for 'em."

"I hope I get a good shot at Druke with my bow this time," Charlotte said.

Every time Preacher heard her cultured tones, he was struck by how the seemingly genteel young woman thrived in such primitive conditions and skewered bad men with arrows. She sounded like someone who'd never done an honest day's labor in her life, but her actions were just the opposite.

He gave in to his curiosity and asked, "I hope you don't mind me bein' nosy, miss, but I was just wonderin' what your last name is and how you came to be out here so far from civilization."

Before Charlotte could answer, a loud growl sounded from outside the cave.

Preacher sprang to his feet. "That's Dog."

The big cur still hadn't been around this morning, but Preacher wasn't worried about him. He knew from long experience that Dog could take care of himself. He knew as well that if Dog sensed danger, he would warn them if at all possible.

Since it was daylight outside, there was no need for the blanket to close off the cave mouth. Preacher picked up his rifle and swept the makeshift curtain aside.

Dog stood just outside the cave mouth, his fur bristling as he stared down the slope. Another rumbling growl came from deep in his throat.

From behind Preacher, Will said, "That's the wolf I saw last night, all right. You're sure he's really a dog, Preacher?"

"I'm sure. Him and Horse are my best friends. They been with me a long time."

"What's he growling at?"

Preacher shook his head. "I don't know. I don't see anything out of the ordinary, but

239

Dog must smell something. I trust his instincts."

Charlotte said, "Druke's men can't have caught up with us already."

"I didn't think it was likely," Preacher said, "but we can't rule it out. Better grab your guns, just in case. I'm gonna have a look around."

Will and Charlotte retreated into the cave while Preacher started cautiously down the slope. "Dog, hunt."

Dog bounded away, then stopped suddenly and whirled around to gaze up the slope past Preacher. A vicious snarl came from him, and Preacher knew it was a warning.

He turned to bring up the rifle and caught a glimpse of Blood Eye hurtling down toward him.

In that instant, Preacher knew the renegade Crow had climbed onto a rocky outcropping above the cave mouth and launched himself from there. He shouldn't have had time to find the hideout, but obviously that wasn't the case.

The next split second, Blood Eye crashed into Preacher and knocked him to the ground. As they struggled, they tumbled down the rocky slope.

"Preacher!" Will shouted from the cave

mouth. He rushed out to go to the mountain man's aid.

A shot blasted. The rifle ball ricocheted off a rock just inches from Will's side. He threw himself backward into the cave.

Partway down the slope, Blood Eye found himself on top of Preacher and lifted his tomahawk for a stroke at the mountain man's head.

The collision with Blood Eye had jolted the rifle out of Preacher's hands, and he couldn't reach his pistols or his knife. He grabbed Blood Eye's wrist instead and stopped the deadly blow as it started to fall. With a grunt of effort, he heaved Blood Eye to the side and rolled after him.

Preacher ended up on top. He tried to drive a knee into the Crow's groin, but Blood Eye twisted at the hips and took the would-be crippling blow on his thigh. Blood Eye scissored his right leg up, hooked the ankle in front of Preacher's throat, and forced the mountain man off of him. Preacher rolled again and came to an abrupt, painful halt as a large, sharp-edged rock dug into his back.

A shot boomed and Dog yelped in pain. Preacher looked around for the big cur, but before he could spot Dog and see how badly his old friend was hurt, Blood Eye dived at him again. Once more, Preacher had to grapple with the renegade.

Blood Eye was in the grip of a killing frenzy. As they struggled over the tomahawk, his face, only inches from Preacher's, was twisted in grotesque lines.

Preacher had never seen a more frightening visage in his life. Blood Eye was like something out of a terrifying nightmare, the sort that made a man bolt up out of sleep with a panic-stricken cry on his lips.

Fortunately, Preacher had never been the sort to suffer from nightmares.

He knew that Blood Eye was just a man, not a monster. He wrenched hard on the Crow's wrist, and Blood Eye dropped the tomahawk.

Instantly, Preacher hammered a fist into the renegade's face. The blow was a short one, traveling no more than six or eight inches, but it packed tremendous power and rocked Blood Eye's head back.

Preacher hit him again, but Blood Eye jerked his head aside just enough to make the punch skid off his cheek without doing any real damage. Like a striking snake, his hand darted up and closed around Preacher's throat, rolling Preacher onto his back.

A huge dark shape loomed up behind

Blood Eye and blotted out the sun. "Hold him still!" a harsh voice ordered.

Druke, Preacher thought. Had to be. He tried to heave himself free from Blood Eye's grip as Druke struck with a rifle butt. Preacher saw it coming at his face, but couldn't get out of the way in time.

The craven blow exploded in his brain like a keg of black powder going off. Preacher's last thought before darkness swallowed him was that it had taken both of them to beat him.

CHAPTER 27

"Stay back," Will warned Charlotte as they crouched just inside the cave mouth. He had tried to get a shot at Druke as the man knocked out Preacher, but Druke and Blood Eye had moved too fast. The two of them had dragged the unconscious mountain man behind a boulder and taken cover behind the big rock themselves.

"There are just two of them," Charlotte argued. "We can take them."

Will shook his head. "From where they are, they've got too good a view of the cave. As soon as we step out, they'll kill us. Druke came pretty close with that first shot of his."

"They don't want us dead. Blood Eye will want to torture us, like he's planned all along."

"That may be what Blood Eye wants, but I think Druke is fed up with all of it and just plans on killing us as efficiently as possible."

"We can't leave Preacher in their hands. Not after he rescued us the way he did. We'd be dead if not for him."

Will's expression was grim as he nodded. "I know. I'm trying to think of some way out of this, but so far . . ." He fell silent as he turned to look up at the narrow chimney above the fire pit.

It was a natural passage through the rock and came out about a hundred yards up the slope. Even as he considered the idea, he discarded it. The chimney wasn't wide enough. His shoulders would never fit through it.

"I could do it," Charlotte said as if she had read his mind. "I could climb out through there, slip around behind them, and take them by surprise. They'd never be expecting it."

Will shook his head. "No, it's too dangerous —"

"More dangerous than waiting in here for the rest of Druke's men to arrive? You said it was just the two of them, didn't you?"

"That's all I saw," Will admitted.

"Druke and Blood Eye must have hurried on ahead of the others, but the rest of Druke's men will be coming along behind them. You know that."

Will nodded reluctantly. "I suppose you're right."

"You know I am. This is our only chance, Will. Otherwise, they'll lay siege to the cave and we'll be trapped here. Sooner or later, they'll root us out, and then . . ." She didn't have to elaborate on what would happen then. Both of them knew all too well the fate that lay in store for them if Druke and Blood Eye got their hands on them again.

At least they just wanted him dead, Will thought.

Blood Eye had something worse in mind for Charlotte, and in the end she would die, too, more than likely.

If she didn't, she would wish she were dead.

With no other way out of the cave, Will reluctantly agreed with Charlotte's suggestion. "All right. There doesn't seem to be any choice. But you have to promise to be careful."

She smiled, came up on her toes, and pressed her mouth to his. When she stepped away from him, she said, "Long past time for such as that, I'd say."

Charlotte's pulse hammered in her head as Will lifted her into the chimney. While he gripped her calves, she rested her moccasin-shod feet on his shoulders and reached up into the opening to feel for handholds.

The roughly circular chimney was barely wide enough to admit her shoulders with her bow and the quiver of arrows slung on her back, and its sides were slick with soot from the fires that had burned underneath it over the past months. Her hands might be stained permanently black by the time she reached the top.

That was a small price to pay for their freedom.

She would do whatever it took to save Will and remain with him. So much had happened, before they left Philadelphia together and since. She had done things that she would have deemed impossible at an earlier time.

No turning back, they had promised each other, and it was true. Nothing could ever again be as it had been before.

Her fingers closed over a rough protrusion in the rock. "I think I've got it."

"Be careful," Will said again.

He maintained his grip on her calves as she lifted herself higher in the chimney and used her other hand to search for a second grip. She found one, made sure of it, and pulled herself still higher.

He had to let go of her then. Instantly, she missed his touch.

But she kept climbing. She braced a knee against the side of the chimney. It was so narrow that once she got her body entirely inside it, she could rest her back against one wall and her feet against the opposite wall and work her way up by that method.

"I'll keep them occupied," Will called from below, and a moment later she heard a shot. He had told her to be careful, but he was taking a bigger chance than she was. Druke and Blood Eye could fire into the cave mouth, and there was no telling where the rifle balls might ricochet.

Charlotte put that danger out of her mind and concentrated on what she was doing. She heard more shots from inside and outside the cave alike but told herself not to think about them.

The climb was slow going, so slow that the hundred yards might as well have been a mile. The chimney had a slight slope to it, which made it a little easier than if it had been straight up and down. The small circle of light that marked the top came slowly, inexorably, closer.

The upper opening provided enough light for her to see the chimney walls as she climbed higher, helping her locate hand-holds and footholds. She moved a bit faster, but still cautiously. If she slipped, it was possible she would fall all the way to the bottom.

Such a plummet might prove fatal. At the very least, she would be badly injured and the situation would be no better than it had been before.

At last, the opening was only a few feet above her. She paused for a moment to catch her breath. Sweat from her exertion coated her entire body. Between the dye, the soot, and the sweat, she supposed she looked a terrible sight, but none of that mattered. She could always clean up later.

If they survived.

Ready to make the last haul, she shoved with her feet and reached up. Her right hand gripped the edge and she pulled herself higher, reaching out through the opening with her left arm as she sought something else to grab.

Something grabbed her. Fingers that felt like bands of iron clamped around her wrist. She cried out in shock and pain as someone with great strength lifted her out of the chimney.

Her exclamation turned into a scream as she saw Blood Eye leering down at her.

"Charlotte!" Will shouted at the other end of the passage. "Charlotte!"

She had no chance to respond to him. As

Blood Eye hauled her out into the open, he brought his other arm around in a vicious backhanded blow that cracked across her face and drove her head to the side. He hit her in the stomach then flung her on the ground.

Charlotte groped for the knife at her waist, determined to put up a fight even though it was probably in a losing cause.

Before she could pull the weapon from its sheath, Blood Eye kicked her in the head. She felt the brutal blow, and that was the last thing she knew.

Something had gone terribly wrong. Charlotte's frightened cry had told Will that much. He rushed from the cave mouth to the spot just underneath the chimney and peered anxiously up through the passage. "Charlotte! Charlotte!"

He was too distraught to maintain the pose that she was an Indian warrior called Gray Otter. He saw something dark blocking the chimney's other end, and then suddenly it was gone, replaced by a small point of light.

The chimney was empty. One way or another, Charlotte had gotten out of it.

Will rushed back to the cave's entrance. As he'd traded potshots with Druke and

Blood Eye, he'd thought both of them were behind that boulder with Preacher as their prisoner. He realized that one of the men — probably Blood Eye — could have crawled backward and used the boulder to shield him from view until he was far enough away to circle around and get above the cave.

Maybe Blood Eye had spotted the place where the chimney opened, or maybe the renegade Crow had just assumed there had to be such an opening and had gone in search of it. Either way, it was obvious that Charlotte had run into trouble and everything was going to hell.

Giving in to the fury that surged up inside him, Will fired at the boulder even though he didn't have a real target at which to aim. The ball *spanged* off the big rock.

A harsh laugh came from behind the boulder. "What's wrong, Gardner?" Druke called. "Lose your little friend?"

Will cursed as he reloaded.

Druke laughed harder. "You better come out of there. You need to take a look at what I can see from here. Blood Eye's got your —" Druke stopped short.

What did that mean? Will thought.

When he got his answer a moment later, he almost wished he hadn't.

"He's a woman!" Druke said exultantly. "I mean she is. Gray Otter's a woman!"

Will groaned. The only way Druke could know that was if Charlotte was Blood Eye's prisoner.

"Better get out here," Druke said again. "I was gonna shoot you down where you stood as soon as I got the chance, but now there's no need. Do what I say, Gardner, or the woman dies!"

Will swallowed hard. As he gripped the rifle tightly, he stepped out of the cave. Druke emerged from behind the boulder and covered him.

"Up here," a guttural voice called.

Horrified by the thought of what he was going to see, Will turned and gazed up the slope. Blood Eye stood next to the chimney opening with his arm around an unconscious Charlotte to hold her up in front of him. His other hand pressed a knife to her throat.

The Crow had ripped Charlotte's buckskin shirt open and torn down the band of cloth around her torso, exposing her breasts.

"I knew you had a squaw with you," Druke said with a smirk, "but I didn't know it was Gray Otter. Throw all your weapons down, Gardner, or Blood Eye will cut her throat. You know he'll do it."

Will didn't doubt that for a second. He was convinced that Blood Eye wanted to have his way with Charlotte, but he would forgo that evil pleasure if he had to.

"All right," Will said. "I surrender."

"Not good enough to say it." Druke gestured curtly with his rifle barrel. "Get rid of your guns and knife, now."

Will set the rifle on the ground at his feet, pulled the brace of pistols from his belt and tossed them down next to the rifle. His hunting knife came last as he dropped it beside the guns. He was no longer armed.

Nothing left to him but despair.

CHAPTER 28

Preacher had always figured when it was his time, he'd be staring into the face of Ol' Scratch himself. After meeting the renegade Crow, he wasn't sure the Devil could be any uglier than that blasted Blood Eye.

The idea that St. Peter might welcome him instead of Beelzebub occurred to him, but given the sinful life he'd led, he considered the possibility pretty far-fetched. But he wasn't facing either, which just went to prove that he could be wrong from time to time. His head hurt like blazes and that meant he was still drawing breath.

He didn't smell brimstone, either . . . although smoke stung his nostrils and he heard flames crackling somewhere nearby. Maybe he was wrong and he was in Hell after all, he thought.

Cold water hit him in the face like a fist. He jerked and sputtered, unable to control his reaction to the shock of the water.

"I thought you were wakin' up," a man's voice said. "Now that I'm sure of it, I better go tell Jebediah."

Preacher forced his eyes open and blinked them rapidly. By the light of a good-sized fire burning nearby, he saw a short, whiskery man in buckskins hurrying away.

Preacher lifted his head, shook it to get rid of the water, and looked around. He was back at Fort Druke, tied to one of those posts where Will and Charlotte had been bound the previous night. At least, Preacher supposed that had been the previous night. He knew he had been unconscious for a long time because it was dark again, but didn't think he'd been out cold for more than a day.

Rather than sitting down with his back against the post like the other prisoners had been, Preacher was tied so that he was standing up. His weight hung forward on his arms, which caused his shoulders to ache and throb.

He couldn't feel his hands, so he knew the bonds around his wrists were cruelly tight.

A few feet to his left, Will Gardner was in a similar predicament. His head drooped forward, and from the limp aspect of the young man's body, Preacher could tell that he was unconscious.

In the firelight, Preacher saw numerous bruises and bloody scrapes on Will's face. He'd been beaten savagely.

Preacher suspected that Jebediah Druke was responsible for that punishment. It was the sort of crude viciousness in which the outlaw would indulge.

Blood Eye went for subtle but more agonizing torture.

Preacher looked around for Charlotte, but didn't see her. His blood boiled with anger as he thought about her being Blood Eye's captive all day. There was no telling what perversions the renegade might have subjected her to during that time.

He spotted several men coming toward him. One of them was the little whiskery gent who had thrown the water in his face.

Next to that man strode Jebediah Druke. He wore a big smile on his face as he approached. It didn't make him any less ugly. Three or four other men followed him, all of them hard-faced individuals who looked capable of almost anything.

"Sam told me you were awake," Druke said as he came to a stop in front of Preacher. "I want to know who you are. I tried to convince Gardner to tell me, but he was stubborn."

256

"You want to know who I am, eh?" Preacher asked as a wry smile curved his lips under the drooping mustache.

"That's right."

"I'm the fella who's gonna kill you and bust up your phony little kingdom."

Druke's smile disappeared as his face darkened with anger. "That's mighty big talk for a man who's tied hand and foot," he snapped.

"Maybe I won't always be. Fact is, if you want to cut me loose, we can settle this here and now, Druke. Just you and me." Preacher paused a moment. "Oh, I reckon you can get your tame Injun to help you, if you want to even the odds a mite."

Druke took a step toward him.

The man called Sam said quickly, "Better take it easy, boss. He's just tryin' to get your goat. No need to give him what he wants. He ain't goin' nowhere until we're ready."

Druke glared at Preacher for a long moment, then drew in a deep breath and blew it out. "You're right, Sam. I planned on killing him first thing, but that was before I knew we were going to take him alive. We can have the same show we planned all along with Gardner and Gray Otter. We'll just have an added attraction now."

"Well, I ain't so sure Blood Eye's gonna

give up that gal," Sam said nervously. "He's had her off in the woods all day and acts like she belongs to him. But we got Gardner and his friend here for sport." Sam shook his head. "Who'd have ever figured that Gray Otter was a gal? She must've killed half a dozen of us! I never heard of no woman doin' anything like that."

Preacher said, "I doubt if she's like any other woman gutter trash like you boys would ever run into."

"You just keep runnin' your mouth," Druke said. "You'll be sorry before it's all over."

"I'm already sorry I run into a varmint like you."

At the other stake, Will Gardner suddenly groaned. He shook his head slowly from side to side as he regained consciousness.

Druke stepped over to Will, took hold of his chin in a brutal grip, and wrenched his head up. Will blinked and grimaced in pain.

"Now you're both awake," Druke said. "That's good. I'm not exactly sure yet what we're gonna do with you, but when I figure it out I want both of you to know."

"Ch-Charlotte . . ." Will said through bruised, swollen lips.

"She's with Blood Eye," Druke replied harshly. "Has been all day. I reckon he's probably put her through the wringer. Even if the two of you were free, you wouldn't ever want her again."

"That's where . . . you're wrong," Will said. "Nothing any of you villains do . . . could ever touch her. Not the real Charlotte . . . the one I love."

"Keep telling yourself that, boy. Keep telling yourself, and try not to think about all the things Blood Eye's done to her . . . and all the things he'll do to her in the future."

Will groaned again, and Preacher said, "Keep your spirits up, son. These fellas are a bunch of talk and not much more."

Druke was about to say something else, but Sam touched him on the arm. "Look who's comin', Jebediah."

Preacher twisted his neck to gaze in the direction the whiskery little man was looking. Two figures had entered the large circle of firelight and came toward the prisoners.

"Charlotte!" Will cried in a choked, horrified voice.

Charlotte stumbled along. She might have fallen if not for Blood Eye's hard hand on her arm. Her face was puffy. Her thick black hair tumbled loose around her shoulders. She still wore her buckskins, but the torn shirt hung open. It swayed a little with each step she took, revealing the valley between her breasts.

The rest of Druke's men began to gather. Most of them eyed Charlotte with open lust. They were careful not to stare at her for too long at a time, though, from fear of offending Blood Eye.

"I didn't know if you'd bring her in to watch the sport or not," Druke said to the renegade Crow as he and Charlotte came up to the group and stopped. "I'm glad you did. After all the things she's done, she deserves to see everything that happens to Gardner and this other fella."

With a sneer, Blood Eye said, "This other fella, as you call him, is Preacher."

Druke pulled his head back a little and frowned. "Preacher, you say? The one who's supposed to be such a ring-tailed roarer? Sticks his nose into everybody else's business? That one?"

Blood Eye jerked his head in a curt nod.

Charlotte looked at Preacher with a miserable expression on her face. "I'm sorry. I didn't mean to tell him —"

"Don't you worry about it, missy," Preacher broke in on her apology. "Whether they know who I am or not, it won't make a whole heap of difference."

"Now that's where you're wrong. I've heard a lot about you. You're supposed to

260

be the toughest man in the Rocky Mountains." Druke laughed. "Well, you don't look like it now."

"I told you . . . turn me loose and we'll see," Preacher said in low, menacing tones.

"Actually, I was thinking about doing that," Druke said.

Preacher frowned in surprise.

Sam began, "Boss, I don't know —"

"Here's the deal," Druke went on, ignoring his lieutenant. "You can fight one of us — not me, but I'll pick your opponent — and if you win, I'll put a bullet in your head and kill you quick. If you lose . . . Blood Eye gets you."

"So I die either way," Preacher said.

"That's about the size of it. But I promise you, a bullet in the head is a worthwhile prize compared to what Blood Eye will do to you."

Druke might actually be right about that, Preacher thought grimly, but he didn't intend to let things go that far. Turning him loose would be a bad mistake. Preacher planned to do more than just win the fight.

A lot more.

But he was willing to play along. "I might agree with that idea on one condition."

"What's that?" Druke asked.

Preacher inclined his head toward Will.

261

"Gardner gets the same reward I do. If I win, you kill him quick, too."

"No!" Charlotte cried in horror.

"It's all right, Charlotte," Will told her. "Preacher's just trying to help me. And he's right, I'd rather have the bullet in the head."

She covered her face with her hands and began to sob. The cool, deadly pose she had maintained as Gray Otter was gone, finally overwhelmed by the horror of everything she had gone through.

"Do we have a deal?" Preacher prodded Druke.

"Sure. Why not? Do you want to know who you'll be fighting?"

Sam laughed. "You're talkin' about Pierre, aren't you, boss?"

"That's right." Druke turned and called, "Pierre!"

The crowd parted. The man who came forward from the shadows and shambled through the gap was huge. Close to seven feet tall, with shoulders as wide as an ax handle and arms like the trunks of small trees, he looked more like a bear than a man. The wild thatch of dark hair and the tangled beard added to the animalistic impression.

"There's your opponent," Druke said in satisfaction. "A little simple-minded, but strong enough to tear a man in half with his bare hands. All you have to do to earn quick, clean deaths for you and Gardner, Preacher, is put him on the ground and keep him there. Still want to go through with it?"

"I'm ready when you are," Preacher answered without hesitation.

"Not just yet. I want you to think about it for a while. Think good and hard about it." Druke turned away and added over his shoulder, "Come on, Blood Eye, and bring the girl. I want to talk to her."

CHAPTER 29

Charlotte thought Blood Eye was going to refuse to follow the order, but the Crow followed Druke, shoving her along with him. They went to one of the cabins, where Druke opened the door and smirked at her.

"Welcome to my home, Miss . . . ?"

Charlotte didn't answer him. There was no real reason to keep her identity a secret any longer, but she had hidden it for so long that a part of her rebelled at the idea of revealing the truth.

Mostly, though, she was numb, unwilling and to a certain extent unable to respond. The day she had spent with Blood Eye had been long and terrible.

The really bad thing was . . . it could have been worse.

A lot worse.

And probably would be in the future, unless some miracle saved them.

Blood Eye pushed her into the cabin. A

candle burned on the table, its flickering light revealing the bunk and other spartan furnishings.

Jebediah Druke fancied himself the ruler of this valley, Charlotte thought, but the existence he led in King's Crown was hardly a luxurious one. She couldn't understand why anybody would fight so hard for such a life.

Of course, the life she and Will led was even more primitive, she reminded herself, and she had enjoyed each and every day of it, even the ones filled with danger. She had responded to the challenges of the frontier more enthusiastically than she had ever dreamed she would.

The fact that she had spent those days with the man she loved had a lot to do with it.

Their idyllic existence was over. Will would soon be dead, along with their new-found friend Preacher, and she . . . would be the plaything of a crazed renegade, at least until he grew tired of her.

There was no way of knowing what fate might befall her after that, only that it would be horrible.

Druke broke into those grim musings. "Do you want a drink? All I have is bust-head whiskey, but it's better than nothing.

265

Although a lady like you might not think so."

Charlotte felt a little stronger because she knew nothing was likely to happen to her in the next few minutes. She looked down at her ripped buckskins. "Do I appear to you to be a lady, Mr. Druke?"

Druke smiled. "You certainly do. You see, I thought you were just a squaw at first. It wasn't until I got a better look at you that I realized you're white. And then when I heard you talk . . . Well, let's just say that you're a far cry from what I expected Gray Otter to be."

Charlotte summoned up a wry smile of her own. "Then I suppose our masquerade was a successful one."

"For a while." Druke's tone hardened as he went on. "That's all over now."

"Indeed it is."

Blood Eye asked, "What do you want of us, Druke?"

"Of you, my friend, nothing," Druke answered. "Your work is over for the time being, depending on how that battle between Preacher and Pierre turns out. Right now, I'm just indulging my curiosity. I want to know Miss Charlotte's story. I want to know how a young white woman from back east winds up pretending to be a savage."

"The only true savages in King's Crown are you and your men," Charlotte said.

Druke sat down at the table, pulled a jug over to him, and uncorked it. He took a long drink, then set the jug down and wiped the back of his hand across his mouth. "Sure you don't want some?"

"Positive," Charlotte said. "And I'm not going to tell you anything, no matter what you do to me."

Druke laughed. "You sound awfully sure of yourself. Shouldn't you know by now that Blood Eye can make anybody talk? It's one of his most useful skills."

"All this talk is the practice of lizards and idiots," Blood Eye snapped. "A waste of time. I take the woman and go."

Druke sat forward. "I'm still in charge here. I know what a dangerous man you are, Blood Eye, but I have more than a dozen dangerous men on my side. You can't handle all of us."

One of Blood Eye's rare smiles curved his thin lips. "If you are so sure of this, Druke, then keep on giving me orders. We shall see."

For a long moment, the two men stared coldly at each other. Charlotte supposed it was too much to hope that they would kill each other and give her a chance to get away.

She didn't want to escape. She just wanted an opportunity to free Will and Preacher. Maybe get her hands on her bow and arrows . . .

Then they would all gladly take their chances.

"Take her and go," Druke said abruptly. "But stay close. In an hour, Preacher and Pierre will fight. Depending on how that turns out — and whether or not I decide to honor the agreement I made with Preacher — your services might be needed."

Blood Eye's hand closed around Charlotte's arm again.

She looked at Druke. "I beg you, sir —"

"Don't waste your time," he said with a harsh laugh. "Get this through your head, girl. You raised hell with me and my men for months. I don't care what happens to you. That's up to Blood Eye now."

Charlotte knew that barring the miracle she had hoped for earlier, she had just been condemned to hell.

Will raged as Druke and Blood Eye took Charlotte away, but tied to the post as he was, he couldn't do anything about it. As he cursed and strained against his bonds,

Preacher felt a twinge of pity for the youngster.

Not too much, though. Will and Charlotte had decided to journey to King's Crown, and somewhere along the way they had come up with the idea for Charlotte to pose as an Indian. They were the ones who had gone to war against Jebediah Druke and earned the man's ruthless enmity.

Preacher could sympathize with that, of course. If ever a man needed killing, it was Druke. And Blood Eye, too. That went without saying.

To Will and Charlotte, trying to help the honest trappers in the valley probably had seemed like some sort of romantic quest. It went right along with William Pendexter's fascination with Fenimore Cooper's writings.

Since their time might be short, Preacher figured it was time he had himself a talk with the youngster.

Will's head had sagged forward again. He muttered bitter curses under his breath as he hung on the post.

"Will," Preacher said sharply, to break through the young man's self-pity and fear for Charlotte. "Will, listen to me."

Will lifted his head and gazed dully at the mountain man. "What is it?"

"I know who you really are. I talked to your pa back in St. Louis."

A confused frown creased Will's forehead. "What? You talked to my father?"

"That's right. He gave me the job of comin' out here and findin' you. He wanted me to give you a message, and since this might be the last chance I get to deliver it . . . Anyway, he wants you to know that he forgives you for runnin' off the way you did. He wants you to go home. He didn't hire me to force you to go back east, which I wouldn't have done anyway, but he wanted to make sure you understood that he'd like to mend the fences between the two of you."

Will stared at Preacher in what appeared to be total incomprehension. After a moment, he shook his head. "What you're telling me is impossible, Preacher. My father never met you or anybody else in St. Louis. He never traveled any farther west than Pennsylvania. And he's been dead for five years!"

The words shocked Preacher. Will certainly sounded like he was telling the truth. But Preacher had seen the evidence with his own eyes.

"Look, I saw that birthmark on the back of your neck, Will. I know that you're really William Pendexter."

Will's eyes widened as he looked over at Preacher. "Pendexter!" he exclaimed.

"That's right. Your pa, Barnabas Pendexter, hired me to find you and give you that message. He staked me when I was flat broke, and he gave me your name and description, right down to that birthmark."

Will surprised Preacher again by laughing. "I have that birthmark, true enough, but Barnabas Pendexter isn't my father, not by a long shot. My name is really Will Gardner, like I told you —".

Will broke off as a large group of men came toward them, led by Druke and Sam. The giant Pierre was right behind them. Several of the men carried burning torches.

Preacher looked for Charlotte and Blood Eye, but didn't see them. He didn't know where they had gone, but there was no time to worry about that.

Druke had decided that he had let the prisoners stew in their own juices long enough.

It was time for battle.

CHAPTER 30

Druke came to a stop in front of Preacher and Will and regarded them with a self-satisfied grin. "So, have the two of you been thinking about what's in store for you? Still hoping for that quick bullet in the head?"

"If that's the best we can do," Preacher said, "I'd rather have that than be carved on by that damned ugly heathen. Where is he, anyway?"

"Blood Eye is around somewhere," Druke replied with a vague wave of his hand. "He always is. But he's usually where you least expect him to be. That's the way he takes you by surprise, when it's too late to do you any good."

"What about the girl? She's still with him?"

"Oh, I think you can count on that." Druke leered. "Unless I miss my guess, he's not going to let her out of his sight for a while. Or out of his reach, either."

Will Gardner — which was how Preacher still thought of him and what he insisted was his real name — lunged forward against his bonds as much as he could and cursed fiercely at Druke. "You'll pay for what you've done," Will raged. "You and all of your vile bunch, including that Indian."

Preacher could have told Will not to waste his breath, but it was too late. Druke stepped closer to the young man and swung a vicious backhand that smashed across Will's face. The force of the blow twisted Will's head to the side. A crimson thread of blood trickled from the corner of his mouth.

"You don't have a say about anything anymore, boy," Druke jeered at him. "Your little ladyfriend is gone, and Preacher controls whether you die quick and easy or slow and screaming."

"Let's just get on with it." Preacher's voice and face were grim as he was careful not to betray the leap in spirits he had suddenly experienced.

Ever since he had regained consciousness, he had wondered what had happened to Dog. He remembered hearing a shot and the big cur's yelp of pain, but nothing about his old friend's fate after that. Although he always tried to hold out hope in desperate situations, he'd halfway accepted that Dog was dead.

But he had just spotted a ghostly gray shape gliding through the shadows outside the ring of firelight, and something about it was familiar enough to have sent that thrill through him.

If Dog was alive and had tracked them, it was like having a secret weapon on his side. If Preacher had his hands free and his old friend to fight at his side . . .

Well, there was no telling what might happen.

"I don't blame you for being eager." Druke flipped a beefy hand at Preacher and told his lieutenant, "Cut him loose."

As Sam started toward the mountain man with a knife in his hand, Druke went on. "Three or four of you men draw a bead on Preacher. If he tries anything funny while Turner's cutting him loose, go ahead and kill him."

"Just be careful you don't shoot *me* while you're at it, boys," Sam added.

"All you have to do to guarantee a quick death is make a grab for the knife, Preacher," Druke continued. "But if you do, our deal is off and Blood Eye gets to see just how long he can keep Gardner alive. Or what passes for alive, anyway."

"I'll keep our bargain," Preacher said as

Sam went behind him. "I'm a man of my word."

"Are you suggesting that I'm not?" Druke demanded.

"I'm just sayin' you'll get your show."

"That's all I asked for."

Preacher barely felt the blade sawing at the rawhide lashings around his wrists. When his arms came loose and swung forward, pain throbbed in his shoulders. He almost fell on his face since his feet were still tied, but he managed to catch himself.

A moment later, his feet were free, too, but he didn't trust himself to take a step just yet. He stood there and let the blood flow back into his extremities. He flexed his fingers and rubbed his hands together in an attempt to speed up the process. The pins-and-needles sensation as feeling returned was devilishly painful, but he knew it wouldn't last long.

While Preacher was working at that, Druke said, "I've had a talk with Pierre. He understands that he's not supposed to kill you, only defeat you. I think he'll honor that . . . but it's always a little hard to be sure what a brute like Pierre really comprehends."

Instead of being insulted by those words, Pierre gave a rumbling laugh. To Preacher the noise sounded a little like a rockslide.

Druke made another motion to his men. The ones carrying torches spread out into a rough circle about thirty feet wide. They plunged the torches into the ground and left them standing upright. They formed a ring with fairly large gaps between them.

"Consider that your prize ring," Druke said to Preacher, "and the prize is death. Step out of the circle, or let Pierre throw you out of the circle, and you lose. Blood Eye gets both you and Gardner to do with whatever he wants. Pierre knocks you unconscious or breaks a leg or anything else that makes it impossible for you to keep fighting, you lose and Blood Eye gets you. Clear enough?"

"What do I have to do to beat that bruiser of yours?" Preacher asked.

"It's the same set of rules. Throw him out of the circle, knock him out, disable him some other way. That's all it takes to win a bullet, Preacher." Druke grinned. "But I'm betting you can't do it."

Preacher looked at the other men gathered around the ring of torches. "Maybe you fellas should do some wagerin'," he suggested. "You might make yourselves a little money."

"By betting against me?" Druke said. "I

don't think anybody's interested in doing that."

"You got 'em buffaloed that much, do you?"

Some of the men looked a little uncomfortable at the way the conversation was going.

Druke scowled and snapped, "Forget it. You won't drive a wedge between me and my men. Now get on with it. You've had enough time to get the feeling back in your hands and feet."

That was true. Preacher's feet and legs still felt a little clumsy, but he thought he could get around all right. His hands were almost back to normal.

Druke pulled out a pistol and pointed it at Preacher. "Move. Get into the circle, *now.*"

Preacher flexed his hands a few more times as he walked between a couple blazing brands into the ring of torches. Pierre lumbered after him.

Preacher walked to the center of the rough circle and stopped. Druke's men closed in around the makeshift arena, so he couldn't see Will Gardner anymore.

He hadn't spotted Dog since that first glance, either. Maybe what he'd seen wasn't really the big cur. It could have been just some phantom of his imagination, he told himself, more of a hope than anything real.

But if it was a hope, he was going to hang on to it stubbornly. He and Dog had been through a hell of a lot together. He wasn't going to give up on the gallant, shaggy beast.

Pierre came to a stop a few yards away. His eyes were dull, but he wore a big grin on his hairy face. He flexed his hands, too, but Preacher had a hunch it was out of eagerness to get them on an enemy.

Preacher looked over at Druke, who stood just beyond the ring formed by the torches. "I don't reckon you'd let a man have a drink before he has to fight for his life, would you? I've worked up a hell of a thirst bein' a prisoner."

"Don't forget, you're not fighting for your life. You're fighting for an easier death," Druke reminded him.

"I don't reckon you're gonna let me forget. What about that drink?"

Druke shrugged. "Why not? Sam, go fetch the jug from my cabin."

As Turner hurried away, Pierre asked, "We fight now?"

"In a minute, Pierre," Druke told him. "I can't really blame Preacher. I'd want to be drunk if I had to fight you, too."

Preacher shook his head. "I don't plan to

get drunk. Just need a little something to cut the dry in my throat."

Turner came trotting back with a corked jug. He handed it to Druke, who moved a step into the ring and tossed it to Preacher. The mountain man caught it deftly, pulled the cork, and tilted the jug to his mouth. Fiery liquor gurgled down his throat.

The whiskey had a bracing effect, but that wasn't the only reason Preacher had asked for it. He lowered the jug, wiped the back of his hand across his mouth, and replaced the cork. He said quietly, "Is the fight on?"

"What?" Druke asked. "What did you say?"

"I asked is the fight on?" Preacher repeated, still pitching his voice low.

"Speak up, damn you!" Druke burst out. "Muttering's not going to do you any good."

Preacher took a deep breath and raised his voice. "I said, is the fight on?"

"Yes!" Druke answered impatiently. "Yes, the damned fight's on!"

"Good." Preacher turned, almost too fast for the eye to see, swung the jug with both hands, and smashed it into Pierre's face as hard as he could.

CHAPTER 31

Pierre went down like a poleaxed steer. For a couple seconds that seemed longer than they really were, stunned silence from the crowd greeted Preacher's unexpected attack.

Then angry yells burst from the men, and several of them surged forward until Druke yelled, "Hold it!" and waved them back.

Preacher still held a small piece of the busted jug. He tossed it aside as he turned to face Druke.

"What the hell was that?" Druke demanded. He looked as outraged as the rest of the men.

"You never said anything about no weapons," Preacher told him. "And you gave the jug to me yourself, so I don't reckon you got any kick comin'."

"You knew you were supposed to fight barehanded!"

"Nobody ever said that. Pierre's out cold,

so I reckon I won the fight."

Red-faced, Druke sputtered for a second. Then his face suddenly lit up with a grin as he looked past Preacher.

That couldn't be good, the mountain man thought.

Slowly, he turned his head to look over his shoulder. Behind him, Pierre had started to climb laboriously to his feet. The big, bearlike man's face bled in several places, and more blood leaked from his nose. Whiskey dripped from his tangled beard.

But he was definitely *not* out cold.

Preacher bit back a curse. Busting a jug in a fella's face would have knocked out a normal man for hours, or maybe even killed him. Pierre wasn't like most humans.

In fact, the man began to grin as if he found the whole thing funny. He pawed at his face with a massive hand to wipe away the mixture of blood and busthead, then paused to pick several small pieces of broken jug out of his beard.

The crowd of Druke's men jeered and roared with laughter, their fury of a moment earlier forgotten as it became obvious that Preacher's ploy had failed.

"Looks like you better think again, Preacher!" Druke called. "The fight's still on!"

"Well, hell," Preacher muttered.

Pierre lowered his head and charged like a runaway bull.

Preacher half expected the ground to shake under his feet, like he had experienced when he was in the vicinity of buffalo stampedes.

Pierre wasn't just big, he was fast, too. Preacher tried to leap to the side and avoid the charge, but Pierre reached out with an abnormally long arm and snagged him. Preacher went down on his back with a bone-jarring, tooth-rattling crash.

He couldn't allow the stunning force to overwhelm him. He forced his muscles to work, and after a glance to make sure he wasn't near the outer edge of the ring, he scrambled away. He needed to put some room between himself and Pierre.

Again Preacher wasn't quite quick enough. Pierre lunged after him and grabbed the mountain man's ankle. He pulled Preacher toward him.

Preacher twisted around and aimed a kick at Pierre's face. After busting the jug without much effect, he wasn't sure if a kick would do any good, but the thought of surrendering never crossed his mind. He wouldn't give up even if the stakes hadn't been so high. It just wasn't something he could do.

His heel smashed into Pierre's jaw. The big man's head rocked back and his grip on Preacher's other foot weakened. Preacher pulled free. He somersaulted backward and succeeded in creating a little space between himself and his opponent.

With his height and long arms, Pierre had an advantage when it came to reach. He came at Preacher again and could have hammered him with punches from those malletlike fists, but he didn't even try to box. Chances were, he had never had to resort to that tactic in the past. He would have triumphed in most of his fights based on sheer size and strength alone. That was why he preferred to grapple with his opponent.

Preacher had to avoid that at all costs. If he let Pierre's arms close around him, the fight would be over.

Now that he had a better idea how fast Pierre was, he could plan his own responses better. He darted aside as Pierre groped for him and snapped a hard left to the big man's nose. More blood flew as the punch landed.

Pierre didn't seem to feel the blow, despite the fact that he had crimson leaking from his nostrils.

It seemed to Preacher almost like he had punched a block of stone. Time to change tactics.

As Pierre wheeled and flung out his arms in another attempt to grab him, the mountain man stepped in and hooked a left-right combination into Pierre's midsection. He put all the strength in his rangy body behind the punches.

Getting that close was dangerous, but he had to risk it. If Pierre had a weak spot — that was a big *if* — Preacher had to find it, and the sooner the better. Every minute that passed increased the chances that the big man would grab hold of him.

The blows didn't seem to have much effect, Preacher saw again as he danced back. If Pierre's head was like a stone block, hitting his belly with its corded muscles was like punching the wall of a log cabin, he thought.

He looked closely at his opponent. Had the man's face turned a little gray? Preacher couldn't be sure. Most of Pierre's features were hidden behind that bushy beard and the forest of hair that fell over his forehead.

The possibility was enough that Preacher had to try again. When Pierre swung a wild, backhanded blow at his head, he ducked under it and stepped in once more. He pounded a straight left to Pierre's sternum to keep him off balance, then swung a curving right to the belly with all the power of his arm and shoulder behind it. He thought his fist sank a little deeper than before.

Pierre's breath *whoofed* out and he leaned forward. Preacher lifted a left uppercut to the big man's chin, barely making Pierre's head move, but it must have stung a little. He blinked rapidly and for a second, didn't seem to be able to focus his eyes on Preacher.

That confusion didn't last long enough for Preacher to take advantage of it. Pierre's gaze locked on him, and with an angry bellow the big man thundered forward again.

Preacher was confident that he could dart around and hit Pierre all night if he wanted to, but his hands ached and by the time he'd put the man down and out, every knuckle in his hands might be cracked and swollen. He couldn't afford to be crippled that way.

So as Pierre charged him again, Preacher waited until the last second before diving aside. He caught himself on his hands and used his feet to sweep Pierre's legs out from under him.

Pierre toppled forward and crashed to the ground like a falling tree.

Preacher muttered a disappointed curse as he rolled over and came up on one knee. He had hoped they were close enough to the edge that when Pierre pitched forward, he would land at least partially outside the ring.

That wasn't the case. Pierre had fallen short by a couple feet.

He was slow to get up, though, so Preacher dived on top of him. He drove a knee as hard as he could into the small of Pierre's back, finally bringing a grunt of pain from the big man.

Preacher got both arms around Pierre's neck and levered his head back. He locked Pierre's throat in the crook of his right elbow and tightened his grip. Pierre reached around and tried to grab him, but Preacher pressed himself close to Pierre's back. The big man couldn't reach him from that angle.

All he had to do was hang on until Pierre passed out from lack of air, he told himself.

Pierre didn't cooperate and make it easy. He pushed himself up onto hands and knees and threw himself to the side, rolling over so fast that Preacher was trapped underneath him. That sudden reversal threatened to crush Preacher under Pierre's great weight.

Preacher didn't let go, even though he

couldn't breathe, pinned to the ground as he was. He summoned up his strength and tried to roll out of the trap, but Pierre weighed too much. He was immovable.

As Preacher lay there and struggled, he heard Druke's men shouting encouragement to Pierre. He drew strength from the jeers and catcalls. He'd heard it said before that you could judge a man by his enemies, and he was proud to oppose men like the scum Jebediah Druke had gathered around him. He could tell that they all thought he was beaten.

They were about to find out how wrong they were.

Drawing on his reserves of strength, Preacher rolled Pierre off of him again. Maybe Pierre had finally started to weaken from being choked, or maybe Preacher was just too damned stubborn to be denied. Whatever the reason, Preacher rolled Pierre onto his belly again. He slid his right knee off Pierre's back and planted that foot on the ground. With that leg for leverage, he hauled Pierre's upper body a foot or so from the ground, giving him the chance to get his left foot down, too.

Pierre flailed backward at him, but the attempts smacked of desperation.

Inch by inch, Preacher straightened up.

Pierre rose from the ground until he was on his knees with Preacher behind him, right arm still locked around his throat.

Pierre pawed at that arm, but couldn't tear it loose. Preacher applied more and more pressure. Some of Druke's men still shouted, but most of them had fallen silent as they watched the unexpected spectacle of the massive Pierre being beaten.

Preacher looked over Pierre's head and saw Druke standing silently at the edge of the circle with a sullen expression on his face. Clearly, he was as shocked as the rest of his men at the way the fight was about to end.

Preacher could tell that it was almost over. Pierre's attempts to break free were feeble. Another minute or so, Preacher thought. . . .

Some of the men near Druke stepped aside. Blood Eye and Charlotte appeared in the opening. The renegade Crow had come to see how the battle played out. If he was disappointed at being cheated of his sport, his impassive features showed no sign of it.

Charlotte looked scared but defiant. Preacher was glad to see that. She had to be ready to fight. Likely they wouldn't be able to get out of here without her help.

Suddenly, Pierre went limp. Preacher's first thought was that the big man was shamming, but then he decided that Pierre wasn't that cunning. Or that good an actor. Besides, he was dead weight.

Preacher let go of him and stepped back.

Pierre fell forward. Judging from the way he landed face-first he was either out cold or dead.

Preacher looked at Druke and grinned. He needed a minute to catch his breath, and he played for it by saying, "Looks like I won."

Druke exploded. "You cheated!"

"Did no such thing, and you know it. Everybody here saw it. Now you got a bargain to keep."

"The hell I do," Druke said with a sneer. "A promise made to a man like you doesn't mean anything. Blood Eye gets you both!"

"No!" Charlotte cried.

Preacher wasn't the least bit surprised by Druke's double cross. It didn't matter, anyway. He'd never intended to stand by and let himself be executed. He was about to open his mouth and yell for Dog to attack. As soon as the big cur tore into Druke's men like a gray whirlwind with razor-sharp teeth, Preacher planned to jump one of the varmints and get his hand on a gun.

He never had the chance. Before he could

yell for Dog, he was as shocked as everybody else when a shot blasted and a black hole suddenly appeared in Druke's forehead. The rifle ball bored on through and exploded out the back of Druke's skull, splattering bits of evil brain matter on the men standing near him.

Jebediah Druke's reign of terror in King's Crown had just come to a stunning end.

CHAPTER 32

Preacher had no idea where the shot had come from or who had blown Druke's brains out.

For a second, he figured that Will Gardner must have freed himself somehow and gotten his hands on a rifle.

But more shots rang out as Druke's men began to yell in confusion and scatter away from the makeshift prize ring. Preacher heard the swift rataplan of hoofbeats and knew that the renegades were under attack by another group.

Maybe word of the massacre of Monkton's group near the pass had gotten around the valley and the rest of the trappers had banded together to wage war on their oppressors. Preacher didn't think that was very likely, but he didn't have any other explanation for the chaos that suddenly erupted around him.

Those thoughts flashed through his brain

as he launched himself forward. He wanted to reach Blood Eye and get Charlotte away from the Crow.

He probably wouldn't have made it in time — Blood Eye had already whirled around and started to drag his prisoner with him — if Charlotte hadn't unexpectedly thrown herself at him and sunk her teeth into his shoulder.

Taken by surprise, Blood Eye yelled and stumbled. That slowed him just enough for Preacher to hit him from behind with a diving tackle.

The collision made Blood Eye let go of Charlotte's arm. As Preacher and Blood Eye fell, the mountain man shouted to her, "Get to Will! Turn him loose!"

Charlotte darted away into the swirling mass of violence and confusion.

Even though he was exhausted from the grueling fight with Pierre, Preacher knew he couldn't lose the opportunity to take care of Blood Eye once and for all. He rammed his right elbow under Blood Eye's chin and forced his head back. Preacher smashed his other hand into the Crow's throat in an attempt to crush his windpipe.

Blood Eye gagged and choked, but didn't give up. He punched upward and landed a blow in the mountain man's face with enough force to knock Preacher to the side. Preacher rolled onto his shoulder and hip and came up swinging his leg in a kick aimed at Blood Eye's head.

Blood Eye ducked. Fresher and faster, he grabbed Preacher's leg and heaved. Preacher went over backward.

He had barely hit the ground when Blood Eye sprang up and swung a tomahawk at his head with blinding speed. Sheer desperation twisted Preacher out of the way of the blow.

As the tomahawk dug into the ground only inches from his head, he clubbed both hands together and swung them, catching Blood Eye on the side of the head and literally knocking him off his feet. Blood Eye came down a yard away and rolled.

Preacher leaped up and would have gone after him, but at that moment a galloping horse loomed up between them. Preacher threw himself backward to avoid being trampled.

As he fell, he caught a glimpse of the bearded, hard-faced man in the saddle. Preacher had never seen him before. He wasn't one of Druke's men.

Still with no idea who the strangers were, knowing only that they had shown up at a very fortunate time for him, Preacher looked around for a weapon. He grabbed one of the torches still standing upright and yanked it out of the ground.

He whirled around, expecting to see Blood Eye charging toward him again, but to his surprise the Crow seemed to be gone. Preacher didn't spot him anywhere in the confusion of men, horses, dust, and powder smoke.

He heard a furious bellow over all the commotion and turned to see Pierre lumbering toward him. Preacher wouldn't have thought that the big man would regain consciousness so quickly, but Pierre obviously had the constitution of an ox to go with the build of a grizzly bear.

Preacher slashed the torch across Pierre's face as the man lunged at him. Pierre screamed and pulled back. He pawed at his flame-seared eyes with his left hand while his right flailed blindly toward Preacher.

Pierre staggered as an arrow suddenly drove deep into his chest. He didn't fall until another feathered shaft appeared as if by magic in his throat. He toppled sideways to the ground as blood gushed from the wound.

Will Gardner and Charlotte stood about twenty yards away. Will had a pistol in each hand, along with a powder horn and shot pouch slung over his shoulder. Charlotte had found her bow and arrows.

"Preacher, come on!" Will called.

The smartest thing they could do was get out of there while all the confusion was going on, Preacher knew. He yanked the arrows out of Pierre's body, figuring Charlotte might need them later.

As he ran toward the two young people, Druke's second in command, Sam Turner, appeared behind them. Preacher would have yelled a warning, but he didn't have to. A huge, furry shape sailed in from the side, crashed into Turner, and knocked the man off his feet.

A flashing swipe of Dog's teeth ripped Turner's throat out.

Preacher was immensely glad to see that he'd been right earlier. Dog was still alive.

The reunion could wait until later. Preacher knew they needed to get clear of the fighting. It seemed likely that the men who'd attacked Fort Druke were on their side, but in such chaos, a friend might accidentally prove as dangerous as an enemy. Better to wait until the shooting was over and then sort things out.

He slid the bloody arrows into Charlotte's quiver, gripped her right arm and Will's left. Raising his voice to be heard over the tumult of battle he shouted, "We need to get out of here. Come on!"

It wasn't far to the nearest slope, maybe half a mile. Preacher hurried in that direction and urged the two young people along with him. Dog ranged in front of them to take care of anybody who tried to stop them.

No one did. Druke's men continued to put up a fierce struggle against the invaders. Everyone was too concerned about their own life or death to pay any attention to the former prisoners as they fled from the so-called fort.

But Blood Eye was still on the loose somewhere unless he had been killed in the fighting. The renegade Crow might well be the biggest danger of all. Preacher knew they couldn't afford to let their guard down until they were sure Blood Eye was dead.

They reached the base of the nearest peak and began to climb. Once they were high enough to be out of harm's way, they could stop and wait for the outcome of the clash below.

If the survivors of Druke's bunch happened to win, which Preacher considered unlikely, then he and his companions would climb higher into the mountains and hole up somewhere until they figured out what to do.

If the mysterious attackers emerged victorious, then Preacher would slip back down into the valley and find out what was going on. He would leave Will and Charlotte in hiding until he was sure the newcomers meant them no harm.

They climbed several hundred yards up the wooded slope and stopped at a rocky outcropping that shielded them from view.

Between all the fighting and climbing, Preacher was slightly out of breath, another sign that he wasn't quite as young as he used to be. He sat down on a rock and blew out a sigh. "Either of you two hurt bad?"

"I'm all right." Charlotte pushed back a wing of dark hair that had fallen forward over her face.

"I'm fine," Will said. "A little sore from the thrashing Druke gave me, but that's all."

"He won't thrash anybody else," Preacher said. "Somebody shot him through the head."

Charlotte shuddered. "I know. I think some of his . . . cranial matter got on me."

"Better wash it off as soon as you get the chance," Preacher advised dryly. "It's liable to eat a hole in your clothes."

As if that reminded Charlotte that her current outfit was hardly modest, she pulled the ripped shirt closed and held it that way

297

with one hand.

Will peeled his own shirt over his head. "Mine's too big and it's got blood on it, but I'll trade you."

Preacher turned his back while they switched garments. Will's shirt was too big on Charlotte, as he had said, but at least it covered her decently. He ripped even more away from her shirt and fashioned it into a crude vest.

"What happened down there?" Will asked. "Who are those men?"

"I don't know. They showed up at a mighty handy time for us, though." Preacher looked at Charlotte. "Good thing you were able to get Will loose."

"I had to kill a man with his own gun and take his knife to cut the bonds," she said coolly. She seemed to be one of those rare individuals whose nerves got steadier the more desperate the action around her. "But luck was with me."

"I'm not sure how much of it was luck," Will said.

The shooting had continued down at the fort, but it began to dwindle. The big campfire still burned, and so did some of the torches, creating enough light for them to see the men on horseback mopping up.

Bodies littered the ground in the aftermath

of battle. One of the riders dismounted and began checking them. Preacher's eyes narrowed as the man came to one of Druke's followers who was still alive.

The stranger lifted a pistol and finished off Druke's man with a shot to the head.

Will and Charlotte were watching, too. She gasped, and he exclaimed, "Good Lord! That was cold-blooded murder. I mean, Druke's men deserve to die and I've shot some of them from ambush myself, but . . ."

"Cold-blooded is right," Preacher agreed. The man who had just carried out the execution turned so that Preacher got a better look at his face. Preacher couldn't make out any details except the black patch that covered the man's left eye.

Something was familiar about him. The eye patch sent a tingle of recognition through Preacher, but at that moment he couldn't remember where he had seen the man before.

For the next few minutes, the stranger stalked around the area and dispatched three more wounded men. Then he said something to a man still on horseback, and that rider turned his mount and galloped off.

"I'm starting not to like the looks of this," Will said.

Preacher felt the same way, but he said, "Let's just wait and see what happens."

They didn't have long to wait. Dog had followed them up the slope and then sat down at the end of the outcropping. He growled as the man who had ridden off came back a few minutes later with another man riding beside him.

The way Preacher figured it, the one with the eye patch had sent a subordinate to tell their boss it was safe to ride in. All of Druke's men were dead.

The invaders all wore buckskins and homespun, coonskin caps, and broad-brimmed felt hats. The latest arrival was dressed in store-bought clothes and wore a stylish beaver hat.

Even at a distance, it was easy to tell that he was rich.

When he took off his hat and spoke to the man with the eye patch, Preacher felt that shock of recognition again, and he had a name to go with it. "Pendexter!"

Beside him, Charlotte let out the same sort of choked, horrified gasp that Blood Eye had prompted from her. Will just stared, stunned.

"You know Barnabas Pendexter?" Preacher asked Charlotte.

300

"I'm afraid I do," she replied in a hollow voice. "He's my husband."

CHAPTER 33

Recognizing Barnabas Pendexter had jogged other memories in Preacher's brain. He knew where he had seen the man with the eye patch before.

"Teach him a lesson," the leader grated.

Preacher caught a glimpse as the man leaned in, clutching a bloody left arm. He had a craggy, big-nosed face. A black patch covered his left eye.

With a shake of his head, Preacher came back from that shadowy alley outside Kilroy's tavern in St. Louis. The man had been in charge of the robbers who had attacked him. It looked like the varmint had recovered from the slashed arm Preacher had given him.

Just a few minutes after that encounter, Preacher had been introduced to Barnabas Pendexter inside the tavern. He realized that encounter hadn't been an accident. Pendexter had known where to find him.

And he had known that Preacher would be broke and in need of a stake to return to the mountains. Pendexter had been Johnny-on-the-spot with the offer of a job and a sad story about how his son had run away to be a mountain man. . . .

Those memories and the theory that sprang from them took only a moment to wheel rapidly through Preacher's brain. He uttered a heartfelt, "That filthy liar!"

"I couldn't agree more," Will Gardner said.

The whole thing was starting to make sense, Preacher thought. He looked at Will and Charlotte. "Pendexter set me up to find the two of you."

"Of course he did," Charlotte agreed. Her voice was still a little shaky from the sight of Pendexter. "That's the sort of diabolical mastermind Barnabas is. He likes to believe he can manipulate anyone into doing what-ever he wants." She paused, then added bit-terly, "With some justification, I suppose. He convinced me that he loved me and that I should marry him, after all. I had no idea at the time that I was just a . . . a toy to him. A plaything, nothing more."

"Seems hard to believe any fella could feel that way about a gal like you," Preacher said.

"You're being gallant. But I was a much

different individual back then. I had no idea what I was capable of."

Preacher looked over at Will. "I reckon you were tellin' me the truth about not bein' Pendexter's son."

"The very thought is revolting. I worked for him, that's all. That's how I . . . got to know Charlotte."

"Will was at the house quite often, discussing business matters with Barnabas. He was Barnabas's chief clerk."

Preacher grunted. "No offense, Will, but you don't really strike me as a clerk."

"Like Charlotte, at that point in my life I had no idea what I might be capable of. But I'd always been interested in the frontier. I'd read novels about it —"

"Pendexter was tellin' the truth about that part of it, anyway," Preacher said. "So the two of you fell in love and decided to run away together."

"Not exactly," Charlotte said. "That makes me sound so . . . brazen. We struck up a friendship. That's all it was at first."

Maybe as far as she was concerned that was true, Preacher thought. But no young man became friends with a woman as beautiful as Charlotte without having a few other thoughts in mind, too.

"Barnabas had started to treat me very

badly. Will was aware of that, and eventually he suggested that if I wanted to get away, he'd be glad to help me." She put an affectionate hand on his arm. "We didn't actually fall in love until we had spent more time together."

While Preacher listened to their story, he also kept one eye on what was happening down below in the valley. Barnabas Pendexter stalked around, checked all the cabins, and circulated among his men. He seemed to be asking them questions, and he didn't like the answers he got. He appeared animated, even angry, as he waved his arms in the air while he spoke to his men.

Will saw that, too. "Pendexter has figured out that you're not anywhere down there, darling. He wants to know how his men managed to let you get away."

"They underestimated us." Charlotte glanced at Preacher. "They can't see us up here, can they?"

"Not very likely," the mountain man said. "I wouldn't mind if we were up higher, but it's dark and we've got good cover here."

Will said, "I'm still not clear how and why you were involved with this, Preacher."

For the next few minutes, Preacher told them about how he'd been attacked and robbed back in St. Louis and how he had met Barnabas Pendexter shortly after that.

"It was his men who jumped me," Preacher said. "That fella down yonder with the eye patch was the one in charge. Pendexter must've known he couldn't hire me to come looking for you unless I needed somebody to provide a stake for me. He also must've found out enough about me by askin' around to figure that I wouldn't take the job even then if I knew I was really lookin' for his runaway wife. So he made up that story about Will here bein' his son. When I agreed to take the job, him and his hired killers trailed along behind and waited for me to find the two of you. Once they were sure I had, they stepped in to wipe out Druke's bunch and grab you both. That's where they didn't quite pull it off."

"No offense intended, Preacher," Will said, "but why go to so much trouble just to trick you into working for him? Obviously he was able to hire a large group of ruffians. Why didn't he just give them the job of finding Charlotte and me?"

"I can answer that," Charlotte said. "As I mentioned before, Barnabas is diabolical. Setting up such a ruse is exactly the sort of thing that would appeal to him. Besides, when he sets out to do something, he likes to use the best available tools for the job."

"Which means he don't consider me anything more than a tool," Preacher said. "If I didn't have enough reasons to dislike the fella already, I reckon that's another one."

Charlotte told him, "Don't be too insulted, Preacher. Barnabas sees everyone that way, as little more than chess pieces to be moved around the board in moves of his choosing."

The faint sound of shouting drifted to them. They looked down on the scene of battle again and saw that Pendexter's men had mounted up. They began to ride out in different directions.

"He's told 'em to spread out and find you," Preacher said. "We'd better get movin' while we can and put some distance between us and them. We'll find a hidey-hole where we can put up a fight if we need to."

"We have a bow, a handful of arrows, a knife, and two pistols," Will pointed out. "How much of a fight can we put up, no matter where we are?"

"That's all we've got right now. Well, that and Dog." Preacher smiled in the darkness. "But there are a lot more weapons in this valley, and unless I miss my guess, they're gonna be comin' to us."

■ ■ ■ ■

Preacher knew they wouldn't be lucky
enough to find another cave like the one
miles from there that had sheltered Will and
Charlotte for months. Anyway, in the end
that hideout hadn't worked out so well.
They had been tracked to it and captured.

As they climbed higher on the mountain,
Preacher kept his eye out for some other
place where they could hole up. Along
toward dawn, he finally found it. They had
come to an almost sheer bluff. He studied
it, thinking the climb wasn't really a difficult one, but it couldn't be done quickly
and anyone who attempted it would be out
in the open, completely exposed to fire from
above . . . or rocks dropped on his head. If
they could get to the top of the bluff, they
might be able to hold out against Pendexter's men, he pointed out to Will and Charlotte, but likely they would be better off if
they were armed with weapons that weren't
quite so primitive.

Will insisted that he be the one to climb
first to check it out. "If something happens
to one of us, Charlotte has a better chance
of coming out of this alive if she's with you,
Preacher."

"I ain't sure but what this little gal is tougher'n both of us," Preacher said with a smile.

"Maybe so, but I want to do this," Will said, over-riding Charlotte's objections. He handed Preacher one of the pistols he'd picked up after the battle.

Preacher and Charlotte spent a tense few minutes at the base of the slope after Will disappeared at the top. It was a relief when he called down to them, "There's nothing up here! No wild animals or anything else that should bother us!"

"All right," Preacher said to Charlotte. "Up you go."

She made the climb and he followed. Reaching the top, Preacher discovered they were in a narrow, steep-sided canyon barely fifty yards deep. A tiny spring bubbled out of the rock at the far end. As the sky in the east turned gray and gradually lightened, they explored. There wasn't much to find except some hardy brush and the spring, which was a stroke of luck.

"I think I can fashion some more arrows from branches," Charlotte said. "They'll be crude because I'll have to whittle them down to sharp points with the knife, instead of putting flint heads on them, and I don't know what I'll do for fletching, but I can

309

give it a try."

"That'll be better than nothing," Will told her.

"And I'll come up with some more guns," Preacher added. "The way Pendexter's men spread out, I ought to be able to jump one or two of them and help myself to whatever they're carryin'. Fact is, I'd better get back down there 'fore it gets any lighter. You two try to get some rest . . . but not at the same time. Somebody's always on guard."

"We understand," Will said. "We've had to be vigilant for a long time now."

With a nod of farewell, Preacher slid back down the slope to join Dog, who had stayed at the base of the bluff. The two of them trotted off into the pre-dawn gloom.

Preacher crouched on the thick lower limb of a pine tree. The needles that surrounded him were a little bristly, but he could put up with that discomfort for a while. The important thing was that the man riding up the slope toward him couldn't see him in the shadows amid the tree's thick growth.

He waited for Pendexter's man to pass underneath him. Dog was hidden in the brush nearby, ready to come at Preacher's call and help if need be.

Preacher wanted to take care of the hired

killer without a gunshot that would draw the attention of the other searchers. They shouldn't have scattered quite so much. If he had given the orders instead of Pendexter or the man with the eye patch, he would have insisted that they stay in pairs.

Lucky for him somebody hadn't thought that through.

Preacher glanced through a gap in the branches toward the mountainside about half a mile away. He knew the canyon where he had left Will and Charlotte was up there, even though he couldn't see it from where he was. He hoped they were all right.

Then he didn't have time to think about that anymore. His unsuspecting quarry was almost in position. Preacher held his breath as the rider, a burly man with a sand-colored, soup-strainer mustache, moved directly beneath him.

Preacher dropped from the branch, doom hurtling down from above.

CHAPTER 34

Will felt exhaustion creeping up on him, but when he looked at Charlotte he could tell that she was even more tired. He had forgotten the last time he'd actually slept, as opposed to being knocked unconscious, but all he'd had to endure were beatings and the threat of being tortured to death by a madman.

The ordeal Charlotte had undergone was . . . worse.

He pushed that thought out of his head. Ever since they had escaped, he hadn't allowed himself to dwell on it. He said to her, "Why don't you find a comfortable place to lie down and get some sleep?"

"I'm really not that tired," she said, which he knew was a lie. "I can stand the first watch."

"No, it's all right. I'd feel better if you slept first."

She smiled at him. "If you're sure . . ."

"I'm sure."

She was close enough to come up on her toes, lean forward, and kiss him. Her arms wrapped around his waist.

When he had thought they were both going to die, he would have given anything to take her in his arms and feel her warm, sweet lips pressed to his again. He drew her closer. It was a wonderful sensation.

She stiffened suddenly and pulled back.

"What's wrong?" he asked hoarsely.

Charlotte shook her head. "Nothing. Nothing at all. We're going to be fine now, aren't we, Will?"

"Of course we are. We'll get out of this."

"Barnabas —"

"Barnabas will never bother you again," he said with his voice as firm as he could make it. "I give you my word on that, Charlotte."

A forced smile appeared on her face. "I'll sleep for an hour or so. But then you wake me up."

"I will," he promised.

He didn't intend to keep that pledge. He would let her sleep as long as she could. Charlotte needed rest.

And he needed to think.

She found a nice grassy spot where some bushes would shade her from the glare of the rising sun and stretched out on her side. She pillowed her head on her arms and closed her eyes, and a few minutes later Will could tell by the regular rising and falling of her back that she was asleep.

He walked closer to the mouth of the canyon. Even though he was extremely curious about what was going on down below in the valley, he knew better than to stand in the opening. It would be too easy for Pendexter's men to spot him there.

He hunkered behind some rocks, close enough to the canyon mouth so that he would hear if anyone rode up to the base of the bluff.

He warned himself not to think about what had happened the previous day, but as dawn crept over the rugged landscape, he couldn't stop the ugly images from creeping into his mind.

Blood Eye had had Charlotte as his captive for an entire long day. It was obvious the renegade Crow lusted after her, and she had been powerless to stop him from doing whatever he wanted.

It wasn't her fault. Not by any stretch of the imagination. Will knew that, and he knew it shouldn't make any difference in the way he felt about her. He didn't *want* it to make any difference. The best thing to do was put it behind them and pretend it hadn't even happened. They had to concentrate on getting out of this mess alive.

But if they got away, Barnabas Pendexter would just come after them again, Will mused with a frown. Pendexter wasn't just evil; he was incredibly stubborn and arrogant, too. He had tracked them down once, and he would find a way to do it again.

It was clear that only one thing would stop his threat from looming over them for the rest of their lives.

Barnabas Pendexter had to die.

That thought occupied Will's mind when he suddenly felt a light touch on his shoulder. He jerked around and his hand went to the pistol tucked behind his belt.

He stopped short when he saw Charlotte standing there.

For a second he couldn't speak. Then he said, "I thought you were asleep."

"I dozed off. But then I woke up and I couldn't get back to sleep. Will, we . . . we need to talk —"

"No, we don't. Everything's fine. We'll get away from Pendexter and find some other place where he'll never bother us again."

"Perhaps we will. But that won't stop you from thinking the things that you're thinking right now."

He shook his head. "I don't know what you're talking about. I'm thinking about how we're going to escape —"

"You're thinking about what Blood Eye did to me."

Will felt his face grow warm. "It's not proper to speak about such things —"

"You believe that he dishonored me. Had his way with me."

"You had no control over what that savage —"

"He didn't." Charlotte shook her head vehemently.

Will frowned, unable for a moment to fully comprehend what Charlotte had just told him.

"He didn't molest me. He . . . he tied me up, and I thought he was going to, but he didn't. Oh, he said things . . . vile, unspeakable things . . . about what he planned to do to me, but he said that first I had to be . . . prepared."

"What the devil did he mean by that?"

"Devil may well be right." A tiny shudder went through her. "While I was tied up, he carried out some sort of . . . ritual, I suppose you'd call it. He chanted and danced around me. It went on for hours. If I didn't know better, I'd say that he was trying to summon up a . . . a demon from the bowels of Hell!"

"Good Lord," Will muttered.

"Exactly. I suspect He's the one who saved me, because I prayed harder than I've ever prayed in my life. Finally Blood Eye stopped what he was doing, and I thought it was all over then. But instead of attacking me, he sat down and crossed his legs and took out a pipe. He put something in it —"

"Tobacco?"

Charlotte shook her head. "I . . . I'm not sure. It looked more like some sort of herb. But he smoked it like tobacco for a while, and then he just sat there. His good eye had gotten rather glassy. I thought he was going to pass out. I hoped he would, so that I could at least try to get free and slip away, but he never did."

She paused while Will tried to digest everything she had told him. The story seemed far-fetched, but her words had the ring of truth to him, and he knew her better than he had ever known anyone else. He didn't think she was lying to him.

"Finally, it started to get dark," Charlotte continued. "Blood Eye came out of his stupor, or whatever you'd call it, untied me, and took me back to Druke's stronghold to watch Preacher's showdown with the giant French brute. You know everything that happened after that."

"Earlier when you kissed me," Will said, "why did you stiffen and pull away?"

"I didn't. You did. I just reacted to what you did. That's when I knew that what you thought had happened was bothering you. I knew that I had to tell you the truth and make you understand that nothing has to change between us. Nothing."

Will took a deep breath. He hadn't been aware of the reaction in him that she described, but he couldn't swear that it hadn't taken place. It was true that bad thoughts had been preying on him. "I'm glad you told me. If things were otherwise, it wouldn't have made a difference. Truly."

"Of course it would have," she said softly. "But they're not. And now that we've cleared the air we can do like you said and concentrate on getting away from here. Away from here and far, far away from Barnabas Pendexter."

He almost told her then what he had been thinking about how Pendexter's death was the only thing that would truly free them. He stopped himself and decided there would be time enough for that discussion later.

Charlotte hated Pendexter, Will had no doubt about that, but she had been married to the man. *Was still* married to the man, legally. He wasn't sure how she would feel about murdering Pendexter if it came down to that.

As for himself, Will knew he could put a bullet in the blackguard's heart and never lose a second's sleep over it. He might even get the chance to do that before they left King's Crown.

That probably would depend to a large degree on how Preacher's mission was going. . . .

CHAPTER 35

Pendexter's man never saw Preacher coming. The mountain man crashed onto his back and shoulders and drove him out of the saddle. They tumbled to the ground as the startled horse lunged ahead.

Preacher landed on top. His target writhed around and tried to throw him off. Preacher hammered a punch to the back of the man's neck.

Pendexter's man fumbled for his pistol. As it came free, Preacher slid the knife Charlotte had given him from the sheath at his waist and plunged it into the man's side. He angled the blade up, felt it scrape against ribs, and then the gasp the man let out told Preacher that the point had reached his heart.

The man spasmed and died before he could even cock the pistol, let alone fire it.

Preacher pulled the knife out and stood up. He took the pistol from the man's limp fingers and then looked around for the rifle the man had dropped. It lay on the ground a few feet away. Preacher retrieved it, too.

He took the dead man's powder horn and shot pouch as well and slung them over his shoulder by their straps. He was almost fully armed again, and it felt good.

The man's horse had come to a stop about fifty yards away. Under the circumstances, the mount wouldn't really do Preacher and his young friends any good, but he walked over to the horse anyway, speaking softly as he approached to keep it from spooking again. He held out his hand and let the animal nuzzle against his palm.

He found two more pistols in scabbards strapped to the saddle, and a search of the saddlebags turned up a hatchet. For fighting, Preacher preferred a tomahawk. A hatchet was better for chopping wood and brush, but he took it, too.

"Come on, Dog," he said as he trotted away from the site of the ambush. The big cur bounded alongside him.

Preacher wished he had time to look for Horse and his pack animal. He was confident that wherever Horse was, the big stallion was all right. Horse could take care of himself, and he would look after the pack horse, too, but Preacher would have liked to be reunited with his other trail partner.

When it was over he would be, he told himself. When Barnabas Pendexter and his hired killers were dead.

Preacher had decided it was very unlikely Pendexter would give up, even if Charlotte and Will escaped from King's Crown and tried to make a life for themselves elsewhere. If everything they said about Pendexter was true — Preacher had no reason to believe it wasn't — Charlotte running away from him again would make him more determined than ever to find her and take her back.

Running away with Will Gardner a second time would just make it worse.

A lot of folks would consider it Pendexter's right to feel that way, given the fact that Charlotte was his wife. For all practical purposes, she was Pendexter's property, to do with whatever he wanted to. That was the way the law saw it.

But Preacher had never held with all the laws and strictures of civilization. He believed in a higher law, a law of right and wrong. That was one reason he had chosen to live his life out in the wilderness, far from all those artificial, arbitrary rules.

He had no doubt that Pendexter would continue on his ruthless quest as long as he had to. More than likely, he would rather see Charlotte dead than let Will have her.

So it was a fight to the end, Preacher thought. Will and Charlotte would live out their lives in peace in King's Crown, or they would die there.

Preacher moved on, sticking to cover as much as he could and hunting the hunters. Even though he had enough guns for himself, it wouldn't hurt to get more so Will and Charlotte would be better armed. In a fight against overwhelmingly superior odds, they could never have too many guns.

A short time later, he spotted another of Pendexter's men following a game trail along the edge of a narrow draw. Preacher circled quickly to get ahead of him and crouched behind a boulder as the man rode toward him.

The sound of the horse's hoofbeats grew louder as the rider approached. He drew even with the boulder, then passed it, and Preacher made his move.

The man caught a glimpse of Preacher from the corner of his eye or something warned him. He turned to swing his rifle around. Preacher reached past it, grabbed the man's shirt, and hauled him off the horse.

A kick to the head as soon as the man hit the ground knocked him out. Preacher considered cutting his throat, but dragged him off the trail into some brush instead. He sliced strips of cloth from the man's shirt and used them to tie his hands and feet. Another piece of cloth went in the man's mouth as a gag.

The varmint might still die if he couldn't get loose and no one found him, but leaving him tied at least gave him a fighting chance. Preacher knew that was more than he would have gotten if the situation had been reversed.

He had just stepped out of the brush when a rifle blasted and a heavy lead ball hummed past his ear. He threw himself backward into the brush as a second shot rang out.

At least two men, he thought as he knelt in the thick growth. That explained how the shots had come so close together.

He had a hunch he knew what they had done. They had followed the hombre he'd just knocked out, using the man as an unwitting stalking horse.

And Preacher had played right into their hands.

Those shots would bring any of Pendexter's men who were within hearing distance galloping in Preacher's direction. It was going to get a little crowded around there.

In fact, it already was. Several more shots

roared and sent him diving to the ground as the rifle balls whipped and crackled through the brush around him.

On his belly, Preacher crawled backward. He paused as he heard the distinctive thud of lead against flesh and looked back over his shoulder at the man he had left tied up. One of the shots had struck the man in the head and blown away a chunk of his skull, killing him before he ever regained consciousness.

"Sorry, mister," Preacher told the corpse, "but it was your own bunch who killed you. They had to have seen me drag you in here and just didn't give a damn if they killed you, too, as long as they got me."

He crawled past the dead man and then angled to the side as he went toward the draw again. Rifle balls still whined and buzzed through the brush like angry hornets as Preacher reached the edge of the growth. The open trail lay between him and the gully.

Preacher gave a piercing whistle. That was as good as a verbal command to Dog. A moment later, a man screamed somewhere nearby, and the sound told Preacher that the big cur was on the attack.

The screams continued and caused the victim's companions to shout in confusion.

Preacher took advantage of the distraction to burst out of the brush and dash across the trail to the draw with a rifle in each hand and four pistols and the hatchet stuck behind his belt.

More shots blasted, but Pendexter's men reacted too slowly. Preacher had already slid down into the draw and was safely out of sight before the shots came anywhere near him.

The gully was about ten feet deep and a little less than that wide, a natural trench in the earth carved out by the torrents that resulted from occasional downpours.

It was dry at the moment. Preacher hurried along toward the men who had been shooting at him.

He might have escaped by going the other way, but escape wasn't what he had in mind. He had the urge to take the fight to his enemies and whittle down the odds a little more.

The screaming stopped, which meant that Dog had finished his bloody work. He would retreat for the time being, since he could no longer take Pendexter's men by surprise.

"What the hell was that, a wolf?"

Preacher heard the voice clearly, no more than thirty or forty feet away from him.

Another man answered, "I don't know, but it tore poor Robinson to shreds."

Carefully, Preacher climbed the gully's side. He had long since lost his hat, so he didn't have to worry about removing it as he edged his head up far enough to take a look.

The two men were standing behind thick-trunked pines that gave them a view of the trail along the draw. Preacher spotted a man's leg sticking out from behind another tree and figured it belonged to the unlucky Robinson, who'd had a fatal encounter with Dog.

"Where do you think that guy Preacher went?" the first man asked.

"He probably took off up that little draw once he got into it. I don't reckon we ought to waste any more powder and shot right now."

"Larrabee won't like it that Preacher got away. Neither will Pendexter."

"Well, I don't see either of them out here riskin' their own hides, do you?" the second man asked.

Preacher figured the man with the eye patch was Larrabee.

"What about Simmons?"

"One of us better go over there and see about him. Preacher probably killed him, but Larrabee'll want to know for sure."

Preacher grimaced. The man was killed by one of his own with all their wild shooting.

The first man said with obvious reluctance, "All right. I'll go take a look. You cover me, though."

"I'll be right here," the second man said.

The first man stepped out from behind his tree. His beard-stubbled face was pulled taut by nervous lines as he darted his gaze back and forth. In a crouching run, he started toward the brush where Preacher had taken cover earlier.

The second man moved out more into the open, as well, and watched his companion.

Preacher let the first man take about five steps before he rose up from the draw with a pistol in each hand and called sharply, "Hey!"

The first man stopped short and instinctively turned toward Preacher. So did the second man.

Neither of them had time to react before the guns in the mountain man's hands roared.

The first man doubled over as the ball punched into his midsection. The second one flew back against the tree trunk behind him as the force of the ball that drove into his chest lifted him off his feet.

They hit the ground almost simultaneously.

Preacher lowered the pistols as smoke curled from their muzzles. The echoes of the shots rolled away across the valley. Preacher cocked his head slightly to the side as he heard something else.

The drumming of rapid hoofbeats.

Time to get moving again, Preacher thought with a grim smile. He whistled for Dog and lit a shuck out of there.

CHAPTER 36

The sound of sporadic shots echoed through the valley all day. An hour might pass between bursts of gunfire, and as that interval stretched out, Will became more convinced that Preacher's luck had run out at last.

If the mountain man was dead, Will thought, it would be up to him to get Charlotte out of King's Crown and find a safe place for them elsewhere.

The problem was that there might not be a safe place anywhere in the West as long as Barnabas Pendexter was alive.

In a way, it surprised Will that Pendexter had come along in person on the hunt for Charlotte. Pendexter had never been the sort to get his own hands dirty at anything. Will had seen that for himself back in Philadelphia as he had come to realize the shady nature of many of Pendexter's business enterprises.

But as the man's chief clerk, he knew perfectly well that nothing illegal could ever be traced back to Pendexter. If the authorities ever became interested in some of the less than savory activities that put money in Barnabas Pendexter's pockets, it would be someone else who took the blame and wound up in jail because of it.

Possibly even Will himself, which was one more reason he had been willing to help Charlotte escape from her marriage and leave civilization behind.

Out on the frontier, anyone could make a fresh start.

Unfortunately, evil existed even there. Jebediah Druke and Blood Eye were proof of that.

Druke was dead, and Blood Eye might be, too. Will would have felt better about that if he had seen the Crow's body with his own eyes. He couldn't stop worrying that Blood Eye was still out there somewhere, plotting his revenge.

"You look like you're a million miles away from here," Charlotte said from behind him.

Will turned to her with a smile. He wasn't going to tell her that he'd been thinking about Blood Eye. There was no reason to remind her of the ordeal she had gone through the day before, even if it hadn't been as bad as it might have been.

"I was just hoping that Preacher will get back soon. All that shooting down there has made me pretty concerned about him."

"I'm sure he's fine. He has Dog with him, and anyway, those men Barnabas hired will be no match for Preacher."

"Not individually, but if there are twenty or thirty of them . . ." Will didn't know for sure how many men Pendexter had brought with him. They had never gotten a good look at the group in the daylight. By the time the sun rose that morning, the hunters had been spread out across the valley.

"I still say not even thirty men will be able to run Preacher to ground."

"I hope not."

Both of them had gotten some sleep during the day, so even though their slumber had been fitful, they weren't quite as exhausted as they had been when they'd reached the canyon shortly before dawn. The spring water was good and they had drunk deeply from the pool, but neither had been able to find any food except a few berries.

That wasn't going to keep up their strength for very long.

Charlotte sat down on the rock next to Will where he had been perched on sentry duty. The warmth of her hip against his through their buckskins felt good. Without thinking about what he was doing, he slipped an arm around her.

She leaned her head against his shoulder. "Do you ever regret running away with me and coming out here?" she asked softly.

"What? Good heavens, no! I could never regret being with you."

"Even if it costs you your life?"

"I've always known the cost might be high. It always is for the things in life that are truly valuable."

Charlotte snuggled closer. "This past year, I've felt more alive than I ever thought I would, Will. Even with all the hardships and danger, it's been worthwhile for me."

"For me, too. We can't let ourselves think that it's over. We've still got a fighting chance."

As he said that, he turned his head to press his lips against her glossy black hair. He was leaning toward her when the arrow slammed into his back and drove him forward off the rock.

Preacher had led his pursuers on a merry chase during the day, but it was almost over. By his count, with some help from Dog, he had killed fourteen men and cut Pendexter's force down by a little more than half.

Sending that many men across the divide in one day was a sobering thing. Preacher had spilled a lot of blood in his lifetime and taken the lives of more men than he could count, but he didn't deal out death callously or lightly. His conscience was clear — as he had said many times before, he'd never killed a man who didn't need killin' — but all that humanity weighed on a man. It surely did.

If everything went according to his plan, he would kill even more before the day was over.

With every exchange of gunfire, the net had drawn closer around him. He had worked his way back toward the canyon, disposing of as many of Pendexter's men as he could while at the same time drawing them on.

He had seen something earlier in the day that had sparked an idea in his head. He knew approximately where on the mountainside the canyon was located, and several hundred feet above it were a number of boulders that looked like they were poised to roll down the slope. It had occurred to him that if he could lure all of his enemies to the area in front of the canyon and then climb up there to start an avalanche, he might be able to wipe out all of Pendexter's force at once.

Of course, there was considerable risk in that plan. If Will and Charlotte stayed in the canyon, they would be in the path of the falling rocks, too. Preacher needed them to stay there to exchange shots with Pendexter's men and make them believe they were laying siege to the canyon, instead of being lured into a trap.

Preacher thought the back end of the canyon, where it narrowed down to the spring, would be fairly safe because of the way the mountainside bulged out above it. When they heard the avalanche's rumble, Will and Charlotte would have to abandon their position at the mouth of the canyon and make a run for the other end.

It was the best chance they all had of getting out of there alive, Preacher decided.

He reached the base of the bluff that led up to the canyon. Some of the hunters might be watching him at that very moment, but he didn't care. They needed to know where he was going. He paused and whistled a birdcall, the signal he had told Will and Charlotte he would use when he returned to the canyon.

No response came from above.

Preacher frowned. It was possible they

hadn't heard him, so he whistled again. Still nothing. Maybe they had mistaken his signal for the call of a real bird, even though with all the shooting that had been going on in the valley, none of the birds still around were making any noise.

Preacher felt the hackles on the back of his neck stir. Something was wrong. "Come on, Dog," he said quietly. "We'd better get up there."

They climbed the bluff without much trouble, even though Preacher was weighed down somewhat by the four rifles slung over his shoulder and the half-dozen pistols stuck here and there around his body.

When they reached the top he unslung one of the loaded rifles and held it ready as he scanned the canyon. Dog padded forward, equally tense, and suddenly stopped and growled.

"I see him." Preacher broke into a run toward the shape of a man sprawled behind some rocks.

Will Gardner lay on his side. His face was pale and the shaft of an arrow protruded from his back. A pistol lay on the ground beside his limp, outstretched hand.

Preacher didn't see Charlotte anywhere.

He dropped to a knee beside Will. "Keep watch, Dog." He rested a hand on the young man's chest.

Will was breathing.

Preacher checked the arrow, saw that the head hadn't penetrated too deeply. He drew the knife, made a couple cuts, and carefully worked the arrowhead out of Will's back. Fresh blood gushed from the wound, but that wasn't necessarily a bad thing as long as the bleeding didn't continue for too long.

Preacher was worried about Charlotte, but he had to concentrate on saving Will's life. He made a hurried search for some moss with which to pack the wound and found enough to staunch the crimson flow. As he was binding the moss in place, Will groaned and started to stir.

"Take it easy," Preacher told him. "I'll help you sit up in a minute."

"Charlotte . . ." Will gasped. "Blood Eye!"

It was what Preacher suspected had happened. He had known all along that Blood Eye might still be a threat, but he couldn't handle everything at once.

When he had patched up Will as best he could, he lifted the young man and propped him against one of the rocks. Will was washed out and haggard, but he seemed to be thinking clearly.

"Blood Eye got into the canyon somehow and attacked us from behind. I'd been trying to keep watch for him, as well as for Pendexter's men, but he was too sly. And I was . . . distracted."

A gal as pretty as Charlotte could certainly distract a young fella, Preacher thought. "Did that ugly varmint hurt Charlotte?"

"Not that I know of. In fact, she got a shot off, and I'm pretty sure she wounded him. He was already hurt. He had a lot of dried blood on his side."

"Got winged during that fight last night," Preacher said. "What happened then?"

"The rifle was empty. She tried to use it as a club against him, but he knocked it out of her hands. She struggled with him . . . kept him from coming after me . . . I was able to crawl into cover behind these rocks, but I couldn't get a shot at him, not with Charlotte so close to him. He . . . he dragged her away."

Will's voice was bitterly self-reproachful as he went on. "He dragged her away, and there wasn't a damned thing I could do about it. I tried to get up and go after them, but I passed out. The next thing I knew, you were here."

"The shape you were in, if you'd caught up to him he likely would've killed you. But the fact that he ambushed you, didn't press the fight, and dragged Charlotte off tells me

that he's probably hurt pretty bad, too."
Preacher paused. "You reckon you can
stand up and walk, Will?"

"Don't . . . don't worry about me. Just go
after Blood Eye . . . and Charlotte."

"Well, I'd do that, except for one thing."
Preacher already heard the sound of hoofbeats coming closer down below.

Will clutched the mountain man's arm
arm and asked raggedly, "What are you talking about? You have to find them! You have
to . . . save her!"

"That's what I plan to do," Preacher
promised the young man, "but right now
we've got company comin', and if we don't
give 'em a warm welcome neither of us will
get out of here alive!"

CHAPTER 37

Preacher helped Will to his feet and steadied him as he hobbled over to the canyon mouth. He lowered Will to the ground behind a place where the rock jutted out and provided a little cover.

As the mountain man unslung the other rifles and placed them on the ground beside Will, he said, "What's left of Pendexter's bunch will be here in a few minutes. You've got make 'em think we're all still here and keep 'em occupied. Fire one of these rifles, then a couple of the pistols. Reload one gun, fire a couple more, then reload again. Keep switchin' back and forth between the rifles and the pistols."

"I . . . I think I can do that," Will said. "I'm a little lightheaded right now —"

"That's from losin' so much blood. You'll be all right. Just don't let those no-goods make it up the bluff. I'm countin' on you, Will."

"Charlotte counted on me, and I let her down."

"Don't go to thinkin' like that. We'll find Charlotte, and she'll be all right. But right now we've got to take care of that other bunch."

"If I see Pendexter, I'm going to kill him. I'll put a rifle ball in his head."

"Be my guest," Preacher said. "He's got it comin'."

"What are you going to be doing while I'm holding them off?"

Preacher pointed up the slope above them. "See those big rocks up yonder? I'm gonna start them rollin' in this direction."

Will's eyes widened. "You're going to start an avalanche? But won't that get me, too?"

"Not if you take off for the other end of the canyon when it —" Preacher stopped short as he realized that in Will's condition, the young man wouldn't be able to run fast enough to get out of harm's way if he waited until the avalanche started.

"Tell you what," Preacher resumed. "I'll give you a signal when to take off for the other end of the canyon, so you'll have enough time to get there before the avalanche rumbles through."

"But won't that allow Pendexter's men more time to reach the canyon, too?"

"Can't be helped. I'll howl like a wolf when it's time for you to pull back."

Will nodded grimly.

"Dog" — Preacher pointed to the other end of the canyon — "go on back there and stay."

Dog whined as if he didn't like the command.

"I don't care. There ain't nothin' you can do to help me now. Go on."

With a disgusted look on his face, Dog padded away toward the spring.

Down below, about a quarter mile away, a number of riders emerged from the trees on the other side of the open area at the base of the bluff. Preacher recognized Barnabas Pendexter as one of them, along with Larrabee and a dozen other men.

Preacher picked up one of the rifles. "I'll help you get the ball started, Will. We got plenty of powder and shot, so don't worry about burnin' too much of it. Keep the lead flyin' as thick and fast as you can, son, and we might have a chance."

"I won't let you down, Preacher," Will said in a voice choked with emotion.

The range was long, but Preacher drew a bead on Pendexter, anyway. Maybe he could make a lucky shot and cut the head off the snake first thing. "Let 'er rip," he told Will.

The young man had braced one of the rifles against the rock. He fired, and Preacher squeezed the trigger a couple heartbeats later. The twin reports echoed across the valley.

Not one of the men below toppled from his saddle, so Preacher knew the shots had fallen short. But they had served their purpose by getting the bunch's attention. Gray smoke puffed from rifle barrels as the men returned the fire.

Preacher quickly reloaded the rifle and set it beside Will. "Here we go." He sprinted for the far end of the canyon as shots continued to ring out behind him.

Dog jumped around eagerly as Preacher passed him. The mountain man didn't slow down. The slopes above the canyon weren't sheer, but climbing them presented a challenge. He grabbed handholds and started pulling himself up.

A moment later, he was surprised to come upon a trail that hadn't been visible from below. It blended into the rocky background. Mountain goats must have made it, he thought. He'd been accused in the past of being half mountain goat himself, so he scrambled up the trail faster than he had expected.

At the canyon mouth, Will kept up sporadic bursts of rapid fire. It sounded like two or three people were defending the canyon. Eventually Pendexter or Larrabee might figure out it was only one man with several weapons on hand, but Preacher doubted if there would be enough time for that to happen.

One way or another, it was going to be over soon.

The trail turned into a ledge that slanted up to the cluster of boulders that was Preacher's objective. They were only about twenty yards away.

He paused to look down. He could see all of the canyon from there except the area at the back where the spring was located. It confirmed his hunch that the boulders might pass over that part of the canyon as they tumbled down the slope.

He couldn't see the bluff leading up to the canyon at all, but he could see the trees where Pendexter's hired killers had been a few minutes earlier. They had advanced beyond that point and might have reached the base of the bluff.

Preacher threw back his head and let out a wolf howl.

At the canyon mouth, Will twisted his head around sharply and looked up toward the boulders. He pushed himself to his feet and started toward the canyon's far end in a shaky run. Every few steps, he used the butt of one of the rifles he carried to brace himself up, like a makeshift crutch.

Preacher headed for the boulders once again.

He was about ten feet from the nearest one when Blood Eye stepped out from behind it with Charlotte's neck held in the crook of his left arm and the knife in his right hand pressed to her side.

Preacher stopped short. He still had the knife and the hatchet, but neither of those weapons would do him any good at the moment. Blood Eye held Charlotte in front of him like a human shield. The renegade Crow's one good eye glared murderously at the mountain man.

"I figured we'd run into each other again," Preacher said.

"You are fated to die at my hand," Blood Eye rasped. He was in bad shape, but his hatred kept him going and continued to make him a danger.

"I don't think so. Charlotte, are you all right?"

Blood Eye's arm was so tight across her throat that she couldn't talk. Preacher didn't see any fresh bloodstains on her buckskins, though, so he was hopeful that Blood Eye hadn't hurt her.

"I waited for you, white man," Blood Eye said. "Now we finish it, eh?"

"Fine with me. Let the girl go, and we'll settle it, just like you want."

With every moment that went by, Pendexter's men had more of a chance to reach the canyon. If Preacher didn't get that avalanche started soon, they might overrun Will's position and shoot him full of holes.

Blood Eye urged Charlotte along the ledge. They came closer to Preacher. Only a few feet separated them from the mountain man.

"Yes," Blood Eye said with a hideous grin. "I will let the girl go."

A sudden shove sent her off the ledge. Charlotte screamed as she found herself with nothing but empty air underneath her.

The shocking, unexpected move horrified Preacher just enough to freeze him for half a second, giving Blood Eye the time to leap at him. The knife in the renegade's hand flashed up and then down as it streaked toward Preacher's chest.

Preacher grabbed Blood Eye's wrist and turned the blade aside at the last instant. The point ripped a fiery line across his ribs. He pivoted, hauled Blood Eye around with him, and rammed the Crow against the rock face that rose beside the ledge.

Preacher heard a sharp crack and knew at least one of the renegade's ribs broke under the impact. He kept his left hand clamped around Blood Eye's right wrist and strained to hold back the knife.

At the same time, his right hand shot forward and locked around Blood Eye's throat. The two men stood on the ledge separated by only an inch or two. Their bodies trembled as they strained against each other. Even though they hardly moved, it was a clash of titans.

Blood Eye's lips drew back from his teeth in a grimace. Blood leaked from the corner of his mouth. Preacher heard the Crow's breath bubbling in his throat and knew that the jagged end of a broken rib had punctured one of his opponent's lungs.

The renegade was drowning in his own blood.

Blood Eye spat crimson in Preacher's face. He couldn't say anything, not with Preacher choking him. They swayed slightly back and forth as powerful corded muscles struggled against each other.

"You're finished," Preacher grated. "Go ahead and die!"

Blood Eye suddenly weakened, and Preacher rammed him against the cliff again. Blood gushed from the Crow's mouth, flooding down over Preacher's hand. He twisted Blood Eye's wrist, shoved hard, and buried the knife in the Indian's chest. The renegade stiffened. His good eye widened and bulged.

With a bellow of rage, Preacher wheeled around and threw the dying Crow off the ledge. Blood Eye flew through the air and crashed down on the slope. He tumbled limply for a few yards and then stopped in an untidy sprawl.

"Help!" Charlotte cried.

Preacher looked down and saw her clinging to the ledge. She'd been able to twist in midair and grab it as she fell.

He lunged to where she was dangling, reached down to take hold of her wrists, and lifted her to safety. She clung tightly to him for a moment.

Then she stepped back and looked up into his rugged face. "Will . . . ?"

The shooting was still going on down below, so Will wasn't dead. He might have a chance.

Preacher looked over the ledge again and saw Pendexter's men advancing up the canyon, firing toward the end of it. "Come on," he snapped as he sprang to the nearest boulder. "You can give me a hand."

He put his shoulder against it and shoved. Charlotte joined in the effort. The boulder made a grating sound as it shifted on the rock. The two of them heaved against it again and again.

Suddenly the huge rock tipped away from them. Nature did the rest of the work as gravity took over and pulled it more off balance. With a rumbling roar, the boulder struck another and knocked it into motion, as well.

Preacher ran to a smaller rock and heaved it down the slope for good measure. More and more boulders tumbled down the mountainside. One of them rolled right over Blood Eye's body, leaving a gory smear on the rock.

The Crow wouldn't cheat death this time, Preacher thought in grim satisfaction.

He grabbed hold of Charlotte's hand. "Come on! We gotta get back down there!"

CHAPTER 38

Will's situation had quickly turned desperate.

He had done everything Preacher said, even though every time he'd fired one of the rifles the recoil had made pain throb through his wounded back. He had held off Pendexter's men until the signal came for him to retreat then had moved toward the back of the canyon as fast as his battered body would carry him. He had waited for the avalanche that with any luck would wipe out their enemies.

But the avalanche hadn't come. Dog growled and barked as if he sensed that Preacher was in danger, and Will's blood seemed to freeze in his veins when he heard a woman's scream from higher on the slope.

Charlotte!

He would have run back along the canyon where he could look up and see what was going on, but several of Pendexter's men reached the canyon mouth and opened fire on him. Will crouched behind a rock beside the little spring-fed pool and returned their shots.

All he managed to do was slow down their charge, and more and more of them reached the canyon with each passing moment. They poured through the gap, and he knew it was only a matter of minutes before they over-ran him.

Until that happened, he would fight.

With his ears ringing from all the shots, he couldn't hear much, but he felt the earth tremble underneath him. He looked up, and suddenly the sky was blotted out by a cloud of falling rocks and dust.

"Dog!" Will cried as he threw himself as far back as he could go. The big cur pressed against him, no longer growling or snarling. He sensed that what was happening was too big for him to fight.

A roar became louder and louder until Will wondered if it was the sound of the world ending.

Preacher and Charlotte hurried along the ledge. Reaching the end of it, they looked over the edge. Dust hung so thick in the air that they couldn't see into the canyon.

"Will!" Charlotte cried. "Will, can you

hear me?" She scrambled down ahead of Preacher.

As the dust clouds began to thin, Preacher looked over his shoulder and saw that tons of rock had slid into the front part of the canyon — right where Pendexter and his men had been the last time Preacher saw them. His fervent hope was that they were still there, buried for all time under that mass of rock and dirt.

Charlotte dropped the last six feet or so and landed lithely. The area in front of the pool was littered with small rocks, but the brunt of the avalanche had missed it as Preacher had thought it would.

He heard her cry out again, "Will!" Then a sound came to his ears that lightened his heart.

Dog barked a greeting.

When Preacher reached the ground he saw Will and Charlotte embracing and kissing. The young man appeared to be all right. Better than all right, in fact, with the woman he loved in his arms again.

Dog bounded over and reared up to rest his paws on Preacher's shoulders. He licked the mountain man's grizzled face until Preacher laughed.

He scratched the big cur's ears. "We done it again, you hairy old varmint. Escaped death by the skin of our teeth."

"Not quite." Barnabas Pendexter came out of the clouds of dust with a pistol in his hand. Larrabee, the cold-blooded killer with the eye patch, was beside him and also pointed a pistol at Preacher, Will, and Charlotte.

Pendexter was covered with dust and grime and didn't look so elegant. Blood trickled down his face from a long scratch on his cheek, and his sleek dark hair was askew. The light of madness burned in his eyes. "I've come for you, Charlotte. Your loving husband has come for you at last."

She looked at him with horror and rage on her face. "Loving husband? You never loved me, Barnabas! You just wanted to use me, to bend me to your will like a slave!"

Pendexter sneered. "Such is my right."

"You had no right to beat me as you did. You had no right to keep me a prisoner and make my life a living hell!"

"You'll come back home with me now," Pendexter said as if he hadn't heard her. "Everything will be just like it was before, you'll see."

"Nothing will be the same. I'll die first!"

Charlotte plucked one of the pistols from behind Will's belt. She twisted toward Pendexter and brought the gun up in both hands. Her thumbs looped over the hammer to cock it.

"Kill the men!" Pendexter screeched to Larrabee.

Preacher was already on the move. He darted to the side and pulled the hatchet from behind his belt. His arm flashed back and forward even as Larrabee fired. Preacher felt the heat of the pistol ball as it passed close beside his cheek.

The hatchet revolved through the air and landed with a solid, meaty *thunk!* in the middle of Larrabee's forehead. The keen blade drove through his skull and into his brain.

At the same time two more shots roared. The ball from Pendexter's pistol passed between Charlotte and Will and chipped stone from the wall behind them.

Charlotte's shot punched into Pendexter's chest, staggering him. His eyes opened wide. His jaw sagged. He managed to rasp, "Charlotte, how . . ."

"It wasn't difficult at all," she said as his eyes rolled up in their sockets.

His knees unhinged and he collapsed in a limp heap of dead flesh.

Charlotte dropped the gun and sagged against Will. She started to cry as he held her.

"It's over," he told her as he comforted her. "It's all over now."

"Is it, really? You swear?"

Will looked over at Preacher as the mountain man bent to wrench the hatchet out of Larrabee's skull. The man with the eye patch was dead as he could be.

Preacher gave Will a curt nod.

The young man stroked Charlotte's hair. "I swear. Just like I swear to love you for the rest of my life."

As far as Preacher was able to determine, Pendexter and Larrabee had been the only survivors of the avalanche. If any of the other men had lived through it, they had done the smart thing and taken off for the tall and uncut.

Climbing out of the canyon over the debris left by the avalanche wasn't easy, especially for Will with the arrow wound in his back, but they managed and by nightfall had found a good place to camp beside a stream.

With Jebediah Druke and his men all dead and the threat of Barnabas Pendexter ended for all time, Preacher figured it was safe to build a fire.

By its light, Charlotte cleaned and re-dressed the wound in Will's back. "You're

355

going to be all right," she assured him.

He smiled. "Of course I will be, with you to nurse me back to health."

Preacher had shot a rabbit and it was roasting over the fire. He looked up as he heard steady hoofbeats somewhere nearby.

Will and Charlotte heard the sound, too. Both reached for the guns they had close at hand.

Preacher stood up and held his rifle ready. A moment later, a broad grin broke out on his rugged face as two large, familiar shapes loomed through the shadows and came into the firelight. Dog let out a welcoming yip.

"Figured you were around somewhere," Preacher told Horse. He set the rifle aside and went to greet the stallion. The well-loaded pack animal followed closely behind.

Preacher stroked the stallion's nose. "You've been just waitin' for things to settle down again, haven't you?"

Horse tossed his head as if agreeing.

Preacher was glad they were all together again.

As they ate the cooked rabbit, he asked Will and Charlotte, "What are the two of you goin' to do now? I reckon you can go back east if you want. The only reason you came out here was to get as far away from Pendexter as you could, wasn't it?"

356

"Not entirely," Will said. "Like I told you, I've always been fascinated by the frontier. Even though a lot of terrible things have happened, most of our life here has been good."

"Very good," Charlotte said as she hugged his arm. "I think we might stay for a while and see if we can earn our living as trappers."

Preacher chuckled. "You mean Will Gardner and Gray Otter?"

"No. I mean Will Gardner and his wife Charlotte." She looked over at him. "I really would like to be properly married now that we can, Will."

"I'd like that, too." His voice was husky with emotion. "We'll have go to back to civilization to do it, though."

"Just for a short time. I think I can stand it if you can."

"Oh, I can," he assured her. "I certainly can."

"What about you, Preacher?" Charlotte asked as she turned to the mountain man.

Preacher reached over to scratch behind Dog's ears. "That money Pendexter paid me was for a stake so I could get back to trappin' once I'd found his runaway son. Reckon I did that job as well as it could be done, so there's no reason I can't use those supplies with a clean conscience."

"If it's trapping you want," Will said, "you should stay here in King's Crown. It's one of the best places for beaver pelts you'll ever find."

"Yeah, I know, but I was thinkin' I might move on and try my luck somewhere else."

"Too many bad memories here, I suppose," Charlotte said softly. "Yes, I understand the feeling. Preacher may have a point there, Will. Perhaps it would be better if we made a fresh start elsewhere."

"Whatever you want is fine with me. Someplace new and clean."

"That's one good thing about the frontier," Preacher said. "No shortage of hills to see the other side of."

He would continue answering that call of the unknown as long as the blood flowed in his veins.

J. A. JOHNSTONE ON WILLIAM W. JOHNSTONE
"WHEN THE TRUTH BECOMES LEGEND"

William W. Johnstone was born in southern Missouri, the youngest of four children. He was raised with strong moral and family values by his minister father, and tutored by his schoolteacher mother. Despite this, he quit school at age fifteen.

"I have the highest respect for education," he says, "but such is the folly of youth, and wanting to see the world beyond the four walls and the blackboard."

True to this vow, Bill attempted to enlist in the French Foreign Legion ("I saw Gary Cooper in *Beau Geste* when I was a kid and I thought the French Foreign Legion would be fun") but was rejected, thankfully, for being underage. Instead, he joined a traveling carnival and did all kinds of odd jobs. It was listening to the veteran carny folk, some of whom had been on the circuit since the late 1800s, telling amazing tales about their experiences, that planted the storytelling seed in Bill's imagination.

"They were mostly honest people, despite the bad reputation traveling carny shows had back then," Bill remembers. "Of course, there were exceptions. There was one guy named Picky, who got that name because he was a master pickpocket. He could steal a man's socks right off his feet without him knowing. Believe me, Picky got us chased out of more than a few towns."

After a few months of this grueling existence, Bill returned home and finished high school. Next came stints as a deputy sheriff in the Tallulah, Louisiana, Sheriff's Department, followed by a hitch in the U.S. Army. Then he began a career in radio broadcasting at KTLD in Tallulah, which would last sixteen years. It was there that he fine-tuned his storytelling skills. He turned to writing in 1970, but it wouldn't be until 1979 that his first novel, *The Devil's Kiss,* was published. Thus began the full-time writing career of William W. Johnstone. He wrote horror (*The Uninvited*), thrillers (*The Last of the Dog Team*), even a romance novel or two. Then, in February 1983, *Out of the Ashes* was published. Searching for his missing family in the aftermath of a post-apocalyptic America, rebel mercenary and patriot Ben Raines is united with the civilians of the Resistance forces and moves to the forefront of a revolution for the nation's future.

Out of the Ashes was a smash. The series would continue for the next twenty years, winning Bill three generations of fans all over the world. The series was often imitated but never duplicated. "We all tried to copy the Ashes series," said one publishing executive, "but Bill's uncanny ability, both then and now, to predict in which direction the political winds were blowing brought a certain immediacy to the table no one else could capture." The Ashes series would end its run with more than thirty-four books and twenty million copies in print, making it one of the most successful men's action series in American book publishing. (The Ashes series also, Bill notes with a touch of pride, got him on the FBI's Watch List for its less than flattering portrayal of spineless politicians and the growing power of big government over our lives, among other things. In that respect, I often find myself saying, "Bill was years ahead of his time.")

Always steps ahead of the political curve, Bill's recent thrillers, written with myself, include *Vengeance Is Mine, Invasion USA, Border War, Jackknife, Remember the Alamo, Home Invasion, Phoenix Rising, The Blood of*

Patriots, The Bleeding Edge, and the upcoming *Suicide Mission.*

It is with the Western, though, that Bill found his greatest success and propelled him onto both the *USA Today* and the *New York Times* bestseller lists.

Bill's Western series include *The Mountain Man, Matt Jensen, The Last Mountain Man, Preacher, The Family Jensen, Luke Jensen, Bounty Hunter, Eagles, MacCallister* (an Eagles spin-off), *Sidewinders, The Brothers O'Brien, Sixkiller, Blood Bond, The Last Gunfighter,* and the upcoming new series *Flintlock* and *The Trail West.* May 2013 saw the hardcover Western *Butch Cassidy, The Lost Years.*

"The Western," Bill says, "is one of the few true art forms that is one hundred percent American. I liken the Western as America's version of England's Arthurian legends, like the Knights of the Round Table, or Robin Hood and his Merry Men. Starting with the 1902 publication of *The Virginian* by Owen Wister, and followed by the greats like Zane Grey, Max Brand, Ernest Haycox, and of course Louis L'Amour, the Western has helped to shape the cultural landscape of America.

"I'm no goggle-eyed college academic, so

when my fans ask me why the Western is as popular now as it was a century ago, I don't offer a 200-page thesis. Instead, I can only offer this: The Western is honest. In this great country, which is suffering under the yoke of political correctness, the Western harks back to an era when justice was sure and swift. Steal a man's horse, rustle his cattle, rob a bank, a stagecoach, or a train, you were hunted down and fitted with a hangman's noose. One size fit all.

"Sure, we Westerners are prone to a little embellishment and exaggeration and, I admit it, occasionally play a little fast and loose with the facts. But we do so for a very good reason — to enhance the enjoyment of readers.

"It was Owen Wister, in *The Virginian* who first coined the phrase *'When you call me that, smile.'* Legend has it that Wister actually heard those words spoken by a deputy sheriff in Medicine Bow, Wyoming, when another poker player called him a son-of-a-bitch.

"Did it really happen, or is it one of those myths that have passed down from one generation to the next? I honestly don't know. But there's a line in one of my favorite Westerns of all time, *The Man Who Shot Liberty Valance,* where the newspaper

editor tells the young reporter, 'When the truth becomes legend, print the legend.'
    "These are the words I live by."

The employees of Thorndike Press hope you have enjoyed this Large Print book. All our Thorndike, Wheeler, and Kennebec Large Print titles are designed for easy reading, and all our books are made to last. Other Thorndike Press Large Print books are available at your library, through selected bookstores, or directly from us.

For information about titles, please call:
    (800) 223-1244

or visit our Web site at:
    http://gale.cengage.com/thorndike

To share your comments, please write:
    Publisher
    Thorndike Press
    10 Water St., Suite 310
    Waterville, ME 04901